Stairway To Heaven

Love United #4

Stairway To Heaven
By
Melyssa Winchester

For more information regarding the cover please visit rolffimages at http://www.fotolia.com

The story within these pages is dedicated to the Dean girl to my Sam girl, my very best friend and a woman I appreciate more than life. Jennifer Kendrick, this one's for you.

Prologue

Three Months Prior

Michael

For as long as I have existed there is one thing I have known beyond a shadow of a doubt.

Every step taken has been in preparation of this very moment. The wars waged, the feelings and emotions that have been laid out for the world to see, every single motion scripted in an effort to bring us to this very second. The day the light would go against the darkness and reign supreme despite every effort made by the other side to change it.

We were always meant to stand here in this church and face Lucifer. Even though we have not always known that Ryan would be the person to bring about his end, he was meant to stand here as well. It had to be him. There would be no other being in existence that could do it and do it he did.

The battle has been over for only a few minutes, the effects painfully obvious. Not only with my brothers and me, but also through the two humans that stand with us. We are all weighed down under what has taken place and as long as we exist after this moment, I know that it will be something that is never forgotten.

There is only one person missing from what should turn out to be a very large celebration. Gabriel. I am unsure of why he is no longer standing with us, but knowing my brother, it is because he is off doing right by the humans that we had broken away from only hours before. He would never be able to move forward and celebrate everything that happened without first making sure they were okay.

It is one of the things I respect and love about him. I only wish I could embrace him just once in this moment. We have done what we set out to do all along. We took down our fallen brother and we had done it as a team. Even though there had been moments along the way where things looked bleak, we had risen above it and come out on top. Right now, I want nothing more than to share that with the brother that helped me get here.

Something is not right. With as happy as this moment should be, it is not appearing that way for Ryan and Serenity. As they look across the church at me, their faces are masks of sadness and pain. I have to assume that it has something to do with how they both came to feel about the very man they destroyed here today, but I sense that there is more to it than that. As if there is something more they are aware of that I am not. Of course, I could just read them both and none would be the wiser, but I find that just like my brother before me, I want them to bring it to me on their own.

My time on the planet has changed me just as Gabriel predicted. In times past, I would have balked against the changes or even the assumption of change. In this regard, it is surrounded by a positive light, so I will embrace it rather than run from it. All of us standing here now have changed everything, not only for the world, but for Heaven as well.

Making my way over to where Ryan and Serenity stand deep in conversation with my brothers, I find it hard to mask my excitement, a sensation I have not felt for quite some time.

"Gabriel should be here for this. It saddens me that he has chosen to check in with the humans rather than be here for this moment of true celebration."

"Uh—Mike, that's not where he is." Ryan says as he turns to face me, his face displaying a level of pain I haven't witnessed during our time together.

Why does he look so upset? Is he really that affected by ending Lucifer's reign?

It is only when I really look at him, taking in everything about him, that I land on his eyes and notice they have returned to their very human shade of light blue. It is a most unexpected turn of events. It seems as though doing away with Lucifer, changed him, finally killing the darkness he held inside.

Another cause for celebration, yet something that judging by the boys face, he is unaware of.

"What do you mean, Ryan? Of course that is where he is. It is only for the humans that he would leave a moment such as this. I see we have another event to celebrate as well, which only makes me want him here even more."

"Michael, you must listen to Serenity and Ryan now. They have information that you need to hear as it pertains to our brother."

"Wait, what other thing do we need to celebrate?" Serenity cuts in, her eyes moving rapidly between me and the man she loves.

Ignoring Raphael's statement, I turn to Serenity with a smile. If there is one person, other than Ryan, who would want to celebrate what I noticed, it was her and I didn't want to waste any more time keeping it from her. The celebration needed to begin.

"It appears that in ending his reign, Ryan has had the darkness removed from him. The very thing he wanted for months has now come to pass. He is now free to be who he was always meant to be. Not only have we defeated the darkness in its most evil form today, we have also banished it completely from the purest angel in existence."

Where I expected them to at least show some shred of happiness at the information I had given, they did not and in that moment, I remember my brothers earlier words. Before I could turn to him and ask him to explain, Serenity spoke and everything came to light.

"Michael, we know about Ryan, but it's not because of what happened to Lucifer. That's what we need to talk to you about."

"What do you mean? How else could the demon have been lifted from him other than through ending the very being that put it there?"

"Gabriel…" She chokes out before tears begin to fall from her eyes. "Gabriel did it."

"I am unsure of how that is even possible? Did Gabriel figure out a way around the old power?"

"No man, he didn't." Ryan picks up, releasing his hand from Serenity's and making his way over to where I stood.

"Then how is it possible? Is this Father's doing?"

"No, it's not his either." Ryan said sighing, finally coming to a stop directly in front of me, his body tensed for a reason I cannot even begin to understand. "Shit, I don't want to do this. It's hard enough dealing with it happening right in front of me, but explaining it when I don't even get it myself, I don't think I can do it."

Raphael began to move forward and something in his expression as he made his way forward, told me everything that I needed to know. They needed to tell me something that happened while we had been fighting and it wasn't going to be good.

Something that Gabriel had done.

"Where is our brother, Raphael? If he is not with the humans as I believe him to be, then why is he not here with us now?"

"He's not here because he's gone, Michael." Serenity says quickly before she began to sob, Ryan immediately reaching out and pulling her into his body.

"Gone how?" I finally ask after a few minutes of silence that surrounds Serenity's now muffled cries. Just what are they trying to tell me?

"He sacrificed himself in order to save me, Michael. He didn't warn anyone, just came to Serenity the way they planned and told her what to do to save me."

None of this is making sense to me. I understand what it is that Ryan is saying and even why Serenity is crying, but what led up to that point is blank and before I can come to terms with what I'm hearing, I need answers.

"You both need to start from the beginning."

"Gabriel found me earlier," Serenity began, breaking away from Ryan and finally turning her tear stained face to mine. "I told him what Lucifer was planning for Ryan and he told me that he had a plan that could fix it. He wanted me to mislead Ryan and do as Lucifer wanted, at which point he would enter the room and heal him."

"Gabriel entered into a plan with you that he did not inform the rest of us about?"

"It seems that way, Mike." Ryan spoke up, his arms never once breaking away from Serenity as she continued to force the emotion down.

"After Ryan threw himself on the blade, he came and told me that in order to save him, I had to do exactly what he said because normal healing wouldn't work. I had no idea what he was asking me to do, so I went along with it. It's only when Ryan came back that I learned the truth."

"Learned what truth? What did my brother ask you to do?"

"He asked me to remove his light and place it into Ryan."

The minute the words fell from her lips, I finally allow myself to process exactly what happened and the minute the realization hit, I felt the very light around me begin to fade.

"He's dead..." I state, my voice fading off as my mind became flooded with the pain. My brother, the only angel in the world that truly understood me, is no longer here. In his desire to save the world he had given himself up to it.

I hear Serenity begin to sob again, but instead of reaching out to her the way I want to, understanding now just why she is reacting so strongly, I do the opposite. I turn my back on her. I couldn't bear to hear her pain, not when I could feel my own rising to the surface. No, I had to get away from her, from the others and just be on my own. I couldn't deal with this here, not where everyone can see.

"Michael, what are you doing?" Raphael asks as I began taking the first few steps away from them.

"I can't be here anymore, not after everything I have learned. I am sorry if it is not the desired response all of you need right now. If what you are telling me is true and I can sense in my soul that it is, then I need to be far away from here before I do something that I may never be able to take back."

With my final words said, I do the only thing left I can and focusing all of my power on the very light of Heaven and all it contained, I vanish, leaving them all to grieve for my lost brother without me.

Chapter One

Present Time

Graham

I'm not okay.

This tough as nails bullshit I'm trying to portray is finally starting to crack. No matter how strong I believe I am, it's not enough to combat everything that's happening to me. Everything that's been happening for months, though I'm only admitting now that it's something I can't get control of on my own.

It started after I was saved by Serenity in the church. I physically healed and everything seemed to be normal for awhile, but then the headaches came and with each day that passes they only seem to get worse. It's when I get them that the visions haunt me. My senses go haywire and I can smell, taste and feel things that are much better left forgotten. I swear it almost feels like I'm right back where I was months ago and Lucifer is controlling me again.

That's not true though. Three months ago, Lucifer was finished off by Ryan, Serenity and the angels. They went face to face with the Devil and came out on top. It's just too bad that in ending him it did nothing to stop the agony I've been living with.

Entering Hell only seems to add to it. I keep replaying Ryan's words in my head. The fears he had when we went on our mission to get Serenity back. He'd been worried that I might not come out alright and he wasn't wrong. Only I wasn't right going in, so in reality it just made it all worse.

If that isn't enough, Gabriel's dead. The angel that tried so hard to get me to see my worth went to his death fighting the son of bitch that did this to me. He'd given himself over in order to save Ryan, Serenity and me and I didn't even get the chance to say goodbye.

There's so much more I want to say than just goodbye, but right now, a goodbye would be enough. Well, a thank you and then a heartfelt goodbye. I owe him more than he would ever know and even though I hate the way I'm feeling and things I'm experiencing, I would do it all over again. I hate that he had to be taken away in order for it to happen the way it was meant to. Gabriel should be here just as much as any other angel, celebrating, instead of being locked away wherever angels go to die.

I don't want to think about this. It's only going to make the headaches come back. I've successfully moved the last of my things to Stephenville and I plan on being here for the duration, following my dream with my art and living the way I know Gabriel would want me to. There's no way I can let anything stand in the way of that; no matter how strongly it forces itself on me.

That's the thing. I'm powerless against it once it starts. I can feel the memories on the surface and as much as I want to look away, I can't do it. I have to witness it all over again, even though it breaks my heart to do it. I have to relive the moment Ryan told me Gabriel died.

*****

"Graham, you got a second? There's something I need to talk to you about."

11

"Where's Serenity?" I ask immediately, hating that he's standing here alone and that he looks so god damned sad. Did something happen to her and he's here to tell me she's gone?

"She's gone back to the room to be with Emma. She couldn't be here for this man; she's having a rough time as it is. So, can I come in or not?"

Moving out of the way, I motion for him to come in and once he does, I shut the door behind him.

"Alright so what's going on and why do you look like your dog just died?"

He flinches at the words and I immediately want to take it back. I wasn't trying to be an ass, but it looked like I was doing it without even trying.

"Something happened to Gabe tonight and it's not good."

I honestly didn't care what happened to Gabriel, as long as in the end he was alright. I want to know what happened with Lucifer more, even if it's a dickhead move. I needed to know if we still had anything to fear from the bastard that had been riding around in my skin. Nothing else matters. Not even the angels.

"What happened to Lucifer?"

"He's dead, but honestly Graham, you need to just sit down and listen."

I've seen Ryan look a lot of ways over the last year and angry is definitely one I knew well. I'm also used to him being pretty in your face when he wants you to do something, but this was different somehow. He looks like what he had to tell me is physically hurting him, which meant that even though Lucifer had been finished off, something far worse happened.

"Well if Serenity is alright and you're here, I can only assume this visit has something to do with the angels. So what happened to Gabe?"

"He's dead, Graham."

I felt my mouth drop almost as if I had no control over it and all breathing I'd been doing ceased. I want to believe it's a sick joke, but with the tortured way Ryan is looking at me now, I know that's not going to be the case. It's very real. The angel that had come to me in an effort to get help in saving Serenity is gone.

"What the hell happened? How is that even possible? Can angels even die? What the fucking hell went on in that church? What did Lucifer do to him?"

Ryan threw his hand up in the air in an effort to slow me down, but I was having no part of it. The questions were only coming so quickly because I had nothing to go on. If he wanted them to stop, he better tell me everything and soon.

"Lucifer didn't do anything. He had another plan that none of us knew. Gabriel was able to get to Serenity before I did and they worked out a plan together. The only problem is, he didn't explain everything that he was going to do and she went in blind."

"Wait, what are you trying to say?"

"Gabriel sacrificed himself to save me. He had Serenity strip him of his light and give it to me. He disappeared after that."

"Angels can't die..." I manage to spit out as my mind went over everything Ryan is trying to tell me.

"Yeah, they can die man, just like demons can. Though with the demons, they end up in Purgatory or right back in hell in the chambers."

"So, where do angels go?"

"According to Raphael and even Lucifer when I followed him, they cease to exist. They just disappear and don't end up anywhere. It's actually what he wanted for Michael. He never spoke of wanting the same result for Gabe though."

"Why would he do that to save you?"

"Because it was either Lucifer killing me or Serenity, and you know Gabe, he didn't want that happening."

"So what does this mean now? You're Gabriel?"

I understand what happens to angels when they die, but trying to figure out what it meant having Gabriel's light inside of Ryan was causing me to draw complete blanks. I had no idea what that could mean other then the two of them joining.

"No. I'm not Gabriel, but his power destroyed the demon in me, returning me to what I should have been all along, though I'm not quite on board with that yet. I'm pure angel now, with Gabriel's light inside me. That's it."

"How is Serenity handling this?"

"She's not and that's another reason I'm here. I need your help. Well no, I don't, but she does."

There is no question of what my answer would be if he would ever get around to asking the question. I know losing Gabriel would break her and if Ryan's here now asking me to help her, well, I would do whatever it takes to make sure nothing ever touched Serenity again.

"Just tell me what you want me to do and I'm in."

*****

The problem with remembering is, the things you say you're going to do and the ones you end up doing can turn out drastically different. It's been three months since that conversation and I haven't done a damn thing other then sit in this room when I'm not in class and mope.

I pulled away from everyone after learning of Gabriel's death and no matter how much I want to throw myself back in, I can't seem to do it. Not even for the woman that I've spent the last six years of my life loving. I'm letting her down, but I just can't face the world yet.

I spend most nights with a bottle of whiskey and the stereo turned up all the way, drowning out the headaches and the memories. The problem is, in self medicating this way I'm only making everything that I'm trying to escape from that much worse. In trying to block out the sensations from my time with Lucifer, I only bring them on stronger. I can feel, see and even smell the blood as it's being drained out of Serenity, even though that happened well over a year ago. I can see the darkness blazing in her eyes in the church as she told me to fight and come back to her.

I want to drink until it takes it away from me, except the only way that's going to happen is if I drink myself to death. Despite the mild appeal it holds, I can't bring myself to do it.

So I move forward, spending my days working on my art, which is beginning to look a lot like the darkness I'm living with and drink until I pass out in my own puke. I push the feelings, emotions, memories and sensations to the background as best I can.

It's time for me to admit one simple fact.

Serenity is better off without me.

Chapter Two

Ryan

Right about now I would kill for an angel to pop into my room so I could pick his brain and get some of the answers I've wanted for the past three months. Unfortunately, that won't be happening, at least not anytime soon. I need to start figuring out shit on my own again, but this time, it's not like times before. It's harder because it's not me I'm trying to figure out.

She is trying so desperately to hide the way she feels from me, content to paste on a smile and move forward in the belief that it's what I want from her. The problem is, it's nowhere near what I want. Not even close. All I really want is for her to open up to me again, instead of trying so damn hard to be what she thinks everyone wants her to be.

Something happened that day in Green Haven, the last time either of us came face to face with Lucifer and it's been haunting her ever since. At first I thought it had to do with Gabriel and the loss she felt, but the more time that goes by it's easy to see it's more than that. A whole lot more and a whole lot worse than mourning Gabriel could ever be.

As much as I don't want to believe it, she's mourning Lucifer and there are times when we're together where it almost feels as though everything else has become secondary to it. It's not jealousy that makes me think that way, but things said and done during our moments alone that do it. She's not the same Serenity as before he took her from us and even with the bastard dead and gone, he still somehow manages to ruin our lives.

I have to admit, there was a time right after it happened that I went to a pretty dark place. Lucifer, for the longest time, was the only real father figure I had and living with the fact that I'd been the one to end him, turned me inside out. I had this beautiful woman by my side, but I found myself so lost in my own agony and grief over the situation that somewhere along the way I let her go in favor of becoming lost in it.

Serenity can't do that. She won't ever admit it to anyone and it doesn't take the power of mind reading to know it, but she's stuck. She can't move forward even if she wants to. I'm not sure if it's because of the branding Lucifer put on her heart or if it's just something different in the way she is, but she just can't handle it right.

When I finally got my head on straight, I tried to help her. God, there were a lot of nights for the first few weeks after I came out of my dark cloud that we spent awake and talking our feelings through, but even doing that, it didn't help her heal. All talking seemed to do for her was make it more apparent in her mind and really, that's the last thing I want.

This is why I want to talk to an angel so badly and in this case, Gabriel. I was never fond of the connection they shared, even if it wasn't reciprocated on Serenity's end, but there couldn't be any denial of his ability to be what she needed, especially in times like this. What I want to be for her and can't, he would have no problem with, which only made me miss him that much more.

He gave me a gift giving up his life for mine and it wasn't his power and the light that made him who he was. No, he gave me the bond he shared with the woman I love, which only makes everything between us more powerful now. I can feel her in ways that I've been unable to before. I can reach the part of her soul now that I only dreamed of. We're connected in every single way imaginable, except in the way that matters most. I can't heal her broken heart and even worse, I can't bring Gabriel and even Lucifer back to her.

When I brought up the idea of our wedding being not only a chance for us to finally do it the right way, but also a way to honor Gabriel, she'd been all for it. There had been no stopping her. It seemed like a great thing, watching her change from the morose woman I'd been witnessing over the last few weeks; to the strong woman I know and love so deeply. I thought this would be the thing to carry her through.

I was wrong.

Now she's just going through the motions, pretending more each day. It's gotten to the point that even if I do want to bring it up, I can't, because I don't want to push her away completely and I think she might be pretty close to that.

So left with no other alternative and hoping with everything in me that it works, I sit on the bed, close my eyes and focus on the purest thing that I can. I do the one thing that I haven't done in months.

I pray.

Serenity

When I was a little girl, I used to dream about what I would wear on my wedding day. With the way my life is, I suppose it should have been surprising, me being able to think in terms of the future that way, but find me a little girl in the world that doesn't dream of that day. It's something that's been around since the beginning of time.

The voices would not deter me from what I truly believed would one day happen to me. It was so powerful back then that I had every single detail mapped out. I knew exactly what my dress would look like and even imagined the church with visions of my father being the one to walk me down the aisle. There's one thing I could never imagine though and that's what the guy I married would look like.

I knew the kind of man he would be, but never his look.

He would have the softest heart, yet be one of the strongest people I know and he would accept me, differences and all. He would want to make me his entire world in the same way that I would make him mine. A strong sense of self and protectiveness previously unseen in anyone before him, he would be my dream come true.

Ryan is all of those things and as I stand in this dress shop, looking for the right dress, hoping that the way I see it in my mind can actually be recreated in fabric, I find myself amazed at just how close to my childhood fantasies I've come. Some of the details are different, but the things that really matter are all there. I have Ryan and god willing I would have my perfect dress and be able to marry in the perfect church.

I'm sure I should be more affected by the fact that I don't have someone to walk me down the aisle, but I'm not. My dad made a choice all those years ago and even if he did magically come back now, I'm not entirely sure I would want him to be the one to walk with me as I face what looks to be a beautiful future.

I know who it should be and as hard as I've been trying not to focus on it, it's back again, hitting me square between the eyes. The person that should be with me the day I marry Ryan, is Gabriel, but the reality is, he won't be able to do that or anything ever again. Even with as much as I love Michael, he could never do what Gabriel was able to and the fact that he won't be there with me on my special day just hurts.

There was a time not all that long ago where I found him to be the most infuriating, annoying, downright pain in the ass angel ever created and now it's the complete opposite and it has nothing to do with what he did for us.

Gabriel sacrificed himself and it wasn't done for the greater good the way most would expect. No, he did it in an effort to make sure that the love between me and Ryan lives on, despite Lucifer's attempts to end it and us. He looked at a situation where there was no positive outcome and had taken it upon himself to make it happen and there's nothing I can do or say to adequately explain just what it means to me.

Not only did he have me remove the light inside of him, leading to his untimely death, but in doing so, he did something for us that's irreversible. The bond that existed between us, lives on through Ryan now. In his love for me and also hope for a brighter future for the planet he'd been sworn to protect, he gave himself completely over and in the end, saved us all.

So instead of having my beloved be the one to walk me down the aisle, it will instead be me taking the walk alone.

I should be happy with the gift I've been given, but I'm not. At least not in the way everyone wants me to be. I know I'm not dealing with everything right. The others have already begun moving on from it, yet I seem to be completely stuck. I can't move forward while it still feels like the best parts of me are missing. For months, Gabriel had been the one to calm me, talk me through the craziness happening inside my head and most of all, reminding me exactly who I am. Now he's gone and no amount of prayer can bring him back.

I keep going because it's what's expected of me, but in the quiet moments, like right now in this dress shop, I miss him and with each breath I take and exhale, the hole in my heart seems to rip apart even more. I foolishly let myself believe somewhere along the way that I didn't need him, but I was wrong. I would always need him, even when it wasn't in the cards to have him anymore.

Going ahead with this wedding is important to me because this is the one way I can honor the gift Gabriel gave me that day and as much as I want to say that I find strength in it, I can't. He isn't the only one I'm missing. He isn't the only one that my heart can't seem to let go of and the knowledge of that only brings more pain because I'm letting Gabriel down.

No matter how hard I try, I can't deny it anymore.

I miss Lucifer.

Chapter Three

Michael

There he goes again. He is praying, but much like all of the other times over the last three months, it will remain unanswered.

I know that it is not the way that we are supposed to operate as it pertains to the humans, but what the majority of the world does not seem to realize is that we have lost one of our own and for a lot of us, the sting of that has not worn off. Until such time as it does, any prayer sent up urgently, the way Ryan's is now, will not be answered and remain in a growing list that will be seen to at a later date.

If such a date even exists.

The only one that is seemingly unaffected by Gabriel's passing seems to be Father. I do believe that he feels of course, but because of his wealth of knowledge as it pertains to not only the undertaking, but existence in general, he has dealt with his feelings before the rest of us here in Heaven have had the chance to. The one time I broached the subject with him, shortly after coming home after the fight, he explained it to me.

Gabriel has not been the only casualty Heaven has felt over time, though to me it seems to be one of greater importance. Even though he had given me an adequate explanation for his ability to move on, I am just not sure I am buying it. Even the humans mourned their children that were taken too soon, right up until their very last breath, so why was Father so easily moving on?

*****

"Father, there is something that is most troubling to me."

"What is it, my son?"

"We have been home from the fight for almost two weeks now and while the rest of us seem to be completely destroyed with the level of grief we feel, you seem most unaffected."

"There is an easy explanation for that, if only you allow yourself to look at the bigger picture."

"Is this where you tell me that I need to get over Gabriel's passing and instead focus on the fact that in his death we were also able to eliminate the problem of our fallen brother?"

"It has nothing at all to do with Lucifer. Michael, I am aware of your feelings toward me where he is concerned and that you are still untrusting in terms of my true motivations, but I assure you, he is the least of my concerns at this point."

"Then what is the bigger picture?"

"I have known for a very long time that things would take place in this manner."

"He was always meant to sacrifice himself?"

"No, that was not always his path. The truth of the matter is, Gabriel, in his final days seemed to realize something that I was under the impression only I knew. If he had not perished in that church then it was to be Ryan. I learned of his sacrifice a few short hours before he followed through on it and have been able to handle my emotions regarding it since."

"You never thought to tell us? That we might want to know what our brother was planning?"

"No, because if I had done that then things would not have happened the way in which they did and not only would have Ryan been a casualty of war, but so would you and your remaining brothers. Gabriel shifted the original plan and in doing so, gave us a much better ending."

I am most confused by what he is telling me now. With the way he is making it sound, it is as if we were supposed to lose against Lucifer during the undertaking Father had set in motion. I cannot even begin to understand how that is possible.

22

"We would not have lost, but we would have been severely wounded, Michael. Serenity would have been the one to finish Lucifer, as she was always meant to, but we would have lost Ryan in the fight. That is all that you need to know."

"So we are just supposed to take that, accept it and move on, even though we are now without our brother?"

"You must allow yourself the time to grieve, Michael. I would never dream of taking that away from you. Despite what you believe, I still do feel the loss of Gabriel every second that we are without him. I have just learned to manage it. In time, you will reach that point as well."

I don't ever want to reach a point where I do not feel the loss of my brother. Gabriel, for all of his doubts and perceived failings had been so much more than just a brother to me during the time spent together, both with the humans and against Lucifer. There would never be a moment where I would not feel the weight of the loss heavy on my heart.

"It might be that easy for you, given that you knew everything going in and adapted to it, but I can tell you that it will never be that way for me. I will never be alright with losing him and you shouldn't be either."

*****

What I said to Father had been true. Even now, with all of the time that has passed, the heaviness on my heart has not ceased. It is still as heavy as the moment that Serenity stood before me, informing me of his demise and unlike what my father believes, it is not lessening with time passage.

It is no secret that Gabriel has always been the more emotional of the brothers, feeling more for the people in his charge and taking it all on when things did not go according to plan. He is the one that questioned every move made in an effort to not only understand it, but to make sure that it was the right direction to take. He had been called a hindrance on more than one occasion by Raphael and Uriel, who both found his way of being to mirror that of Lucifer and put distance between them because of it.

That is something that he most definitely was not. He may have thought like Lucifer during our time in Heaven, but that is where the similarities end. After working so closely with him as we guarded over his beloved Serenity, I came to learn that he was so much more than any of us ever really gave him credit for.

Gabriel is plain and simply the brother that you want to have around, always. Life without him is just something that is not possible, even if I am living without him now.

One believes that when you die, you go up or down, that there is no in between or even that sometimes you pass away and cease to exist. The reality is, there are multiple options and the last one is the one Gabriel faced the minute he gave himself up.

When Ryan died, he would not cease to exist the way my brother had or at least the half demon I believed him to be, wouldn't have. He would have died and immediately gone to Purgatory. Gabriel did not have that option. As an angel and one of the highest orders, upon his death he would cease to exist. Where our brethren that ventured into Hell remained there after their torturous deaths, meeting their end in the darkest place imaginable, Gabriel had given up his light and just vanished.

How badly I wish that this was just another case of a being of our nature being dragged into Hell, because then I could just formulate a plan of action and head down to save him. As it is now, there is no plan I can make to bring him back and it breaks my heart. Even as I stand here thinking about it, I can hear him calling me names because there had been a time where I didn't even believe I had a heart, much less something that made me feel. How I long to have him here with me to actually do as I imagine him.

There is another reason that I cannot answer Ryan's call and it has everything to do with Gabriel, his passing and what all of this means moving forward. In giving his light over to Ryan, he had not only given his own life away, but wiped Ryan of the darkness that lived wild inside of him. He purified him. As much as I like Ryan and see the potential for greatness in him, I just cannot accept him as a new brother. The Gabriel substitute.

Until I can get over that, I cannot be the one to answer his call. As pure an angel as the man is, now that he has Gabriel's light flowing through him, he is still very much human, which means he still has no access here unless someone like me gives it to him. If he really wants his prayer answered that bad, it will have to come from Father or not at all.

I have nothing left in me to give anymore.

Serenity

I'm tired of feeling so broken.

I swear, no matter how many steps forward I seem to take in my life, I always seem to end up coming back around and taking twice as many back. It's a sick cycle. It's one that unless I find a way to get a grip on it, will be the end of me. Take away the fact that I'm a ball of energy made of Heaven that got thrown into a human body and I'm supposed to be super strong and all you're left with is the broken mess that's left.

This all started when my dad walked out on us. That is my first experience with being completely torn apart. After years of trying to handle that, especially at the age I'd been when it happened, I finally thought I got ahead of it. I came to terms with the fact that he left even though at the same time I adopted the idea that everyone leaves. I just continued moving forward, never giving myself the chance to look back and it's served me well. Time really does heal when it's out of sight, out of mind.

That's what I thought anyway, until Graham went missing. When that happened, it all seemed to come back around, reminding me how fragile I am when it comes to the people and events in my life. Even knowing what I am and what I would mean to the world couldn't stop it. It ran me over like a freight train and even though time has passed since, its effects are long lasting. When we got him back, it healed the brokenness in my heart. I no longer felt empty, instead feeling alive again, even though everything that happened after that left something to be desired.

Flash forward to now and it's like Graham and my dad all over again. I'm torn apart inside and with each passing day, going through the motions, it makes itself more apparent. There really is no hiding it. Everyone knows what I'm going through and I know they are doing everything they can think of to help me, but no one really gets it.

All I know is that I'm really sick of feeling this way. I thought when everything ended that day in Green Haven, I would be able to move on, finally getting the chance to celebrate the happier moments that were to come and not the life and death situations I spent the last year and a half dealing with. Turns out that what I believed to be true before is still very much in effect.

I'm not allowed to be happy.

There always has to be something that comes along and turns my world upside down right around the time that things should be looking up. Gabriel's sacrifice and Lucifer's demise, added to everything else, remind me constantly that for whatever reason, my life is not destined to remain in a shelter of happiness.

I have bright spots of course. I'm not completely devoid of things in life that truly make me happy. Ryan, Emma and Graham are three very real and big things, but even knowing I have them, I can't bring myself to embrace them, not entirely. Which is what brings me to where I am and what I'm about to do.

I haven't seen her in well over a year, but if I want to begin to heal and be the person I know Gabriel wants me to be, than I need to start here. It all starts here really because just like my dad leaving and Graham going missing, she also played a pretty big part in the brokenness inside me and it's time I deal with it.

My mom really wasn't that bad of a parent, despite everything she put me through over the years. She tried. It couldn't have been all that easy having a daughter that talked to spirits and had an aversion to hospitals. She made the best of it, in the only way she could, but out of everything that I've gone through with the angels, my human friends, Lucifer and Ryan, she still played the biggest part in breaking me.

I'm not even sure what I'm doing here really other then needing to see her, explaining to her what putting me in the center all those years ago did to me and making her finally see what her actions caused. I want to be the strong person that Gabriel always told me I was and I think it starts here. It can't make anything worse.

I want to think about something other than what's going to happen when she opens the door, so while I stand here on her doorstep, I focus on the one non depressing thought that crosses my mind with everything I'm seeing. The minute I do, a smile creeps across my face and I know I've done what I set out to do and I have only one person to thank for it.

Ryan. My boyfriend, fiancé and husband. I guess that means I've got three people to thank. Well, a whole lot more since the people I'm picturing are the hockey players that caught us making out in the penalty box months before.

Before everything went to shit.

Well, so much for that memory.

The door opens and I come face to face with the very person I'm here to see. The reality slams back into me at full speed and there's a second where all I want to do is turn and run up the driveway, as far away as I can possibly get from her.

"Serenity!" she cries. "What are you doing here?"

"Something's happened and I know it's weird, me showing up like this, but I really need to talk to you."

When I went over what would happen when she opened the door, that is definitely not what I planned on saying, but there's no going back now.

"Well come on in, you'll catch your death standing out there like that."

You have no idea. I think as I follow her inside, following her into the living room after taking off my snow covered boots. The urge to run still high as we both go through the motions of making ourselves comfortable, but I don't do it. I'm not all that strong right now, but I still have enough in me to get through this.

"So what is it that you want to talk to me about?"

"Why did you put me in the center?" I ask, getting right to the point. "I know I was different, but why couldn't you just accept me for my differences instead of trying to fix what only you thought was broken?"

There's this part of me that as I wait for her to answer wonders if the answer she's going to give will be truthful or not. Rachel Richards has always been the queen of evading questions or giving answers she thinks everyone else wants to hear and I'm really hoping that isn't the way it happens now. I need her to be honest with me because it's the only real way I can begin to move on and heal, not only for me, but for Ryan too. He needs and deserves to have the best wife possible and I'm determined to give it to him, even if it hurts in the process.

"That's not an easy question to answer."

"I don't care if it's easy, Mom. I just want the truth."

I can tell by the look on her face that she isn't going to lie to me. Even if I didn't have the abilities that I do, it would be obvious. She's been lying to me and doing her classic evade for the last twenty-one years. The time for evading and running is over, for both of us.

"When your father left, I needed someone to blame and you became that person. It was wrong of me and there isn't a day that goes by that I don't regret the way I treated you. I'm just not sure at this point there is anything that can be done to fix it."

Yep. She's definitely telling me the truth. Not only can I see it in her mind, the self hatred she has for herself, but it's evident in her body language. When she answered the door, she had been relaxed and bright and now before my very eyes, she is tense and sad. Her body is hunched and her eyes planted on the floor. I know that expression better than anyone, wearing it myself frequently over the years, which means I know exactly what it means now.

"That day in the funeral home with your grandmother, gosh, you gave me all the ammunition I needed. It was like in doing it; I was free to hate you."

"Why?"

"It wasn't the first time I've heard it. It's the first time that you had ever said anything like it, but there was a person before you that did it and once it happened with you, it was proof that you really were his daughter. The loathing just grew at that point."

I didn't want to be affected by her words, but I was. They cut me deep, not only because she was being completely truthful, but because she'd given information that I never knew before. Not only did I have this ability that my grandmother liked to call a gift, but I wasn't the only one. Dad had it too and my mom kept it from me, choosing instead to believe me to be a freak and try and get me fixed.

"Your father started talking to nothing about a year before you were born. The first few times it happened, I blew it off and assumed I was hearing things or that he was on the phone. It wasn't unheard of, since for a long time, he was glued to it, but it got to a point where I couldn't make excuses for it anymore."

"So what did you do?"

"We talked about it. He couldn't explain it to me anymore than you could, even though you sure tried. He eventually

29

checked himself into a clinic, believing himself to be crazy. The same way I always thought you were. If he thought he was, it must be a genetic thing and you had been exposed as well."

Getting answers to things should have made me feel better, but all it did was lead to even more questions and this time I wouldn't walk away before getting the answers. I deserved to know.

"Where is he and don't tell me that he just took off because I'll know it's a lie."

"Why do you want to know all of this now? Serenity, as much as I want to work through our issues, what does knowing this do for either one of us, other than bringing up shit better left buried?"

She gave me answers just in the questions. For years I believed that my father had taken off and left us, but with the way she's trying to avoid answering the question, instead choosing to ask a bunch of her own in an effort to change the subject, I got all the answers I needed.

"He didn't take off, did he?"

She shook her head and I exhaled the breath I'd been holding. Son of a bitch. Everything I have ever known and believed is again being proven wrong. Yet another person in my life lied to me.

"Where is he?"

Green Haven Psychiatric Hospital. He's been there since the day after your third birthday."

There's that damn town again. No matter how much I want to escape it and the memories that my time there brings to the surface, it looks like I never will. We didn't move to Green Haven until I was sixteen, yet somehow my father checked himself into the hospital there thirteen years beforehand.

I thought I could do this, I really did, but the more she tells me the more I can feel my mind reaching the overload point. I'm angry with her, yet understanding because she not only had one person in her life that talked to voices, but two. I'm happy I know about my father yet sad because she took the choice of knowing him and what she perceived to be his illness away from me. I don't know what to do anymore and it's only made worse when she speaks again.

"I'm sorry, Serenity. Sorry for not telling you about your father and more than that, I'm sorry for treating you like you were the reason for it, when you were far from that. You deserve better than I gave you."

She's right about that. I did deserve better, but the way I felt about it when I showed up here today, I still feel now. She'd done the best she could with the information she was given. Other then two and a half years spent in a facility much like the one my father is also in, I still got to live my life, even if it was a far more depressing one then it could have been.

"It's okay, Mom. You did the best you could."

"You saying that just shows that I didn't. You turned into the person you are now because of you and you alone. I had nothing to do with it."

If only she knew how wrong she is. I turned out the way I am, not because of something I managed on my own. I did it because of the people I surrounded myself with and because of who I really am. I want to be able to tell her that, but I can't. It's going to have to remain a secret, because even if I did want to tell her everything, I know she won't understand it and it would damage everything that is being rebuilt from my visit today.

She can never know who I really am, which means I need to get on with the other reason I showed up today. It's the only way to turn this around before the heaviness pulls me under completely.

"There's actually another reason I'm here and I'm hoping that despite moving twice, that you'll be able to help me."

"If it's got something to do with any of your stuff, you know I didn't throw anything away. I figured that would be your call when you were ready. What do you need?"

"Do you still have that pink dress from the dance with Graham?"

Michael

It was only a matter of time before Father caught on to what I have been doing where Serenity and Ryan are concerned. As I stand before him, the scowl on his face burning a hole straight into my very soul, I realize just what I've been doing locking myself away and it leaves me unsettled.

I am acting no better than the fallen angel we put an end to all those months ago. I am no better than Lucifer.

"Michael, you believe me to have called for you in order to lay blame at your feet or to berate you for that which you have done in recent weeks and that is not the case at all. You, much like your brother before you, must let go of the dark place you find yourself in and focus solely on what needs to happen next."

"What is it you believe needs to happen, Father?"

"You need to make your way down to Ryan and Serenity and make your presence known."

"What is to be accomplished doing that?"

"You will begin to heal."

I am unsure how spending time with the humans is supposed to help me heal from the hole that is paramount in my heart, but where I would have walked away before at the mere mention of it, now I am willing to at least hear him out.

"I am of the belief that in being here, surrounded by the other angels and your brothers that you are not adequately getting a handle on what Gabriel's passing has done to you. Seeing them as they are, happily moving about now that Lucifer has been defeated adds to the ache. I can feel it from here."

"You would not be wrong, but what do you suggest I do about it?"

"Ryan and Serenity are grieving much the way you are, my son. I do believe that right now, you need them. That is evident in the amount of calls Ryan alone has made to you, not to mention the few from Serenity herself. In order to come to terms with what has happened, for all of our sakes, I think that you need to give yourself the proper chance to mourn by joining them on Earth."

"You want to banish me to time on the planet because you believe it will help me? You know that standing by your side and overseeing things has always been what brings me the greatest amount of joy. Doing this feels like a punishment, Father and I do believe I have had enough of those."

"Do not look at it that way, Michael. This is the farthest thing from a punishment that I can think of. I know that you do not enjoy surrounding yourself with the human way of life, even though you still manage to do as I ask and continue to care for them from a distance, but in this regard I do believe you need to experience Gabriel's loss as a human would."

I can't agree with this. His suggestion might have merit, but it did not mean I had to like and follow it. We have reached a point in our relationship now where even Father knows not to push his way of thinking on me because I am not afraid to go my own way. I want nothing more than to do that very thing now, but something is in my way, preventing it.

Gabriel.

He spent large amounts of his existence being judged for being the one that felt more than the rest of us. For showing his emotions to the point where he wore them on his sleeve the way humans describe. It was never a weakness, at least not for him. It made him who he is and it is the way he was that I loved most about him, even when he found himself riddled with doubt.

Gabriel would want me to do this. If the roles were reversed he would do it in an effort to heal from my loss. So as much as I want to turn away from this suggestion, remain in Heaven, blocking out all reminders of the brother I lost, I could not do it. I would bend to my father's suggestion because in doing so, I would be doing what Gabriel wanted most.

For me to be right back where I belong, surrounded by my family, even if it is the human one.

"You will do as I suggest? Am I reading you correctly, my son?"

"You are, Father. While I do not believe that it will help, I realize that it cannot do any harm either. If being with Serenity and Ryan is where you believe I need to be, then it is where I shall be."

"Then I do believe you know what you need to do next."

He's right. I do know what needs to be done. The time for shying away from the world around me, running from the reality of the situation, is over. It is time to embrace everything again, much the way I would have if Gabriel had been here standing beside me.

It is time to answer Ryan's call.

Chapter Four

Ryan

There's one thing that still makes no sense to me and no matter how much I call to Michael in an effort to get answers, the confusion continues.

When the angels came to me in Serenity's dorm room and told me that my true calling was to end Lucifer and that I'm really pure angel, I was supposed to be sent back to Heaven. Yet I'm still here in my human existence and it looks like there are no plans to change it.

It might be another side effect of what Gabriel did for me, but I can't help wondering if there's more to it. If maybe Lucifer isn't dead, or banished the way we all assume him to be and still out there biding his time until we come face to face again. That can really be the only explanation for why I'm not living out the remainder of my life among the clouds.

Going down that road does nothing for me. I hate thinking like that because I watched as I slammed the blade in him. I saw his essence drain from the vessel until it disappeared into the ground of the church. If he somehow survived that, then I'm pretty sure no one would ever beat him. I also hate thinking about it because when I do, Serenity can sense the emotions it brings and we start arguing. With the wedding coming up so fast, the last thing I want to be doing with her is arguing. The intent is to get her down the aisle, not scaring her off.

Then there's what happened to my eyes. I know that's because of Gabriel. Whatever he did took away the demonic part of me and while I'm thankful for it, it feels weird not having it there. Looking in the mirror and seeing the clear blue looking back at me makes me think that I'm seeing someone else. It's weird. I'm pretty much avoiding mirrors as much as possible since it happened because I honestly can't come to terms with it. Everything changed that day, for everyone, but no one more than me. I feel like a completely different person and I'm not sure what to do with it.

Serenity had been the one to bring it up to me in the church, the change in my eyes, but sometime between explaining what happened with Gabriel to Michael and even before that, I'd put it out of my mind. When we made our way back to my room that night, both of us covered in blood, Lucifer's and our own, deciding to take a shower together, it's when it hit me again. She'd understood of course and had even gotten me to see her side of things, but I still can't help feeling that accepting Gabriel's gift, I've allowed myself to become someone else entirely.

*****

"I hope it's okay, I just grabbed the first couple of things I saw." She says, handing me the jeans and t-shirt, closing the door behind her.

"It's fine. Anything is better then what I'm wearing now. I'm not sure how much longer I can look at it..."

Of course I mean the rip in my shirt and the blood that stains all the way through. A feeling she knows all too well given that she mirrors me, my blood covering the outside of her clothes, complete with rips in exactly the same spots.

My blood is all over us.

When did this become my life?

"I know, Ry, so we're not gonna think about it or look at it anymore. Come here." She says, motioning with her hand and as I follow her instruction she places both of her hands on the shirt

and begins pulling up until it's off and discarded on the floor behind us.

I want to do the same for her, but I know with the way my nerves are and the buttons on her shirt that I won't get it off her fast enough.

There isn't a time when looking at Serenity, let alone touching her, doesn't spark a primal reaction in me, but now, it's the last thing on my mind. I just want to clean off the blood and the pain of everything we just went through.

Looking away from her and coming face to face with my own reflection in the mirror, I see it. My eyes.

"Holy shit..."

"What?" she asks after removing her own shirt and pants, standing beautiful as ever in front of me in only her bra and panties, her face a mask of confusion.

"Please tell me you can see this."

"I will, if you tell me what you mean." She answers, coming to rest where I'm standing over the sink, leaning in just as I am, both of our faces staring at our reflections in the mirror.

"My eyes. The black lining, it's gone."

"I know, Ry. It's been that way for awhile now."

"How long?" I ask, turning to face her. "Just how long have I been walking around without it?"

"Since Gabe..."

When I don't say anything, she speaks again, this time her tone softer than before.

"Gabriel did more than save you, Ryan. He took the darkness away."

"Yeah, I see that..."

"How does it make you feel?"

I'm not entirely sure how to answer that. For the last year of my life I wanted nothing more than to be rid of the darkness that I was damned with, but now that it's gone, it's like I miss it because I feel empty. The exact same way I felt when Serenity was taken from me.

"Wrong," I say continuing before she can question it. "It just makes me feel wrong. I shouldn't even be here right now."

She places her hand on my shoulder, sympathizing with my answer and I immediately grab her and pull her into my arms, needing more than ever to feel her body connected to mine in whatever way possible.

"He did the wrong thing didn't he, Ser? Saving me. I mean it was wrong. He saved the wrong person."

"What is that supposed to mean?" she asks, moving her body even closer into mine instead of away the way I'd been expecting. "How could saving you be wrong?"

"It's wrong because he was your guardian. He should have been more concerned with you. Not some useless half demon."

Her body tenses under my fingers and I know I hit a nerve. In demeaning myself, I upset her.

"I hate what Gabriel did because it took him away from us, but that is the only thing I hate about it. Wanting to do right by you and heal you, especially with the whole demon thing, I can't hate him for that. Your eyes might have changed, but you haven't, Ry and Gabriel knew that."

"You should be standing with him right now, you know? Not me. You both should have let me die."

"I am standing with him..." is her whispered reply.

"What?"

"I said, I am standing with him. The very best parts of him are now a part of you Ryan, right where they belong. You're telling me that you can't see that? There is no one alive more deserving of Gabriel's light than you."

*****

Deserving of his light or not, I wasn't dealing with it well. I no longer miss that part of myself, but I still can't get used to the fact that the person I've been for the last twenty one years is gone, in favor of this supposed new and improved version.

Everything Serenity said made sense though, so I was going to deal with it, even if it was only for her and the way she sees me.

She should be back anytime now. When she left earlier to run errands, she made a promise that she would be back with more than enough time for our date. Shaking off the residual dark thoughts, I again step in front of the mirror, this time determined to see everything the way that she does. It's the only way we're both going to be able to move forward. If I want my Serenity back, then the first step to getting that would be to accept the Ryan I am now. I have to let that other part of me go.

This time as I stand here, her words from a week ago come across my mind and I finally allow myself to smile. Yes, it was definitely time that I start seeing things the way that she does. Anything less is unacceptable.

*****

"You wanna know a secret?"

"I didn't think we had secrets, Ser. You wound me." I smile before throwing my fist into my chest, over my heart that is beating manically. The same way it always does whenever she's anywhere near me.

"Very funny, smartass! I meant a secret, as in something you didn't know before that I think I'm finally ready to tell you."

Truth be told, I want to know every single thought that crosses her mind, every emotion she has ever felt, good or bad, every single part of her that up until this very moment I haven't been privy to. This is one of the times I wish she would just use her abilities and read my mind, so she could have her answer that much quicker.

"Do you remember the day you showed up in Psych?"

"Vividly, pretty girl, but what about it?"

I'm not exactly proud of those early moments when we first met, so I'm hoping that she's going to bring up a good secret from that time and not something that really did have the potential to wound me.

"You told me your name and held out your hand for me to shake and I swear I stopped breathing for a few minutes. I mean full on loss of breath. Add that to my heart stopping and I'm surprised I'm even here cuddled up like this. I was such a goner."

"Really?" I ask, realizing that this actually is a secret, since the way she looked at me that day didn't speak to any of what she just said. In fact I was pretty sure she loathed me on sight. "That's not the way I remember it at all."

"Well, how do remember it?"

"You looked scared to death at first and then after that, you looked almost annoyed. Like my being there was a pain in the ass."

"The only pain in the ass that day was me, believe me. I saw your eyes and then these," she says running her fingers over both rings in my lips. "And I was pretty much done. You were so freaking beautiful."

"You were? Pretty girl, you're killing me over here."

Slapping me lightly on the arm she leans up, softly kissing my lips and I'm reminded again just how much I love this woman. Not about how fast it moved, or what we were actually supposed to mean to one another, only what we meant now.

I am the luckiest guy in the world.

"You know how beautiful you are; don't even try to deny it."

"So you like the snake bites, huh?"

She lifts her hand to slap me again and I back away, faking a flinch before laughing and bringing myself closer again, this time kissing her nose and watching as she lowers her hand, smile planted firmly across her face.

"Yes, but I loved your eyes more. They were blue, yet that day looked almost cloudy white. It was trippy."

Well that's a word I've never heard about my eyes, but it's definitely something I like hearing. If my wife thinks my eyes are trippy, I'm more than okay with that. I'm over the moon.

"Well these trippy eyes are all yours, pretty girl. For as long as you want them."

"So, forever works for you?"

*****

Knowing how she's been feeling lately and the load she's carrying, I focus on moments like that a lot. I want to remember the moments where she seems most happy because the more time that passes, they seem almost few and far between.

That is what this date night is about. I want to get dressed up, even though I hate having anything to do with a suit and tie and I want us to experience a night together. One where it's just us and not the other things we've been carrying around for far too long. I want to get back to just being the guy that fell in love with a girl.

She knows I love her, but tonight isn't about that. No, it's about something much stronger and something that I haven't had the chance to make her feel since everything happened three months ago.

It's time to make her feel wanted.

Michael

I know that now is probably not the best time to be popping in on the boy. He had sent the prayer up numerous times over the last few days and in my grief stricken haze, I hadn't even given him any indication of hearing it. I don't think wasting any more time is wise either, which brings me to where I stand now. I am in his room, waiting for him to return from his position in the communal bathroom. Once he returns, I can finally get back to what I should have been doing all along.

Looking after my family.

As I wait, I do as I have done so many times before and recall the last conversation I had with Father. It was then that he gave me some information he thought I finally deserved to know and even though I feel better knowing it, I can't help but feel betrayed that it had taken him as long as it did to lay it at my feet.

*****

"Before you go, there is something that I believe you should be made aware of."

"It is regarding the human known as Serenity's father."

Serenity's father. The man that walked out on her in early childhood and who had made no attempt to see her in the years since. Just what is it that Father needs to tell me as it pertained to this man?

"As we did with Ryan, it would appear as though we did the same with Gregory. He is human, but not in the traditional way. He is most like Graham Hudson, except he has abilities that for a great deal of time went ignored by me."

So another man is paying for Heaven's mistake? How many more of these would we find along the way? There could be no greater screw up then that of Ryan and now it appears as though we have done much the same with our very own lights, father.

"How long have you known of this?"

"For quite some time my son. I brought it to Gabriel's attention before the final battle and it was going to be after that when we dealt with it."

"So because Gabriel is no longer here, you are finally bringing it to my attention?"

"That is not what this is about, Michael. It is time to handle the situation. Whether it is you or Gabriel, it still needs a resolution."

"Does Serenity know?"

42

"Her mother has just recently told her. In an effort to get answers, Serenity thought it wise to visit her mother and in doing so learned of it."

"That's why you want me to go down there again, isn't it? You never do anything without a reason behind it and I am beginning to sense that me handling Gabriel's loss in a more productive manner is not a strong enough reason. It is this isn't it?"

He nods and for the second time in as many months, I turn away from him, unable to even stomach looking at the man that I call Father anymore. Everything that I had at one time believed as it pertained to him, is quickly turning out to be a lie and I'm left feeling lost. Is there anything he has been entirely truthful with me about since I joined him? Or has it all just been one lie after another?

"I did not lie to you, Michael. I merely did not inform you of the information that I learned. It was during the period at which you had lost faith in me and as such, Gabriel was told in your place."

"Well maybe now you see the very reason why I lost faith in you to begin with. I will handle this as it is a heavenly screw up, but Father, from now on, you are on your own."

*****

"Some things never change huh, Mike?"

In taking my mind down memory lane, I had forgotten where I am. At the sound of my name from across the room, the reality is slammed back into me. I am here to make amends.

"I am sorry that it took me so long to come, but I am here now."

"What are you talking about?"

"You called for me, or rather, you called for Heavenly guidance. Your call did not go unnoticed, I assure you, but as I am also sure you are aware, we are under a great deal of pressure at present."

His eyes lower and he frowns before my very eyes, telling me all that I need to know. He did very well understand what is going on in Heaven though he didn't want to be the one to bring it up.

"How is everyone handling it?" he asks, his voice a whisper.

"We are doing the best we can, but his loss is felt deeply and it may never be the same again. Gabriel, whether they want to admit it to themselves or not, was the heart of us all and without him, it seems as though all we can do is drift."

It wasn't all of Heaven that felt this way of course, I was speaking only for myself, but I knew in telling him this, he would understand. He had felt loss like this before even though eventually his had been brought back to him. Something Gabriel would never be.

"I know that it's not the same, but that's actually what I was praying to you about. I think the drifting is happening here too and I'm worried about it."

"I assume we are not speaking about you, but of your beloved?"

His reaction to hearing Serenity referred to as his beloved did not go unnoticed. His body goes rigid and his brow furrowed. It is obvious that referring to her in this way is going to take some getting used to. It did not make it any less true, but until such time as he could get a handle on it himself, I would refrain from using it.

"Yeah, this is about Serenity."

"What have you witnessed that has you concerned about her well being?"

"She seems to be moving from one moment to the next, robotically, or as you said, drifting. The time we've spent talking about Gabriel and about how she feels about Lucifer's death, it doesn't seem to change anything. I'm afraid that if something doesn't change soon, we're going to lose her—again."

"Lose her how?"

"She will go inside herself and this time, no matter how hard we fight to bring her out of it, we won't be able to. She's not the same girl that she was before that night in the church, Michael."

"How does she react as it pertains to you?"

"She's the same as always. It's in everything else that she shows how broken by all of this she really is. I don't question her feelings for me. I just want her to be okay and she's not okay, even if she lies and tries to make people believe she is."

"I am afraid that there is nothing that I can do in that regard, Ryan. I would like nothing more than to answer this prayer, but Serenity needs to come to terms with all of this in her own way. Just the same as I need to do as it pertains to Gabriel's passing."

"I know you can't solve it Mike."

"Then why did you call me?" I ask, genuinely confused to why I am here if not to answer his urgent prayer.

"I prayed for her to be her old self again yes, but I also prayed because I didn't want to handle it all on my own anymore. I wanted someone to talk to and just like you've done before, here you are. So thank you."

"You do not owe me a thank you as I have not done anything of real consequence. I feel that my being here now with the information I have recently come to learn is only going to cause even more pain, something none of us need more of."

Now it is his turn to be confused and I do not blame him. Just once I would love to be able to pop in on the young man and not have to talk to him about issues that cause pain, whether they're Lucifer related or personal in nature. If my fallen brother is long gone the way he appeared, then why aren't any of us happier about it?

"What do you mean by that?"

45

"I have information that pertains to Serenity's father and it is nothing good."

"Did something happen to him?"

I nod and again try to shake away the betrayal that still runs hot at what Father has done in keeping it from us.

"He's been locked away in a psychiatric hospital since the day Serenity turned three. The man didn't disappear as she has been led to believe. He has been hidden away for being just as his daughter is. He is another one that we have let slip through the cracks."

"Does she know?"

"She does, though she learned of it right around the same time as I did. While she is able to push it out of her mind in an effort to move forward with the date night you came up with, the sting of it is still there and I am afraid that when she sees me and learns everything, she may turn away even more then you say she already has."

"Learns what exactly?"

"How long Father and Gabriel knew and kept it from her."

No more words need to be spoken because as the gravity of what I am saying sinks into the man before me, it is evident that he knows just as I do that when Serenity found out Gabriel had known and not told her, we would have to face the fallout and just what that could mean.

We could be faced with losing Serenity forever.

Chapter Five

Serenity

After asking my mother about the dress I'd worn the night of the dance and learning it still fit, there were still memories attached to it so I decided it was time for a shopping trip. In order to move forward with Ryan the way I so desperately want to, I need to start over with everything, even the clothing I held onto over the years.

That dance with Graham though seemingly uneventful to any of the people that night and to the rest of the world now, was groundbreaking for me. Up until that point, I avoided all social outings, more comfortable staying in and lounging in sweat pants than getting dressed up and pretending to care what the rest of my classmates had to say, or rather what they wanted to whisper about me when they thought I wasn't listening. That night was my chance to step out of my comfort zone and step out I did.

Even standing in front of my mother's full length mirror, staring at my reflection, I can remember everything as if it happened yesterday. I can still remember the way I freaked out about my hair, wanting to look perfect for the boy next door. I remember the way my body started sweating the minute he wrapped his arm around me and walked me into the gym, never letting go for a second. The way it felt dancing with him and feeling as if I was the only girl in the room as his eyes never strayed from mine.

No, I couldn't wear this dress on my date with Ryan. This dress needed to be put away, just like the memories of a simpler time before everything imploded on me and even more than that, before the half demon with a heart of gold entered my world and turned it upside down in the best way.

After talking with my mom about it, she offered to take me shopping and even though I was still coming to terms with everything, I let her. I wanted this date with Ryan to be perfect, our first one without the threat of the end looming over us. There is no way it could go any less than perfect. I wouldn't allow it.

"Oh, Serenity! This one is absolutely stunning!" she calls from across the store and as I look up from the racks I've been standing in front of for the last ten minutes, seeing the dress she's holding delicately in her hands, I realize she just might be right.

Just like the dress I wore with Graham, its pink, only this dress is completely different in every other way. As I make my way over and really look at it I see that it's made of pure satin, it's long, just the way I like them or at least the way I like them when I have to wear them at all. It's got a halter neckline and the bodice cut away just slightly and the more I take it in, I realize the straps are thin yet are made of gems that even under my mother's fingertips seem to shine with the light. This is the dress. I don't need her to tell me or for the sales lady to come over and tell me just how lovely I'll look in it. I already know because I can see myself in it and also Ryan's face when he sees me walking toward him wearing it. There is no doubt, this is the dress. No more searching needed.

Ryan McGregor, prepare to have your heart stopped.

"This is the one, Mom. We don't need to look anymore."

I watch as she smiles and I can't help but think back to the last time we went dress shopping. The way she smiles at me now makes me long for a do over. I want to go back in time, knowing everything I know now and approach these moments with her differently. I want to see her smile at me this way again. It's the only way to erase the scowls of times past.

"Do we need to find you shoes to match?" she asks, bringing me out of my thoughts and back to the task at hand. Shoes, I already had those. Emma is the queen of shoe shopping and I had no doubt she had a pair that would go perfectly with this.

"No, the sheer amount of heels Emma owns should cover me that way for a very long time."

"Some things never change huh?"

"Not with Emma." I answer laughing. I didn't talk to my mom about Emma much, but in the times I did, it always had to do with shopping, the boys she told me about or something equally as shallow, so right now her statement couldn't be more true.

When did my life take this turn? Is it possible to be able to get what I've been missing all of these years just by opening myself up to it? Or is this destined to fall apart like everything else?

"Serenity, where did you go?"

"Huh?"

"You laughed about Emma and it's almost as if you completely spaced out. Is everything okay?"

Well she was right in her earlier statement. Some things never do change, especially with me. I still have the ability to space out when I find myself lost in thought and even my own mother is catching on to it.

"Yeah Mom, I'm fine. I was just thinking."

"About the boy you're going to wear this dress for?"

"Something like that, yeah." I answer back, almost too quickly. I hadn't been thinking about Ryan at all, but it beat explaining the alternative. I was still on shaky ground with her and letting her know what I'm really thinking might end up making a mess out of what was turning out to be a really good day so far, minus the earlier news.

"I know I don't have the right to ask this of you given everything that's happened between us, but do you ever think I might be able to meet him?"

A few days ago I would have known the answer to this question without hesitation. She would never come anywhere near Ryan because I didn't want him to be tainted by her the way I had been, but now my answer is different and I knew it beyond a shadow of a doubt.

"Yeah Mom, you'll get to meet him."

Again, she smiles and something strange happens inside of me. It warms me. For the first time in forever, I no longer hold any ill will towards my mom.

"Does he realize the treasure he's been given?"

"He does, but honestly, I'm the one that's been given a treasure."

Ryan is more than a treasure to me and no matter how many dresses I buy and dates I go on with him, it won't change. Ryan is my gift, my happiness, He is everything, all wrapped up into a neat little ball.

It's fitting for the little ball of light from Heaven that she falls in love with an angel.

Ryan

When Serenity went missing for those two months before we went in to save her, I spent a lot of time writing. A lot of it was just thoughts, things that I was feeling on the surface that I needed to get out before they threatened to turn me into something I never wanted to be again. Some of them sounded a hell of a lot like song lyrics, though I never did put music to any of it, so maybe they're just poems, either way, I spent a lot of time doing it. The words flowed easily almost as if, in closing my eyes and picturing her, the way I feel about her and the emotions she awakens in me, they wrote themselves.

When she walked into the restaurant, standing by the door and speaking to the maitre d, all of those words that had been so easy to come by before seemed to vanish into thin air. From the way her hair looked as it flowed down around her shoulders, to the dress she wore, I am just knocked on my ass in speechlessness.

When I told her earlier that I wanted her to dress up, wanting to take her somewhere special, I expected her to wear a dress, but not this dress. Wow, if I didn't already know who she is, I would be thanking God for sending me an angel right about now. There is no other being alive, angelic or otherwise that could compare to the dove making her way over to me now.

No doubt about it, I am the luckiest SOB in the world.

Standing up and moving over to where her chair lay empty, I pull it out just as she reaches me and as she takes a seat, allowing me to move her chair back in, I breathe in her scent. The familiar strawberry and vanilla of times past greets me and I can't help but inhale as much of it as possible. Just like there is no other person alive that can compare to her, there isn't a scent alive that can compare to that of Serenity McGregor.

My wife.

"Are you going to stand back there all night Ry, or are you gonna join me?" she asks, the grin on her face so big it reaches right up into her eyes as they begin to twinkle in the corner.

God I love this woman.

"Sorry, pretty girl. I just needed a minute there."

"Cat got your tongue?"

"More like woman took my breath away, but your answer works too."

As I take my seat, I get a full view of the blush as it travels its way across her cheeks until her entire face seems to be bathed in rosy red. It doesn't matter how many times I see it, it's always like the first time.

"You know I could say the same about you. I had no idea your wardrobe extended past hoodies and jeans."

"Very funny. I'll have you know I own a lot of different things."

"Sure you do, baby. You keep telling yourself that. Just remember, I've seen the inside of your closet and I'm a master at wading through bullshit."

Even in one of the fanciest restaurants in all of Stephenville, dressed the way we are, we still manage to keep ourselves grounded in the way we've always been with each other. It always comes back to the ease of humor before the heaviness of the feelings sets in. I can't help but hope that it stays this way forever. I always want moments like this with her, no matter what the location.

"You'll always have them Ryan. It's unacceptable not to."

She's been doing that a lot more lately, feeding off my emotions the way she used to, but this time using them to read my mind just enough to comment on the very thing I'm thinking. She still looks at the ability to read my mind as a flaw, but I see it differently. I enjoy it when she does it because where the words wouldn't always come out of my mouth the way I want, they sure sound perfect in my mind. It's my way of making sure she knows exactly how I feel.

"Why did you want to do this?" she asks, changing the subject.

"Do you remember the day I took you to the church and I had a couple reasons for it?"

"I remember every single thing about that day Ry, how could I not? It was one of the most beautiful days of my life."

"Well, the reason I wanted to do this is sort of like that."

"How so?"

"I've never actually dated before. You're my first in every way possible and from what I've seen with other people and then in movies, well, date nights seem normal."

"So you wanted to do something normal for a change?"

"Yeah, I guess I did. We've been through hell and back Serenity and somehow, for whatever reason, we're still standing and it's about time I treated the woman I love to a real date and not just one where we're hiding out in our rooms waiting for the apocalypse."

"Yeah, that pesky apocalypse, always ruining the fun." she answers with a grin which I can't help but return.

There was a point where I thought we'd never be able to sit back and make jokes about everything we'd been through. Yet here we are doing just that and it's the most natural thing in the world.

As I watch her take a sip of the water in front of her, I take her in. I know that everything we've been through is still paramount in her mind and that as much as she's here with me joking, she's also locked in her grief for Gabriel and Lucifer and trying to hide it from me. I don't want to turn the night around, considering how well it's going, but I do feel like I need to say something. Somehow let her know that she doesn't have to fake anything with me.

Before I can do it though, she lifts her eyes back up and I'm frozen in place. There is a knowing look in her eyes that means she's again reading me and even without saying a word she's letting me know that she gets it.

"Tonight is about us, Ry. Let's just forget everything else for awhile, alright?"

Answering her back with a look of my own, I smile before tapping the menu.

"Whatever the princess wants, she gets. So Princess Serenity, what dost thou want to partake in for dinner?"

Chapter Six

Michael

I am most unfamiliar with the feeling that runs through me. In actuality, I am most unfamiliar with anything that pertains to emotions or feelings because I am trained to be a warrior, not one born of empathy. There is only one brother that is familiar with these annoying sensations and he is the brother that is no longer with us.

If this were happening to Gabriel, he would know what to do and how to adapt, but sadly I am the one that has to deal with it and I am not fond of it in the slightest.

When Father came to me before my departure, I hoped that it would be something pertaining to his needing me in Heaven a little longer, but instead it was an information sharing meeting and one that now, as I stand back in Green Haven for what feels like the hundredth time, I am preparing to deal with, though I find myself conflicted.

There is an anger burning just under the surface and one that is solely directed at my father for what he kept, not only from me, but Serenity all of these years. Finding out mere minutes before leaving to embark on a trip of healing that the human father is very much alive and well and he had known about it all of this time, is just too much to take. It is made worse knowing that my deceased brother knew about it as well and had chosen to follow Father blindly in keeping it a secret.

I am disappointed in the both of them and having never experienced it in its full form before, I have no idea what to do with everything that swirls around within me. I am not only upset with them because they kept it from me, but also because for years Serenity blamed herself for the man disappearing. To find out now that he hadn't vanished at all and that both her beloved and his father had known about it the entire time is just unsettling. It is almost as if I can feel her betrayal as if it is my own.

That is what it all comes back to of course. I feel betrayed and given what I am already attempting to deal with coming back here, this is the last thing I want to feel. Now that there has finally been a level of peace reached, the last thing I want is to turn away from the very light that has guided me since the moment of my creation. That is exactly what I want to do though. I want to turn away from Father, from the light, all of it because much like Gabriel before me, I feel more than I should.

I long for the days when human emotions were spoken about between the brothers like fables, stories that you tell in moments of boredom in an effort to gain a laugh or two. I loathe feeling the very thing I spent years making fun of. It's not helping that as I feel these things, I can hear Gabriel's voice in my head calling me on my lie from months ago.

Green Haven Psychiatric Hospital. This is where I find myself now, about to come face to face with Gregory Richards. The very man that left her at a young age and been the first person to turn her entire world on its axis. I am here to see for myself if he does in fact hold the light within him and also to find out if Lucifer had done anything to the man or even learned of his existence at all.

Armed with the information that he hears voices of the dead, much like his daughter, calls for action. Father, while knowing of the man, had not checked in on him in years and left him to rot in the very human version of Hell. If he did hold the light inside him, he had been left behind and for that I felt that my father had let him down.

We all did.

I owe it to the man and even Serenity herself to get answers once and for all. I had been her guardian during her first two lifetimes and even though I didn't get to do the third, I felt an obligation with Gabriel no longer here, to make sure that she knew everything in this lifetime. It is the only real way all of us can move forward after everything we have been through. I just wish I didn't have to do it because of an omission on my father's part.

Were the Richards chosen because of Gregory's ability or was it really as random as Father led us all to believe?

Appearing before the man, content that he had been medicated enough not to remember much of the visit, I allow myself to take in his surroundings and also the way in which he appears. As higher beings, we are trained not to get emotionally involved in any situation, but the look of this man now as he sits in the wheelchair, his head dipped to the side, drool pooling in the corners of his mouth, that is exactly what I feel.

This man had been tossed aside and left to rot and it only made the betrayal I felt rise even more inside of me. Made of the light or not, this man deserved better than he had been given and even if it took me years to see it happen, I am determined to make up for it, or at least try to.

"Gregory—it is of grave importance that I speak with you. Do you think you can manage that in your current state?"

Lifting his head from its resting position, he turns his gaze upon me and nods his head once before opening his mouth to speak.

"I wondered when one of you would come."

"Who is it that you believe me to be?"

"You are an angel of course. Even with the darkness of the room, I can still see the bright light that surrounds you."

Where I expected to find the man unable to communicate, I am taken aback with how well versed he seems to be. His time in this place could not have been easy and it had surely worn him down until he was only a shell of his former self, yet he still managed to keep his wits about him. Maybe he is born of the light after all.

"I am here regarding your daughter."

"Serenity…"

The way his name falls from her lips in a whisper, his voice rising at the end, speaks of his feeling toward the woman known as Heaven's ball of light. Even with all of the time apart he still knows of her and thinks about her in a loving manner. At least that part of him had not been touched with the overload of medications the humans saw fit to load into him.

"She has just recently learned of your existence. For the last nineteen years she has believed you to have vanished from her life."

"I always knew that would be how Rachel dealt with it."

"You remember all of that time?"

"I remember everything, angel. What I do not understand is why you are here now. After all of these years, why is it now that you choose to deem me with your presence?"

"I have only just learned of your existence as well. I am here in an effort to garner information for your daughter."

"Well, what is it that you want to know?"

"You have the ability to speak with the dead, am I correct in that assumption?"

"Yes, you are correct. I can also talk to beings celestial in nature."

"For how long?"

"As long as I can remember. The world thinks I'm crazy. Can't exactly argue much with them either, all things considered."

"I am sorry that I did not learn of your condition sooner, but I am here now and I need to ask something of you. It is of grave importance otherwise it would not even cross my lips."

"What do you need?"

"There is a light that surrounds you and though my Father will give me no other information to go on, I need to know if you are made of that very light or if you have just been blessed."

"God's keeping secrets is he?"

"It would appear to be that way. I cannot speak to why my father has chosen to do things this way, but in an effort to help you moving forward I need to become one with you."

"Do whatever you have to; I only have one question before you begin."

I would venture to assume that this man has more than just the one question for me, but given his current state and what ran through his very human blood stream, I would answer anything and everything he needed before joining with him. He deserved that and so much more.

"What is it that you wish to know?"

"How soon can I see my angel?"

Chapter Seven

Serenity

I'm not entirely sure how I got to this moment, but I am sure of one thing. I never want it to end.

When Ryan suggested that we dance, I wanted to laugh him off. I mean doing something as trivial as dancing is some kind of joke right? We couldn't be doing something as normal as slow dancing together after everything we've been through. Life was never that good to either one of us. Even as he swept me up into his arms the minute we touched the dance floor, I kept waiting for the other shoe to drop.

It really couldn't be this perfect.

Except, that's exactly what it is and there really isn't any other shoe waiting to be dropped. We didn't have to watch our backs anymore. For the first time in the year plus that we've known each other, we are finally free to be ourselves and enjoy our lives. There is no dark and dangerous evil waiting around the corner, threatening to break us or end us. All we are surrounded by is the light.

He doesn't realize this, but this is definitely one of the things I've been dying to experience. When I wasn't hanging with Graham or Emma and I was alone, I would spend a lot of time listening to music, even going so far as to dance around my room with my hairbrush, singing along to the words, secretly wishing I had someone that would want to dance with me. Ryan without even realizing it is making my dreams come true and it's made even sweeter by the fact that he doesn't even know he's doing it.

Being swept around the floor with him now, our bodies connected as closely as possible, I'm reminded again of our first time. How easily we seemed to fit together. The way it feels now with his arms wrapped around me, leading me as the slow rhythm of the song plays, is exactly the way it felt the night we spent together. He has no idea how safe I feel with him, how completely at peace he makes me and no matter how many ways I come up with to explain it, they never seem good enough.

There's something more between us and it's noticeable when we're touching the way we are now. I have nothing to compare it to because in times before when we've been intimate it was never there, but it's definitely there now. It's the beloved bond, I know it as easily as I do the very real feelings I have for the man I'm dancing with. I just have no idea if he feels it too.

An electric charge between us that I swear I keep checking to see if it's physical visible. We are like two magnets, being pulled toward one another and even though we're as close as two people can get, it's so powerful that it seems to crave an even tighter connection. I don't know as much as I'd like to about the bond , but I do know I never felt anything quite this powerful with Gabriel.

"Someone is way too quiet."

Looking up at the sound of his voice, I'm met with his megawatt smile and my cheeks flush. It doesn't matter how often I see it, it always seems to have the same effect. The minute my eyes catch sight of any part of him, I'm lost.

"Just thinking about how perfect this is."

"And wondering when it's going to blow up in our faces?"

Damn. Sometimes I forget just how close we are. He knows me too well.

"Yeah, a little."

"Well, it's good that I know something you don't know." he replies with a grin, again making my breath catch in my throat.

"What's that?"

60

"I'm going to give you a lifetime of moments just like this one and make sure that they never end."

There it is again. The way my heartbeat seems to slow when he speaks to me like this. His voice is low, as if what he's saying is for my ears only. Usually it happens when he's bending into me, whispering in my ear, but it's interesting to see that it seems to carry over into just about everything he says.

I can definitely get used to this.

"Can I ask you something?"

"You can ask me anything." I say. Once upon a time, he said the very same words to me when I was trying to remember him. A memory he also remembers as he grins again and this time it reaches right up into his eyes and they glow back straight into mine.

"Do you feel different?" he asks and shakes his head. "Shit, that doesn't make sense. What I meant to ask is, with us, does something feel different?"

"Magnetic even?"

The way he looks at me, I know what he thinks. He's assuming that because of the way I answered, that I've read him again. When it comes to us, I don't have to read him at all because I'm feeling all of the exact same things.

"I didn't read you, Ryan. It's actually something I was thinking about before you started talking."

We begin moving off the dance floor as the song ends, Ryan's arm placed tenderly across my back as he guides us back to our table. It's only when we're seated again that he speaks.

"Did it feel like this with Gabe?"

"No, it didn't."

"Is it just an 'us' thing or do you think it's the bond?"

"It's the bond. I've never felt this with you before. Why do I get the feeling you're not happy about it?"

He moves so quickly it takes me a minute to catch up, but the next thing I know he's leaning across the table at me, his hands resting on top of mine and his eyes are no longer the cloudy blue I've come to adore so much, but a grayish white.

"I'm confused by it Ser, that's all. Please don't think I'm not happy about anything I feel when I'm with you."

He might have said the right words, but they don't quite reach his eyes, which means he isn't being entirely truthful and it turns my stomach realizing that even after everything we've been through, he's still keeping things from me.

"I don't believe you."

"You're kidding me, right?"

I really wish I was kidding because with what I see with my own eyes and my disbelief of him now, I know it's only going to take what has so far been the perfect date night and blow it straight to hell.

"No, I'm not kidding. I can see it, Ry. There's something else going on and it's making the words you say, no matter how perfect they are, wrong."

He removes his hands from mine and falls back into his seat and the magnetism I felt earlier seems to go with him. It leaves me feeling empty even though he's still directly in front of me. I feel the loss immediately and I hate it. I want desperately to go back to five minutes ago. I want a do over.

"Do you remember the other day when I said that I felt like someone different?"

"Yeah, of course I do."

"Well that's what you're sensing. I swear to god, Serenity that is *all* it is. The way I feel about you, the pull that has always been there between us, I was really hoping that it was that but magnified because of everything we've been through. Knowing that it's something to do with this beloved bond just reminds me that I'm not entirely me anymore."

It's no secret that deep down he feels like he's sharing space with Gabriel because of the light that now lives inside of him. I understand it completely, I just wish that he could see it the way I do. He isn't sharing space with the angel and everything he is experiencing is still uniquely his, especially everything he feels between us. It's just magnifying what was already there.

"It's all us, Ryan. You're still you and I'm still me. Sure, you've got Gabriel's light inside of you, but it's not him. It's just the light. It makes everything that you already were that much more powerful."

"How strong is it for you?"

I want to jump across the table the minute he asks the question, that's how happy I am that he asked it. It means that he's willing to see what I've been trying to tell him for months.

"When we were on the dance floor, even with as close as I was to you, it wasn't close enough. It's like my body wants to join with yours. It wants to meld together. "

I have no idea if the way I'm explaining it is good enough, but with the way his lips lift just slightly, it's obvious that it's good enough for him.

"We're meant to be one..." he replies.

"I think that's exactly what it is."

"Well, that solves that then."

I didn't think it solved anything, but I wasn't about to bring it up again. I told the truth earlier when I said I wanted to focus on us tonight and I am going to stick by it no matter what.

"You wanna fill me in here?"

"If the bond wants us to be one, then I say we give it what it wants."

"Alright, McGregor, what did you have in mind to make that happen?"

"Something we can't do here. I think it's time I took you home."

As he turns from me, signaling to the waiter that it's time for the check, I catch on to exactly what it is he's getting at. There is only one other way that we can connect with one another that would bring us close enough to becoming one the way both of our souls want.

Seconds turn into minutes as I just let the thought of being with Ryan again envelope all my senses. Before I know it, I feel his breath on my ear, whispering to me as he pulls my chair away from the table.

"Let's go home, Mrs. McGregor."

Placing my hand in his, more than happy to oblige his request, I smile up at him as we begin making our way toward the door. It's only as we're about to walk out into the night air that I hear it. Clear as day it comes to me in my mind and stops me in my tracks.

The one voice I never thought I would ever hear again.

"Serenity, my belle, I need your help. If you can hear me, please come for us. We need you."

Lucifer.

Lucifer

"Serenity, my belle, I need your help. If you can hear me please come for us. We need you."

I have tried, to no avail to connect to Serenity a total of five times now and just when I think I might be making some headway, I find that I haven't gotten any closer at all. My power is at an all time low, what with losing all of the old power that ran through my veins for the years that I had connected with it and being left with what remained when I became one of the fallen.

In order for everything to materialize in the manner at which I want, I need to connect with her again. It has always been about her. She is at the center of it all, especially as it pertains to me and what I want in the end. When I told her that I would never give up on her, I meant it. Even if I have to spend the duration of my existence pushing my power forward until it wears me down, I will do it until I succeed.

There is no reason for her to help me at this stage of course, especially after everything I have put her through but I am hoping that the branding I put on her heart months ago still remains and at the very least she will listen to reason if and when I do reach her. All I need is her to understand what I want to do moving forward and believe in it. I will do the rest.

I will prove to her that I am worthy of this.

Now that I have faced my own death, experienced every excruciating moment of it in graphic detail almost as if on a continuous loop, I believe I might understand her more than ever before. I made her face this exact fate when I attempted to take her life the first time and while I did not succeed and she is still able to live on, there can never be an undoing of the events of that day and the damage that I did. It really is no wonder that she hates me, only responding to me when she finds herself branded.

I want to remove the brand that I placed on her heart and I want to stand before her as I do it, earning her trust and forgiveness because only through her will I be able to obtain what I think Gabriel would want.

Redemption.

I know now why this is called the true death. Unlimited amounts of time spent going over every move I have ever taken, both dark and light in nature and focusing on the motivations I had while doing them. It is in itself the truest form of torture, one that even I could not recreate when I made my home in Hell so very long ago. Every single moment in time, in a continuous loop in my mind with no breaks in between. It really is meant to end me.

It reminds me in a way, of what I put the Hudson boy through when I flooded him not only with memories, but also sensations that only he as a human could feel. Right now, what I experience on a minutely basis is much like that and it turns my stomach.

I wasn't always that way. There was a point where I was the angel that Father relied on as it pertained to the very humans I ended up torturing. Even with all of the questioning I did, he still leveled me with his trust in such a way that I felt like Heaven's most treasured son. What a difference time can make, as now I am sure I am nothing more than Heaven's biggest mistake.

There is only one person that never saw me that way though and despite the way that I treated him, I remember the times with him fondly and it is those moments with Gabriel that I am most haunted by since being caged here for an eternity alone.

When Father laid out his plans as far as the humans went and I began to turn away from him, not wanting to be just another monkey and follow blindly, Gabriel had come to me and it was in that meeting that I believe we finally stood united on the same page. He understood me more than even he was willing to admit.

*****

"Lucifer, may I have a moment of your time?"

"If you are going to tell me how wrong I am going up against Father the way that I have done, then please leave now. I am in no frame of mind to hear it, even from you."

"Why do you question Father this way?"

"It is what I do or have you not witnessed that for yourself already, Gabriel? I have never been content following along blindly. I need more."

"Brother, it is one of the things I respect most about you. I just want to understand why in this instance you choose to disobey Father this way, knowing what it could mean."

He didn't want to speak the words, but it was no secret what he is getting at. Father did not enjoy being questioned, or challenged and I had done both this time, which meant I would face the ultimate punishment all because I could not follow blindly. If I remained on this path I would be removed from Heaven and the power of the light held within it.

It is a risk I am willing to take.

"I am well aware of what it will mean if I continue down this path, Gabriel. You can say it. He will banish me from Heaven and all that it holds within it, but I find myself unable to care in the way that I probably should. All I do know is that I cannot agree with this."

"But that is what I do not understand. Why can you not agree with it?"

"In doing so, it will mean the end of all that we hold dear. Holding the humans in the same regard as we as angels are is wrong and will spell disaster."

"That does not answer my question, brother."

"Michael and Father believe that I am acting in this manner because I am jealous, but I assure you that is not the case. I am merely concerned about what this undertaking will mean for Heaven as a whole. I enjoy the life that we have created here, so why mess with something that continues to work?"

"At some point even Heaven has to evolve, Lucifer. If it does not then our existence will become rather boring."

"So you believe this to be Father's attempt at evolving? Gabriel, you have always been one of the smartest beings I know, but you have to see how wrong that answer truly is."

"I am unsure how I am wrong. What do you believe this to be?"

"A power play. Father wants to rule over these pesky humans and make them worship him as some kind of superior being, when in reality he has his own failings just as we all do. Add to that the fact that he wants us to accept these new beings as family and treat them as such and it is just too much."

"You believe Father to be flawed?"

"Gabriel, you have reached an all new level of naïve if you are unable to see that for yourself. I believe that if you take a step back and really witness the way everything is happening, it will make sense to you, that which I am saying."

I learned not so long ago about the old power that Father held, of which he did not want to share with us. It is power that gives him the ability to create the world and it is power that in the end would be his undoing.

"Lucifer, that sounds like a threat."

"It has nothing to do with me, Gabriel. Father will be the cause of his own undoing. These humans that he has so much faith in, they will betray him and when they do, everything he has worked so hard for will fall around him. He does not need me, it will all be him."

I can tell with the light diminishing around him that he is taking my words to heart and the seed of doubt has been planted. It had not been my intent, but if Gabriel could see the truth even a little then it meant I wasn't being the spiteful child everyone believes me to be.

"You can see it, can't you? That is why the conversation has suddenly became one sided."

"If what you say is true, what can we do? How are we supposed to fight against our very creator?"

"We stand and we fight until he backs down from this horrible undertaking."

"Do you really think that we can get through to him going up against him that way?"

"I do. So the only remaining question is, are you with me, Gabriel? Will you help me put an end to this once and for all?"

"Yes, Lucifer. Anything that keeps Heaven the way that is now, I will fight for."

*****

I had only needed a seed of doubt and in that conversation I had gotten it. What I didn't admit to Gabriel then and that I continued to deny long after I had been cast out by Michael, is that it did have to do with jealousy. Father had always kept us close to him, including us in everything, but when it came to the humans he did not do that and in the end it built a brick wall between us and had broken me.

Loving Father had been the one thing that I could do better than any other, despite all of the questions I leveled in his direction. To have something else become more important than the bond he shared with not only me, but my brothers too, well it was too much to handle. I could not let them become more important.

That is exactly what happened of course and Gabriel, while pledging to stand beside me through it all had turned on me, but I could not hold it against him. No, this was all on Father and once I fell, that feeling of revenge built in me until it was so large I couldn't get a handle on it anymore. It became my entire reason for being. I needed to watch it crash and burn in front of my very eyes, bringing the so called God with it.

In an effort to protect Heaven, my family and the other beings of light, I had turned into the very thing that would bring about all that I originally feared. I became the very thing they all had to stand and fight against and now as I sit here, cold, locked up and alone, I know that it is time that I see exactly what my role in all of this was and make it better.

It's time for me to go home.

Focusing with what remains of my power, I try one more time to call to the ball of light that holds my heart, reaching out to the very part of her that even without power is still owned by me. I speak to her heart, only I try the one tactic that until now I have been avoiding.

I lie.

"Serenity, you must come quickly. It's Gabriel, he needs your help."

Even as I utter the words, lying to her in this way, I know the proverb that is spoken of so casually on earth is actually pure truth.

The road to hell really is paved with good intentions.

Chapter Eight

Michael

There is no question that of all the deserving people in the world that had been placed in situations such as this, Gregory Richards deserved more than all of them to have his one request granted. We still needed to discuss the past and present in detail, but I want nothing more than to give him this, despite knowing that in doing so I would be causing Serenity further distress.

We are still dealing with the loss of my brother and putting any new pressure on her would do nothing but push an already broken woman even further away. As it pertains to the man sitting before me now though, there is a small part of me willing to risk it in order to have something come from the tragedy we have faced.

"There is much we need to discuss before getting to that point, I am afraid."

"What is more important than a father getting in touch with his daughter? Isn't that what the angels upstairs are all about? Answering prayers?"

I am unaware of any such time at which the man prayed to see Serenity, but it is not at all surprising. With the way Father and Gabriel kept his very existence from me, it cannot be that far of a stretch that they kept his prayers secret as well. He did make a valid point. To the angels above, there is no greater gift then the love of a parent to a child.

"You are correct in your assumption, but there is much that we need to discuss as it pertains to that very daughter

70

before we can move forward. I am not sure how comfortable I feel making this choice without her input."

"Well, if her mother wouldn't have lied to her, I would still have her in my life the way she is meant to be. If you're not willing to help me, can you at least tell me if she's alright?"

It never gets easier with time. Having to stand before a human and give them information that will be most troubling to hear. I would like nothing more than to tell him that his daughter had a fantastic life, full of love and acceptance, but I could not. There was something about this man that told me that even if I did lie about it, he would see through it.

"She has not had the easiest go of her life here, Gregory. In fact, that is one of the reasons I am here now. I believe it is time I told you everything there is to know about the woman you call daughter."

"What did Rachel do to her?"

Humans have always bothered me in this way. When they fall in love, everything is always sunshine and roses, but when they reach a point where the sunshine has gone away and the roses have died, they instantly turn around and place any and all blame on each other, especially when there are children involved. I know with certainty that it is not how Father imagined it when he created the world. It saddens me that we have reached a point now where even with Heavenly intervention; it didn't change the natural human way to push their own accountability down in favor of blaming others.

Rachel Richards is no saint, of that I am sure, but does she deserve the full strength of this man's wrath? I do not believe she does. Heaven is at fault for the lot that this man received in life and also that of his daughter, not the woman who was left to pick up the pieces.

"Rachel is not at fault for your plight in life and if we are to move forward you must heed my words. Believing differently will not bring you that which you want so badly."

"Tell me as much as you can about my daughter. I promise not to bring Rachel into it again. I just need to know…"

"Your daughter did not have an easy time after your departure. She was too young when you left to truly understand what happened to you, so her mother saw fit to explain to her that you had taken off, leaving them alone. It instilled in her an aversion to getting close with anyone for fear that they would leave. It is only recently that she has been able to rise above that and trust again."

I know that my words are not going to be of much comfort to this man, but he needs to hear the truth regardless. In order for all of us to move forward, all of the proverbial cards needed to be placed on the table right from the start. Anything less would spell disaster.

"What you do not know about Serenity is that she is born of Heaven. The daughter given to you twenty two years ago is in actuality a ball of heavenly energy, given to the world in human form in an effort to end the madness that has taken over. She was sent to make things right."

"She's an angel? I am fully prepared to believe that angels are real, but you must think I'm a few bricks short of a full load if you expect me to believe that my daughter, the very real daughter that I made with my wife, is actually a being of Heaven."

"Did you not just call her your angel mere minutes ago? If you can believe in me standing here before you and know where I come from, how is it that you cannot believe that the beautiful girl you've been given is not made of that same light?"

This is another way in which the humans bother me, or rather confuse me as it were. Gregory is the perfect example. He knows beyond all doubt that I am an angel and I am made of Heaven, but the pure, honest and sweet little girl he spent three years raising before he was taken away, he cannot accept as made of the very same place. It makes no logical sense to me, though given everything else I have experienced during my time on the planet; I suppose it should not surprise me.

"Fine, let's say she is an angel—

"She is not an angel, at least not yet. Later in her journey, that is exactly what she will become but until that takes place, she is a ball of heavenly energy, or light as it were." I answer, completely cutting him off before he can go any further.

"Gotcha. So she's a ball of heavenly whatever, what does that have to do with me?"

"Serenity shares the same abilities as you do. She is able to speak with the dead, as well as to heavenly hosts such as myself. She has the ability to sense without question when someone is being untrue with her and has no issue pointing it out. There are a lot of abilities that she is still developing even as we speak, but it has everything to do with you."

"Did I pass that to her?"

"No, but you having the same abilities does bring up a very interesting question. Where do your abilities come from? You have the light within you, I can sense that easily, but to what degree I am unsure. How did the light come to live so strongly inside of you?"

"All I can tell ya is that one day, I was fine and a couple of days later I woke up and everything changed. I could hear voices in my head and even answer them. Rachel caught me doing it and here I am."

"Is this your first encounter with a being such as myself?"

"No. That's how I know what you are."

This is most interesting news and something that Father would definitely want to know. Not only is the human coherent and unlike that of which I had been expecting, but he hasn't been alone as far as the light goes. It's time to find out just who it is that appeared to him and when, so that I can figure out just what my next move should be.

"When did you first encounter a being of light?"

"The first time was before Serenity was born. Then, when she was two and a half, a being just like you came to me and said that Serenity was destined for bigger things and that when the time was right he was going to come and bring her into the light. To be honest with ya, I didn't put much stock in any of it as it all seemed bat shit crazy, but with all you're telling me now, I figure I should have paid it more mind."

There could only be one person in all of creation that would come to this man and say the things that had been said. At first I expected to hear that Gabriel before his passing had come, but it was most definitely not him. While my brother knew of the man and everything that had been mishandled in regards to him, he had not shown up before he was taken, a fact I was sure he went to his grave regretting.

No, this is far worse than Gabriel and it is again another reminder of just how much we had let this man down. If we had known all those years ago exactly what had taken place, maybe we would all be standing in different places now.

Lucifer had come and in doing so; put Serenity directly on the path she is living. His hatred for the light knew no bounds. Even with him dead and gone, this is something Serenity needed to know.

I am just not sure I want to be the one delivering the blow.

Lucifer

There are no words available to explain the way it feels hearing her voice again, even after all the time that's passed. It is no secret that time moves differently in this realm, so for the past four years I have been calling to her and hoping for the first time in centuries that she would finally hear me and answer my call.

"Gabriel is with you?"

There is doubt in her voice and it pains me because I deserve every bit of it. It is only during my time here, having to go over every single thing I've done that I have seen just how deep I immersed myself in the darkness. Much the way that my protégé had always done, it was time for me to own everything, no matter how dark in nature, so that I could move forward with what I needed to do for Gabriel.

When I made the decision to do things this way, I made a promise to myself on the memory of my brother and on Serenity that I would do things differently from here on out. I owed them both that and more, yet in order to reach the true end I believe I am capable of having, I need to follow through on this lie one final time.

It is the only way this will succeed, despite how wrong it is.

"Yes. When he passed, he ended up here with me."

"Why should I believe you?"

"I do not expect you to believe me after all that I have put you through. I ask you to come to me so that you can see for yourself. He is weakened from his loss of light and does not have much longer before he truly fades into oblivion, so time is of the essence."

Gabriel's passing had to mean something more than just giving life to Ryan McGregor. The man's words still haunt me to this very day. He had killed me not for Heaven, but for the very angel that had wanted nothing more than his brother redeemed back into the light by a father that had long since given up.

It has to happen. I would fight for it with everything that remained in me until my time finally did reach its end.

"Where are you?"

The relief that flooded through me at the sound her voice is almost more than I can contain in my current state. The branding is still in place and it is working in my favor, even with so much distance between us. It seems as though I will get what I want after all.

"We are in the chambers of Hell. We are not together, but I am able to see him from my current location. It is not good Serenity, you must make your way here and you must do it quickly."

"How am I supposed to survive Hell when the angels and Ryan could barely do it when they tried?"

"I did not cease in my control during their time here Serenity, but if you are to make your way here then I will make sure you make your way through with no issues. It is of utmost importance that you reach here in one piece. I would never let anything happen to you, especially in the one place I still control."

"Why do you want to help Gabriel now? You've spent years wanting nothing but him dead by your hand. I'm not sure I believe this change in attitude."

She has every right not to believe in me. Every single move that I have made up until the point where Ryan finally plunged the weapon deep into me, has done nothing but bring pain and destruction to not only her, but the world as a whole. I need to earn her trust back and if she would just come to me, I would start by removing her brand once and for all. I would prove myself worthy of her and the faith that at one point she had in me. No other being alive afforded me anything of that magnitude before. I owe her.

"Gabriel above all others held a piece of my heart that I never let anyone else have. I will go to my death doing the right thing by him. I know that I cannot make you believe that, but really hear my words Serenity. I want Gabriel back where he belongs, but the only way that is possible given my current state is through you."

Again the silence floods back in around me, but this time I know that she is not gone. She merely needs time in order to come to terms with what it is I am asking of her. I only hope that she does as I have come to expect and makes her way to me now.

"Tell him I'll see him soon. Oh, and Lucifer. Don't make me regret this."

Chapter Nine

Serenity

When Emma suggested going around town in search of the worlds perfect wedding dress, I had every intention of riding the wave known as my best friend, but I just can't seem to get on her level. I need something like this right now though because with everything I've learned and been through over the last few days, I'm due a break. Shopping with Emma is supposed to give me that much needed reprieve, but it's not.

Even the date night with Ryan, which should have given me a much needed break from the more serious aspects of my life couldn't deliver in the end. Just like in times past, Lucifer couldn't allow us the one night of peace, even in death. A night that started off so magically had turned cold and broken by its end and as I go from shop to shop with Emma, going through the motions and pasting a fake smile on my face, I'm struck with just how much I've changed in the last year.

I didn't tell Ryan about Lucifer and that's the first noticeable difference. I've never been much of a liar or even a person that enjoys lying by omission, but that is exactly what I did. I let him take me back to his room, following through on spending the night with him, all the while holding on to a secret that once it comes out, could be the very thing that splits us apart.

Add to that the fact that I know that my dad didn't just bail on us the way my mother claimed and is locked away in some hospital in Green Haven and nothing about my life seems to be getting better. I've been trying to push the knowledge of Gregory Richards from my mind, hoping that in doing so it really is out of sight and out of mind, but I can't do it. Everything I believed about the man I called my dad has been proven wrong and at some point it's going to grow so big that even I can't block it out and ignore it.

Lucifer's words stick with me. Could Gabriel have ended up in Hell with his fallen brother when according to Ryan, angels just cease to exist when they die? Can I really trust the man that captured me, brought me to one of the darkest places imaginable and branded me in an effort to keep me locked to him forever? How is it possible that he's even alive after what I saw Ryan do to him that night in the church?

This is going to drive me crazy, all of these questions and no outlet to reach out to in order to get the answers. Lucifer has proven on more than one occasion that he is not to be trusted, yet for some reason that has nothing to do with the brand he placed on my heart, I want to believe him so badly, especially about Gabriel, that it physically hurts.

If Gabriel really is trapped there and I'm the only one that can get him out, saving what is left of his slowly dwindling life, than I owe it not only to him, but to every single being in Heaven to go to him and bring him home. I don't think I can live with myself if I don't.

"Ser, you're doing it again."

That's another change I didn't see coming. Emma knows everything now and I'm not sure how to deal with it.

When the time came for her to find out, I always figured that it would be me telling her. It deserved to come from me considering I had been the one all of these years hiding it. I might not have known everything about myself, but I did know that speaking to the dead is something more than a freak of nature thing, which meant that I should have let Emma be a part of it from the start.

"Sorry, Ems just got a lot on my mind I guess."

"Can't get your mind off your husband huh?"

The way she laughs when she says it makes me want to join her, but I can't because I'm not thinking about Ryan. At least not in the way she thinks I am. I can't stop thinking about the fallen angel's voice in my head and what he wants me to do. I can't tell her that though because with her knowing everything, she'll just find a way to talk me out of it and that's something I can't afford.

I will go to Hell and I will save Gabriel, but I have to do it alone. Letting anyone else know about this could put them in a danger that I thought we had finally gotten past. It has to be me and me alone, even if I have to lie to do it.

"Yeah, something like that."

"Well you should really calm the happy there Ser, it's almost too much to handle."

"It's that obvious huh?"

"What's going on? And don't say that it's nothing because I'm not against slapping you. In fact, I've been itching to do it for awhile now."

I spent months lying to Emma and I don't want to do it anymore, but I can't tell her everything swirling around in my head. Not yet anyway. Not until I've done what's needed and bring Gabriel back where he belongs.

"My mom told me something the other day..."

"You went to see your mom?" she asks, obviously shocked that I had done the one thing I swore to her I would never do. We actually made a whole stupid pact about it.

"Yeah I did. I wanted to see if she still had the dress that I wore to the dance."

"Except you didn't just go for that reason, did you?"

"No. With everything that happened with Gabriel and how off I feel, especially where Lucifer is concerned, I thought going back to where the hurt and betrayal started; might be able to help the healing."

"So what did she tell you, because if she made you feel like a freak or crazy, I have no problem hitting an old lady."

"She told me something about my dad." I stop, letting my words sink in, ignoring the urge to laugh at Emma going up against my mother. "Ems, he didn't take off the way she said he did."

"Then what happened to him?"

"She locked him away in a mental hospital."

This is always going to be a touchy subject for Emma. After all, our parents had done the same thing with us before we'd even become teenagers. No matter how much time passed, both for Emma and for me, we would always hate the way our issues had been treated, even if in Emma's case they were valid.

"She did what?"

"He heard voices too, at least that's what she told me and just like she did with me, she put him away and then lied to me about it."

"Please tell me you ripped that stupid bitches head off."

"I didn't. I mean, there was this part of me that wanted to go off on her, but I couldn't do it Ems. I saw the look in her eyes, the real sadness that she has for all the mistakes she made and I couldn't make it any worse. I did go there to heal; going off on her wouldn't have helped me do that."

"So, she locked your father up in a place even worse than the center and you just gave her a free pass?"

I did not give my mother a free pass. I don't think I would ever give her that, but I hadn't done what Emma wanted me to do either. I couldn't. If I'm honest, all I've been since hearing the news is numb to it, so I just forced myself to move forward, despite the damage.

"No. I'm not entirely sure I can ever forgive her for what she did to me, but he's been gone for almost twenty years and despite the way she dealt with me, she stayed."

I can tell that I'm not getting through to her. She's angry, not only for me, but for herself as well. She isn't happy with her parents for what they put her through either and telling her all of this is like throwing her right back into that emotional turmoil. I never wanted that to happen again and it makes me sick knowing that I'm the cause of Emma's now very present attitude change.

"I don't agree with you. I think your mother needs to be told exactly what her mistakes have done and she should pay for them, but it's not my life. I do think you need to go see your father, and soon."

Well there was something we finally agree on. I do need to go back to Green Haven again, despite the sordid history I have with the town and I need to see the man that for years I thought had bailed on me. I'm just not sure I can do it, at least not yet.

There is something far more important I need to do first and despite my need to share it with Emma, I won't. I need to get through this shopping trip, hopefully find the perfect dress and then I can finally focus on what's most important. What's always been most important.

Gabriel.

Graham

I know something that I'm pretty sure no one else knows and no matter how much I drink in an effort to block it out, it just keeps on coming back.

Lucifer though defeated, isn't dead.

He is still very much alive and creating havoc from what I can only hope is his dark corner of hell. The place where he will remain forever for all that he has done to not only me, but to Heaven and the others as well.

I'm not sure how I even know this or why it's me that can hear him clear as day, but I can only assume it's got something to do with the time he spent riding around inside me. Whatever it is, I hate it and I want him to shut up and die the way he should have three months ago.

He's lying to her. He claims that Gabriel is still alive and trapped where he is, but that is so far from the truth it isn't

81

even funny. I know, because just like my body and mind seem to react to the time Lucifer spent with me, they also do the same with Gabriel and I can tell he's no longer with us.

Why he's lying to her I don't know, but she needs to know the truth before she goes into the very place that I almost didn't make it out of. I can't let her go there to save someone that isn't there to be saved. He's using her again, just like all the times before and much like in times past, she's playing right into his hands.

I have the power to stop all of this, if I can just get up from this bed and go to her. We may never be what we once were to each other, but I would always love her and go to my grave in an effort to save her. She needs me now, more than anyone else because I have the answers that can change everything once and for all before there's more blood spilled.

I can't do it though. I'm frozen. As much as I want to save her, I can't throw myself to the wolves again, not when I'm not handling the other times all that well. If she knew I had come this far since the last time we'd spoken, it would break her heart and she would take it all on herself. I made the choices, but she would be the one paying. If she sees me, especially with the hangover haze I find myself in, it would only break what she's trying so hard to fix.

So I have to sit on this. I have to let it play out however it's meant to and hope to God that this time, she sees Lucifer and his lies coming before heading down into something she very well may never come back from.

It's time everyone realizes that I'm not the strong person they believe me to be. I do have a limit to how much I can take. That deep inside me, climbing more to the surface each passing day, is a fear like no other. As much as I want to go to Serenity and stop all of this, I can't.

I'm too afraid.

Chapter Ten

Ryan

I knew it was too good to be true.

Just when I think we've seen the last of it, it has to come right back at us again. It's made worse by the fact that I know it's happening now, that she's holding back from me.

Lucifer has made contact with Serenity and while I'm pretty sure I don't know everything because she hasn't gone into detail about it for me to catch it in her thoughts, I do know enough to know that she's about to do something that if she succeeds, she will never come back from.

I hate these gifts, mainly because I don't think I deserve them. Being able to connect to Serenity on the level we do now, is strange to me, like it doesn't belong. It has always been Gabriel's thing, which is why I seem to find it easier if I believe I'm just sharing space with him. I feel as though I'm possessed and even though it's wrong, it makes it tolerable. It's not the connection in this case that's causing me issues though. It's the fact that I can read her thoughts without even trying.

She isn't the only one keeping secrets. I am too. I can do this and I've done it more than once over the last three months. I've never told her. Lucifer returning is far worse in comparison, but it doesn't make me any less guilty of the very same thing I'm judging her for. Keeping things from each other has never been our style and I don't want it to be now.

Waiting for her to come back from her shopping trip is killing me. I need to tell her that I know about Lucifer and what he wants her to do. I need to make her see that this is just another ploy by the fallen angel to pull us apart. I might have trusted him before, to the point where I believed him to be good, but the time for that passed. He won't ever get me to that point again, no matter how sincere his brother might believe him to be.

The right thing to do is to take it to Michael. Call the angel and tell him what I know, but I don't think I've got enough time for that. I need to handle this with Serenity first. I can't keep taking things to the angels when they might be too hard for me to handle. I'm one of them for crying out loud, I don't need an angel to save the day when I can do it on my own. There's no doubt that Michael needs to know, so at the very least he can tell our father.

Our father.

They say that time heals all wounds and helps in coming to terms with things you have spent a long time distancing yourself from and it appears that it's true in my case. A few months before and even until recently, I couldn't believe I was one of them. A being made of the light, when my entire life has been spent lurking in the darkness right alongside of the man that the beings of Heaven dislike so much.

I could never be a pure angel because deep inside of me, I am or at least I was a pure demon.

The truth is, God made me, just as he had Michael, Gabriel and the others and no matter how much I push it down or for how long, it's always there in the background waiting for acknowledgement. With each passing day I'm noticing that I'm reaching that point. The one where I finally see the reality of what I am and I accept it.

The minute I hear the click of the door, signaling Serenity is back, I pull myself out of my thoughts and focus strictly on her. She's been different since our date two nights before and it's time we get to the real reason why. No more secrets. It's time we both tell each other everything.

"Well, that was pointless." She sighs, placing her bag around the handle of the door and making her way over to the bed, throwing herself onto it, her body shifting until she reached a level she's comfortable with.

"You didn't find it?" I ask, pushing the urge to get right into it down, instead focusing on the reason she had been out to begin with. Her wedding dress.

"No, I found it, but not before Emma dragged me to six different places."

"Well how's it pointless if you found the dress you want?"

I'm not a girl; I don't get the craziness that comes with wanting the perfect dress or even the perfect shoes and accessories. I'm actually pretty damn thankful that all I have to do is wear a suit. I don't think I could handle all the crap that comes along with making yourself look perfect and presentable on a day that really means nothing in the long term. It's not supposed to be about the one day. It's supposed to be about the marriage that comes after it.

"Shopping is always pointless Ry; I thought you of all people knew that."

Well she had me there. I did think it was pointless, but I just assume it's because I'm a guy. Little did I know that the woman I'm about to marry hates it just as much as I do. It's true that you learn something new every day. Serenity always manages to find a way for me to learn about her while having me fall all over again in the process. This is definitely something I can get used to.

"So you've got everything ready?"

"Yeah. It's exactly the way I imagined it to be. It's perfect."

I wish I could agree with her and with the way she's smiling at the thought of the dress being perfect, I really want to do that. I know I can't because it's not and while she may believe that parts of it are, overall she's in denial.

"Ser..."

Looking up from her spot on the bed, she catches my eye and her expression changes, from carefree to serious. Just with the way I say her name I can see her mentally bracing herself for what's about to come next.

"We need to talk about something. Well, we need to talk about a few things. There's something I need to tell you."

I start to feel myself rambling so I stop. I could have easily just said we needed to talk, but just like in times past, I seem to want to blurt everything out in one breath in an effort to get it out of my head.

"Don't tell me you're getting cold feet already, McGregor."

"Not on your life, pretty girl."

"Well, what do we need to talk about?"

Here's my chance. I can tell her everything now. I can talk her out of whatever she's planning to do in an effort to save Gabriel. I can keep her safe with me and we can forget about Lucifer once and for all, no matter if she's branded or not. Our bond is strong enough; especially now that I can combat whatever the hell it is he did to her heart.

"I know, Ser—all of it."

At first as her face scrunches up, obviously confused, I think that maybe she really has no idea what I'm talking about, but the longer I stand at the end of the bed watching her, making no move to join her on the bed, I see the reality of it dawn on her.

Even if she tries to do what she's done before and deflect, attempting to make me believe that she has no idea what I'm going on about, she won't fool me because I've seen the light of realization in her eyes and she can't ever take it back.

"So you really did get all of Gabe's abilities?"

I nod, finally taking a place on the bed across from her and praying as I do that she doesn't balk and back away from me. The day she woke up in this bed and didn't recognize me still stings even with the time that's passed since. The last thing I want is to relive it. It's one of my biggest fears and another thing I've never shared with her.

"How long Ry? How long have you been going into my head without telling me?"

"Don't you mean how long have I known that Lucifer's been talking to you?"

86

I'm not handling this the way I want at all. I can already feel the tension growing inside both of us. I always knew that life with her wouldn't be easy. That we would have to go through trials and periods where we might downright hate each other, but I really hoped it wouldn't happen until well into our married life. Starting before we even walked down the aisle is definitely something I didn't plan for, but I'm powerless to stop.

"He talked to me outside of the restaurant. Are you happy now?"

"You've got the Devil in your head and you think I'm gonna be happy about it?"

"Well, I don't know what else you want me to say. You want to talk about it, how long it's been happening and why I didn't tell you, I'll do it. He came to me that night and again last night, explaining to me that I need to go into Hell in order to save Gabriel, who he says is trapped there with him."

"He's lying to you Ser; please tell me you can see that! Gabriel died; you saw it with your own eyes."

"I saw him disappear yes, but I have no idea if what Lucifer is saying is a lie or not. What if he did get trapped there with him and I'm the only way he can get out?"

For the past three months, all any of us have been capable of feeling where Gabriel is concerned is guilt at not stopping it before it happened. Serenity is taking it harder than most because she followed his requests to the letter that day, never once stopping to question exactly what she was doing, giving his light away the way she did. As upset as I am that Lucifer is using her as a pawn now, I need to take a step back and realize exactly why she's so adamant in doing this.

She believes that she has to save Gabriel because she's the one that killed him.

"Serenity, he's telling you that so you'll go there for him. I know you want to do whatever you think will bring Gabriel back to us, but we can't bring him back baby, he's gone."

As my eyes lock on hers, I see the damage my words, no matter how softly spoken, have caused her. Where minutes before her eyes had been bright and clear, now they were watered down and hazy. I was making her cry, all because I want her to see the truth. The very thing I swore I would never do to her, I'm doing. I'm hurting the only person I've ever loved.

God, I'm a fucking bastard.

"What if he's not?" she asks before wiping at her eyes, wiping the tears that are threatening to fall, leaving only the lingering wetness on her fingers as proof they even existed. "What if he's there and he's exactly the way Lucifer says he is and he dies because we don't save him?"

Gabriel is gone. I know this. I may not be willing to accept it, like Serenity and even Michael, but I know that he's gone and that we need to move on from it. It doesn't mean we forget him, but we can't linger over it when the reality is staring us right in the face. If he's in Hell, caught or not, he still had enough power to break free on his own. He would find a way to contact us.

I just need to make her see this.

"Gabriel is an archangel, Serenity. If he was in Hell, even with limited power, he would be able to reach out to one of us. Don't you think he would have contacted Michael by now if he's really alive and in danger?"

"I'm not an idiot, but you're forgetting something."

"What's that?"

"He doesn't have the light or power anymore. You do."

In an effort to make her see how she's being used, I had completely forgotten that fact and now it was my turn for reality to slam in around me. She had a point. He couldn't reach out to any of us because he didn't have anything to reach out with. He would be as good as human if he was trapped there the way Lucifer said.

"I know you think he's lying to me and I have to admit I think so too, but if I don't do what he asked me to and Gabriel is there and something happens to him, I will never forgive myself."

"You have no idea what you're walking into."

"I'll be walking into Hell, Ryan. I remember my time there; I know exactly what's waiting for me."

I can't argue with her anymore. She does know about Hell, she lived there for months before we got her out. If there is anyone that knows what to expect the way that I do, it's her. It doesn't mean I have to concede on this though. I can't let her do this, no matter what her reasoning for it is.

"I'm not letting you do this."

"You don't have a choice. If you look into my mind you'll see that."

"Shit! I can't do this with you anymore! I tried my best to get through to you, to make you see the truth, but you just refuse to see it. Lucifer is using you and just like before you're going to walk into a trap!"

"Then I guess that's what I'm doing, Ry, because I refuse to walk away from Gabriel."

"This has nothing to do with Gabriel. Yeah, so I have the ability to see into your mind and read your thoughts, something you've been able to do with me for months and it's wrong that I didn't tell you about it the minute I realized it, but now it's time for you to be honest too. You're not doing this for Gabriel, at least not entirely."

"Of course this is about Gabe! Why else would I walk through the very hell I was so desperate to escape, if not to save him?"

"You didn't want to leave, remember? You told me that. You may have been desperate to get out in the beginning, but not when we finally got to you. You wanted to stay with him. You wanna know who you're doing this for, despite your claims otherwise, look no further than the very voice guiding you to do it."

"I'm doing this for Lucifer now? Is that really what you think?"

I don't trust my voice to answer her so I just nod. It's painfully obvious that it's about more than the angel we'd lost that night in the church. She's going to go against what I want her to do because she wants to do the one thing she'd been unable to do since her time with him.

She wants to save the devil.

Chapter Eleven

Serenity

There is one thing I've felt secure in, at least as far as the last year and a half goes and that's Ryan. He has always been the one constant in my life. The one person that no matter how insane everything seems to get, never turns his back on me. With the way things are happening now, I'm walking a very thin line with him and I don't think he can stand idly by anymore. I'm pushing him to the point of no return.

I can't expect him to be okay with this. He's been so great about everything that I've chosen to do up until this point that it's got to come to an end sometime. Knowing how he feels about me and how afraid he is when it comes to losing me again, I get why he feels this way, I do, but it's not enough to change what I have to do.

Even if Lucifer is lying to me and I have no doubt that he is, there is still the lingering question of whether or not Gabriel could have actually survived what happened to him and as long as that question is there, I have to see it through. If that means going deep into the heart of hell and coming face to face with the man that caused all of this to begin with, then so be it.

We're at two different places and until I deal with everything I'm feeling, not only for the angel that I'm so desperate to bring back, but also the fallen one that I've seen into the very heart of, it's going to stay this way. Ryan has come to terms with everything he did with Lucifer and even what he endured after it and that's a place I'm unfamiliar with.

Ever since I started opening up to him a couple of months ago, he's known what my true intentions are where Lucifer is concerned and while he doesn't understand it, he's never pushed me to give up on it. He's remained by my side without question and honestly, I love him for it, but he deserves so much better than what he's getting.

He explained to me what it felt like for him when I was gone, everything he endured on his own, all in an effort to keep himself together until I could come back to him. Add to that how things were when I finally did come home and he's been through more than enough heartache. I don't want to cause him anymore, but that is exactly what I'm doing by not hearing him out, or at least not doing what he wants me to.

I won't back down from this, which means we're at a standstill. The wedding that's due to happen in less than two weeks is in jeopardy, the very relationship we've managed to forge even going through the trials that we have, it's on the edge of a precipice and at any point it could fall. I know what I'm risking, but I can't stop it, not because I'm powerless, but because I just don't want to.

He's right, this isn't just about Gabriel and making sure that he's alright. This is about so much more than that now. It has everything to do with Lucifer and the feelings that have developed over our time together. The ones that Ryan believes are romantic, but are as far from it as you can get. I've seen the real angel buried underneath the darkness and even though he may feel something for me that I do not reciprocate, I do feel obligated to save him because I believe deep down he's worthy of it.

Before Ryan showed up in the room that night to face me down, I struggled with the way I felt because of what I wanted. I wanted to be able to save them both and when Ryan finally put an end to Lucifer, a part of me died with the fallen angel. In order for me to get that back, I need to go face him down once and for all. I need to take that part of me back. I feel like I've let him down and I can't move forward until I do whatever I can to fix it.

"You're going to do this despite everything I've said, aren't you? There is not one damn thing I can say to change your mind..."

"I'm sorry Ry, I know that you don't get it, but I have to do this."

"No, see, that's where you're wrong Serenity. The only thing you *have* to do is stay here with me. Live your life, the one you've been meant to live, planning our wedding and every other little thing that comes next."

God, he makes it all sound so perfect.

"It can be perfect, Serenity; all you have to do is let it be."

There's one thing I hated during my time with Gabriel and it was any time he spent invading my thoughts without giving me warning. The way he could just read them easily used to piss me off so badly that eventually I walked away because of it. It wasn't looking any more appealing coming from the man with his eyes locked on mine now. In fact I'm pretty sure I hate it even more.

That's another one of our issues that is pushing us further apart. I should have known that if he got the beloved bond from Gabriel he would have gotten everything else too. Seeing it in action, knowing that he's been able to do it for god knows how long and hadn't bothered to tell me, broke something inside me. We're both keeping things from each other and all of that has brought us to this moment, where we are more separated then we've ever been before.

So far apart that I'm not even sure there's a way to come back from it.

"Nothing will ever be right again..." I choke out as the realization hits me. As long as there are questions, nothing can ever be perfect. I can't live a life based around what if, especially when it has to do with Gabriel. Lucifer may play a part in all of this, but Gabriel is still the overriding factor and he should be for Ryan too.

"Only because you won't use your brain and think this through. Serenity, all you're doing rushing into things, is acting like me and I can't sit back and let you do it. For once, don't feed off the connection you have to me, think for yourself."

"This conversation is over." I say, sliding over to the side of the bed farthest from him and climbing off. I didn't want to hear anything else now, the damage is done.

"Ser, shit, that's not how I meant it!" he calls to me as I make my way to the door. I continue walking, not wanting to give him the satisfaction of looking back at him. He knows he said the wrong thing, there's no point in letting him see just how wrong it is.

"Don't leave like this, pretty girl, please." He cries out, this time louder than before, causing me to pause, but only for a second. "If you want me to listen and understand then I swear to god I'll do it, just don't leave like this."

Spinning around, but making no movement in his direction, I level my eyes on him and speak one final time before turning around again and making my way from the room for what very well could be the last time.

"I need to do this and I know you don't understand why and that's okay, but thanks for proving what I've known all along. You deserve better than this, you always have."

Michael

With everything I have experienced since my return to the planet, when I came face to face with Serenity and Ryan again, I hoped things would be moving along nicely. As it turns out I was sadly mistaken in my belief.

I've just witnessed the little ball of light walk from the room, this time, much like one time previously, with tears threatening to break through. This can only mean one thing and it is something I am not looking forward to handling. I was supposed to come down here in an effort to heal from the loss of my brother and I seem to be swept up into more turmoil than I can keep track of.

"Son of a bitch!" I hear Ryan scream as I appear in the very spot I watched Serenity vacate only seconds before.

"It's nice to see your penchant for the colorful language has not ceased with all of the changes you are experiencing."

"Not in the mood Mike, so save it."

"I can imagine you wouldn't be given what I just witnessed. I must ask you though, what was this particular fight about? Does she not like your choice of flowers for the wedding?"

I am beginning to see as he scowls at me, why the humans are so intent on the statement of *if looks could kill*. I am sure that if they could, Ryan's would be doing so with me now. It is obvious that my attempts at humor are not hitting their mark the way I intend. As always, humor is only appreciated when they are the ones doing it.

"If you knew what was going on around here, you might not be so quick to make jokes. Not that it's lost on me, the fact that you're making them at all, but not the time Michael."

"Then why don't you explain it to me. I am as you have said before, all ears."

"Do you remember when you said that I had to be the one to finish Lucifer?"

"Of course I remember that, but what does it have to do with your beloved?"

"Stop calling her that!"

"Embrace the gift you have been given, Ryan. There was a time where you had two suitors with bonds held tightly over your love for Serenity and now it would appear as though you have the stronger of the two in your possession. Embracing it is customary in cases such as these."

"I am embracing it Michael, ugh! Can we just stop? This has nothing to do with what I need to talk to you about and it's actually starting to drive me even more crazy, if that's possible."

"Then say your piece."

"If I finished him off in the church then tell me why the fuck he's in her head again!" he demands, his voice raising well above his normal octave, going to a level I have not encountered from him before, even in the throes of his anger.

"Lucifer has contacted Serenity?"

"Yeah and according to him, Gabriel's trapped there and Serenity is the only one that can save him."

I am not sure what to make of what I am hearing, but the more he speaks the more my blood goes cold. Did everything not take place the way it was meant to in Green Haven and Lucifer is still alive? If that is the case why am I only hearing about it now and from Ryan no less?

"I have no idea how that is possible. I witnessed you finish him off with my own eyes, even watching as the power that he held drained from him before he was taken away. If he is able to contact her, there is something more that is going on that we are unaware of."

"I'm starting to think that it's been Serenity all along. Just the way she thought, she has to be the one to finish him."

"You make a valid point but given that the both of you worked together in the taking down of my fallen brother, it would stand to reason that in a way she did follow through as well."

I thought I had seen the end of the insanity after dealing with her father, but as it appears there is much more going on that again I am being kept out of the loop of. If Father had kept this from me after everything that's happened, then Lucifer is going to be the least of his problems.

"There's more, man…"

"Does it have to do with the way she looked when she walked out of here?"

"It has everything to do with that, but there's some stuff you need to know. There are some things we talked about during the time where you had your angel call button on silent."

"Well I'm here now and I'm willing to hear all that you have to say."

"Serenity wanted to save both me and Lucifer that night in the church. I'm pretty sure a lot of it has to do with the brand he put on her, but she told me a couple of months ago that she felt torn between us. She wasn't sure who she needed to save more. So Lucifer doing this, Michael, it's bringing that all around again. She wants to save him and Gabriel, even though I'm pretty sure she knows that stuff about Gabe is bullshit."

I have to hand it to my fallen brother, he had chosen the perfect way to get her attention, even if there is no way it is possible. Gabriel perished the minute his light was taken from him; there is no doubt about it. It is the way it works with us. We do not become stuck in another plain, we just cease to exist.

It does not shock me that she wants to save Lucifer. Even though large spans of time, tragedy and darkness have torn us apart, I do remember the way that he used to be before he let his jealousy get the better of him and I know that is the side of him that Serenity has connected with and is guided by now.

"Lucifer cannot be saved."

"Try telling her that, man. I tried to get her to see reason and she won't have any part of it. Then I had to go and open my mouth and say things wrong—again and well that's what you caught when you saw her taking off out of here. I think this time I've really done it. I've pushed her to the edge."

"What exactly is she going to do?"

"She's going into Hell, determined to save Gabriel."

"She is walking into a trap."

Ryan rolls his eyes at me before nodding. If Serenity is indeed determined to go into Hell in a misguided attempt to save Gabriel then there is only one thing left that both of us standing in the room can do.

Follow her.

Before I can even open my mouth to speak, Ryan puts his hand up, stopping me and proving again just how far he's come in terms of his abilities since being handed the ones Gabriel had given him.

"When do we leave?"

Chapter Twelve

Ryan

"You deserve better than this, you always have."

No matter how much I try to do otherwise, her words keep flooding my brain. That added with the vision of her walking away and I swear I don't think I've got anything left in me to fight with. I guess it's true. I really am whipped over this girl.

There was something so final in what she said that as I sit here waiting for Michael to get back, I can't help but wonder if those are the last words we'll ever say to each other. Not because she wants to go into Hell and it's dangerous, but because we've finally reached a point with all of the bullshit we've had to endure that neither one of us can back down from it.

I don't know what she'd been thinking when she said that to me, but she couldn't be further from the truth. There is no way I deserve better than what I have with her. Yes, it's complicated and it seems as if we're spending more time fighting for our lives and the lives of the people we love, then we are focusing on the real love that burns between us, but I wouldn't change it. Not one single thing. Going through everything that we have only proves to me just how right we are, how meant to be.

If I didn't meet and fall in love with Serenity, I honestly have no idea where I would be right now. I could be dead, sent back to the chambers of hell, or buried six feet under. I could be floating from one location to the next, stripping the light out of souls and drinking their blood the way I had been for months leading up to when Lucifer said he was ready to put me in her path.

Thinking about where I could have ended up depresses me because I know there is no better alternative than Serenity McGregor. She is my wife for crying out loud, this second wedding only a chance for the both of us to do things right for the first time, nothing more. The feelings and the marriage are already there, it's just a show put on by the both of us for the people that couldn't be a part of the last one.

I've spent my life going through the motions, all in an effort to please the only being alive that had ever gotten close enough to me to be considered family. I was feeling like an old puzzle that someone put away, the kind that's missing pieces so it never gets looked at. It isn't until I came across the woman that now holds my last name that I see it clearly. She's the collection of pieces that are missing from my box. She completes it and turns it into the most beautiful picture.

Doing this life without her just isn't something I'm able to accept.

Especially when it's my own bonehead comments that push her away. Going over what I accused her of doing makes my head and heart hurt. There was a time where she fed pretty hard off my emotional state and with this new bond between us and still trying to navigate the ways that it enhances what is already there, I was so sure that she was doing it again.

There's only one other person that knows what it feels like to be me right now and whether I like it or not, I'm going to have to go to him again with what Michael and I are about to do. My hesitation in doing it, has nothing to do with the stunt he pulled when we rescued her from hell. I'm handling that a lot better now that she remembers everything. It's more that he barely made it through unscathed. I don't want to put him through all of it again even if it means saving Serenity.

Graham Hudson has literally lived the worst of it and deserves to be able to move on. I'd actually been hoping to see more of him now that we seem to be getting back to classes and the lives we lead before, but he hasn't been around all that much. Come to think of it, I haven't seen much of Emma either, so I can only hope that the both of them were finally able to admit what is going on between them.

Another reason I didn't want to go calling on Graham again. Even if he had moved off of Serenity and the bond they share, there is still another girl in the picture that's invested, at least partially, in making sure he remained healthy, happy and in one piece.

With as many different reasons as there are for not wanting to ask him for his help moving forward, there is something stronger that outweighed it all. We were all a team, a family even and there is no way any of us could move forward with any plan we had to face, especially ones that involved the darkest parts of the hell we've lived, without doing it together.

Grabbing my jacket off the chair, mentally preparing myself for what I would find when I made my way to Graham's door again, I left for the long trek across campus. There's no more time to debate what the right move is anymore. The right way would always be the one that brought Serenity back to me even if I had to lose her in the process.

Graham

I am not in the mood for this right now.

When I opened my door, I figured it was going to be Emma again. She's been doing that lately. Coming by my room with the excuse that she wants to drop off my English work and then the other reason, she's just checking in on me. I get it, she's worried about me or maybe everyone is worried about me so she's just doing the right thing by checking in, but I don't really want to see anyone.

It wasn't Emma though; it was the last person I expected to see.

Ryan McGregor. The guy I went to hell with. The guy that I haven't seen or heard from since the night he dropped by to tell me that Lucifer was dead and Gabriel had died right along with him. Whatever he was here for now, judging by the look on his face wasn't going to be anything I wanted to hear.

"What did she get herself into this time?" I ask before he can even get the words out.

There's one thing I know about Ryan. Unless it's something to do with Serenity, his expression never changes. It's bland without much feeling attached to it. Bring Serenity or anything to do with her into the equation and it's then that he becomes more active. Given how morose he looks standing on the other side of the door; I can only imagine that the troubles of the past have reared their ugly head again.

Yeah, definitely something I don't wanna deal with given how screwed up I am from the last time it happened.

"How do you know it's about her?"

"Well, I gotta figure with Lucifer up and moving again, she'd have something to do with it."

"How do you know about that? Has she been here? What did she tell you?"

"Man, slow your roll. She hasn't been here. I know about it because I heard the asshole speak."

"If you don't mind, you think you can let me in? I don't exactly want to have a conversation like this standing in your hall."

For a second, I didn't want to let him in. I know the kind of trouble that he would bring the minute he walked into the room and I was dead serious about not wanting any part of it. I've reached my limit for supernatural problems that need my help. Problem is, I know how crazy we would sound if someone came up and heard us talking about it, which means that if I want to appear normal, I had to let him in now.

Once he was in and the door securely shut behind us, I got right down to business. The faster we got the reason he was here out of the way, the sooner I could get rid of him and back to trying to rid myself of the headache from hell.

The irony is not lost on me.

"So, you obviously know about him talking to her and now you know I know, so why are you here?"

"She's going to Hell."

"Excuse me?"

"Lucifer told her that Gabriel is there so she's going into hell to save him."

"Yeah, I know that too. Sorry, I know I should have just told you that."

"You heard all of it?"

"Yeah man, I did and it's all bullshit. At least I think it is. I'm guessing she doesn't believe it and is determined to go there and save the non-existent angel?"

He nods and I sigh. As much as I love Serenity and there is no doubt about that, I really hate when she gets like this. Taking all of this on herself, not talking to anyone about it and then not listening to reason when the truth is staring her right in the face. I actually find myself missing the timid side of her. The girl she'd been when I knew her best because the one she was turning into left something to be desired.

"We're going in after her. If she's determined to do it, then I can't let her do it alone and neither can Michael. The reason I'm here is because you're family, despite our history and we don't wanna move forward without you."

There's this small part of me that feels honored that he thinks of me that way. Considering the fact that I don't have any family left to speak of, it's nice to be accepted into another one, even if it's not traditional. The other part of me is right where I was when he first showed up at my door. I don't want to put myself out there for this cause anymore because I'm not entirely sure I'll make it out alive this time.

"Listen, you know how I feel about her and how much I would love to help you get her out of this, but I don't think I can."

"What do you mean you don't think you can?"

"I haven't exactly been honest with any of you since we got back from Hell."

"If this is about what happened with you and Ser—

Not letting him finish, I speak before he can continue. "This has nothing to do with that."

"Alright man, why don't you explain it to me? Because honestly, I can't believe I'm actually hearing you say you don't want to be a part of this, especially with everything you went through."

"I've been getting headaches for awhile now. At first I blew them off and accepted I had issues, taking meds to try and get rid of them, but the more they came and how much harder they are to deal with, I realized that it had nothing to do with anything natural. What's going on with me is all supernatural."

""What else is going on besides the headaches?"

"If I don't drink myself to sleep every night, the memories he slammed into me take over, along with the sensory overload he flooded me with, even though a lot of it isn't stuff I went through. I can still feel the way it felt for you drinking her blood man. It's bad."

"And you're just telling us about it now?"

"No, I'm telling *you* about it. No one else needs to know. I might not be dealing with it in the right way or the way you might, but I'm handling it. I don't see why anyone else needs to know, especially Serenity."

I know I'm taking a huge risk admitting everything to him and asking him to keep it from the woman he loves, but I really don't care how it looks because it won't do her any good knowing everything I'm going through, especially if she's got Lucifer back on her plate.

"Fine. You don't want anyone else knowing, but that still doesn't explain why you didn't tell me about it sooner. If you've been having the headaches that long, it means it was happening the last time I was here with you and you didn't say a word."

"It's my issue, not yours. You've got the girl of your dreams to focus on and a wedding to plan. It's not like you want to hear this."

He moves closer to me and in a move so unlike me that even I'm shocked by it, I step back from him, not sure what he's planning on doing but wanting no part of a confrontation. I'm too worn down to fight him, if that's what he's looking for. I just want him gone and out of here so I can wallow in my misery alone.

"Man, you obviously need to learn a thing or two about what it is I wanna know. You could have told me this, in fact you should have. Between me and Michael, I'm sure we could have figured a way to fix this for you."

"There's nothing anyone can do, least of all you, even if you do have Gabriel's power now. I'm stuck with this, at least for the foreseeable future. Like I said, I'm handling it."

"Not if you're going to hide out in here for the rest of your life, you aren't. Where the heck is the guy that I fought alongside in Hell? The guy that got his ass kicked by a demon and still managed to get up and fight harder than the angels did?"

"He's dead."

"I don't believe that. The Graham Hudson I know wouldn't back down from a fight, especially when it's something that has everything to do with the girl he's bonded to. He would stand and fight with us."

"I've got no more fight left! Don't you get it? Whatever he did to me and whatever I went through in Hell has drained it all out of me. I can't go there again."

"You're a coward."

"Maybe I am, maybe I'm not. Either way, I can't do this with you guys this time. The guy you knew, if you ever really knew him at all, is dead. Dead and gone and he isn't coming back. So if you need to save Serenity, you better go do it because I want no part of it."

Chapter Thirteen

Michael

There has never been a time that I have felt anything other than peace coming home. With all the dealings that take place on various plains, all of the different avenues we must take in an effort to reinstate an overall feeling of calm, home is a safe place. As I step through the gates now though, it is not a feeling of safety, peacefulness or tranquility that I am filled with. It is as far from all of those things as you can get.

I am filled with doubt and the trust I once had where Father is concerned, is at an all time low. I have not placed blame for this newest development at his doorstep because if I am completely honest, something like this was expected. That expectation had waned with the passage of time, but it was always there under the surface. I just cannot accept that I had taken my focus off it in dealing with other issues that presented themselves.

I am Fathers' most trusted warrior. I should have been better prepared for this. If I had done what I was made to do, maybe he wouldn't have gotten the chance to get through to Serenity at all, brand or no brand. It is a fact that doesn't sit well with me.

Heaven has always operated in this way. Father has always known more than the rest of us and he has always chosen what information was most important to share before passing it on. Keeping everything else that may be just as important locked up tightly inside himself. It has worked well for us, but over the last year, I am finding that I am like my brother in that I can't deal with only half the facts. This is why the doubt has risen inside of me and is showing no signs of slowing down.

If my own father cannot be honest with me, especially in times such as these, then I do not think I can move forward in the capacity that he needs me.

What that means is that I am walking a dangerous line. Questioning him in the manner I have been over the last six months, added to the fact that I am on a search for more answers then he is willing to give means that I am no better than Lucifer.

He questioned Father, he pushed the boundaries, even going so far as to voice his displeasure at what Father planned to do with the humans or rather, how he wanted us to regard them. He didn't fear the reaction his actions would cause and it is now as I am only mere steps away from coming face to face with the man again regarding the very person I am feeling an odd sense of allegiance with, I feel most like him.

I am not the only brother that has walked this path since Lucifer was cast out. Gabriel also walked this line and it is his way of being now that I attempt to summon in order to get through what comes next. If I am to make it through this meeting with Father, especially given what it is that we need to discuss, then I am going to need Gabriel more than ever.

"It appears as though with Lucifer's death the branding did not diminish the way we believed it would."

The distrust running through me is almost too hard to contain as he speaks to me. It is only the people that were in the church that night that believed the branding to cease its control the moment Lucifer reached his true death. Father knew better, so him acting as though he assumed the same thing only makes everything worse and put me even more on the defensive.

He is all seeing and knowing. It is written about in many a religious text and I have seen it with my own eyes every time I stood by his side. Why he is choosing to lie to me now is beyond me, but I am not going to sit idly by and give him the chance. It is time we move forward the right way, or not at all.

"Let us not stand here and pretend that you did not know this would happen because it is just wasted breath Father. You have known from the very beginning that this is where we would find ourselves."

"You are correct."

"You know, I have been trying to figure out why you do the things you do and no matter how hard I try to put the pieces together, they still make no sense. Why would you let us walk into the situation with Lucifer knowing that only a short time later we would be standing here now discussing what to do about his reappearance?"

"Michael, you are aware that I do not upset the natural order. They must take place as they have been written. Any interference can spell disaster."

"Disaster like we are now facing? Serenity, your greatest gift, about to walk into the bowels of Hell yet again in an effort to do what she believes is the right thing, even though you, me and everyone that surrounds us know it to be a ploy?"

"It has always been her, you know this."

"The undertaking again? Really? Did you not sit here months ago and explain to Gabriel and me that the moment in the church was to be the end of it? That she was to reach her full potential in that moment and it would end once and for all?"

"I did say that, but as you can see, nothing went according to plan."

"Because Ryan was the one to drive the weapon deep into Lucifer's non-existent heart?"

"No, that was written about. She played her part flawlessly in terms of taking care of the immediate threat."

"Then why is this happening now? For that matter, why wasn't Ryan taken the minute he did as Heaven wanted of him?"

I do not expect him to give me the answers I seek so desperately. It has never worked that way. So many things he kept from us, it's amazing that he can even keep them straight. As much as I stand by my belief that in order to do the right thing always, we need all the information beforehand, I do not ever expect it to actually take place.

"I only kept the information from you in an effort to keep things moving the way they were meant too. Gabriel is a casualty I do not want repeated, even though he knew a lot more than the rest of Heaven was aware of. The point is to not change the natural order of things and suffer more losses the way that we have been in recent years. I do believe you need to have the answers you want, so against my better judgment, I will tell you."

"Against your better judgment? Don't you mean, you will tell me because you do not have a choice in the matter any longer?"

"There is always choice, Michael. Lucifer wanted us torn apart and even with him trapped where he is now, he is still getting his way. Can you not see that?"

"I see a Father that I love and cherish more than life talking about how he will explain all to me, yet still wasting time on trivial things that have little or no consequence to what we now face."

"Ryan was not taken because I did not want to tear him away from the life he lives with Serenity. Gabriel was right in that regard the first time around. It is nothing but a punishment to give the boy what he prayed so desperately for and then strip it all away from him. Your brother gave up the very light inside of him so that the two of them could live happily ever after and I see no reason to take it away from them now. It would shame Gabriel's memory."

For the first time in the year and a half that we have been going through failed plan after plan, he is telling the truth and saying things that make sense to me. I still have my doubts, but with the truths he is giving me now, it is beginning to lessen.

He still has a long way to go through before I ever truly join by his side again.

"As for why this is happening now, Serenity has been branded and it has not been dealt with. It is because of that very brand that Lucifer is able to use what remains of his dark power to reach out to her. She is still very much in the midst of her undertaking. In doing this, she is taking the first steps to achieving it once and for all, even though she is unaware of it."

"What exactly is she supposed to do? Ryan ended him just as you needed him to, so what is there left to do but wait until the power dries up within him and he finally ceases to exist?"

"That is something I cannot tell you." He answers, his eyes shifting from mine, again bringing the doubt back to the surface. "I know how that sounds, but you must trust in me one final time. This isn't about going to war any longer. We have reached that end quite beautifully already. What happens next is about something more."

Despite my misgivings regarding the way all of this has been handled, I am still very much my father's son. I still stand by him despite the doubts I have and the way I feel myself drifting deep inside. I want to do right by him and help him achieve that which he is setting in motion. It's just becoming harder to do with the secrets he continues to keep.

"What you believe is false, Michael and you would do better remembering just who I am and the power I wield."

"Are you planning on casting me out the way you had me do to Lucifer?"

I have no idea where the words came from, but even if I upset him, I was not going to take them back. In choosing to do things in the manner in which he is, he has brought this reaction in me and it is time that he deals with it instead of me always pushing it down. Nothing would ever change until we confront it.

"Do not be ridiculous, Michael. While you have doubts and I do not enjoy it, I understand in your case why you have them, something I could never quite get with your fallen brother. I will not cast you out for questioning me. I am doing this for all of our sakes and I need you to remember that even when it seems to be something else entirely."

"What part does Gregory Richards play in this? I am sure that you are aware of the conversation that took place between us. That he was visited by Lucifer when Serenity was a young child and it is because of him that Gregory ended up where he did. What do you plan to do to rectify that situation?"

"Gregory Richards has his part to play in all of this and you will come to find out soon enough exactly what that is. Michael, you must let Serenity do what she believes she has to do. It is the only way to reach the end result we all desire here. We will reach this end and achieve true peace once and for all. Isn't that what all of this has been about from the beginning?"

All of this was started hundreds of years before though a lot more of the emphasis seems to be placed on this small span of time. What Father wanted in the very beginning, when he made Serenity to begin with was always ultimate peace for the world and for Heaven. What is above must be below. He was right in that regard. Through each lifetime I guarded the ball of light, it had always been about peace, even though right now peace seems unattainable.

I want nothing more than to get back to the overall goal. Not only because I believe it is what the people of Earth and even the other planets need, but because it is exactly what Heaven needs. We have been under attack for far too long and it is time that the proverbial ball is returned to our court.

"So in order to achieve the peace that you spoke of millennia ago, we must let our ball of light venture into Hell and stand before Lucifer one final time?"

"That is exactly what we need to do, but there is more. You must not let her go alone."

"Well I figured it was a given that she wouldn't be going alone. She doesn't have the first clue what it takes to even enter through the gates there; she is going to need not only me, but Ryan as well."

"There is more information that I have on that front that you need to be made aware of. You must heed what I am about to tell you and be sure to pass it along to the pure angel as well."

Anytime he is willing to give me information, I am more than a little pleased. Maybe the doubts that still linger in me can be erased after all. Extending his knowledge to me now will go a long way to repairing some of it at least.

"Lucifer still resides over his home even though he is trapped. He has pulled the guards down and has given her a free pass for entry. She will make her way to him without the issues that you spoke of when you were there the previous time. He fancies himself to care about her so in an effort to get what he needs, he is using all of his remaining power to keep her protected at all times the minute she enters."

"He's protecting her? Do you realize how ridiculous that sounds given everything he has already done to the girl?"

"I am aware of how it appears Michael, but regardless, he has put it into motion. Showing up with her might set him off, but I do not foresee any issues with you being able to make it through with her. She has the power inside of her needed to create a portal that will take her to Hell. Therefore she does not need you for entrance."

"Yet you still want us to accompany her?"

"Most definitely. I am aware of the excuses that your brother has given as it pertains to Gabriel and also how false they are. I do not want her falling for any more of his parlor tricks. That will change everything in terms of what I have seen. Both you and Ryan must go with her despite their current issues and protect her from anything that deviates from what has been foretold."

"How are we to do that if we do not know what it is you have seen in its entirety?"

"You will know, my son. The answers lie within you. They have the entire time. Trust your judgment."

Chapter Fourteen

Serenity

I have no idea what I'm doing. I don't think I've known what I'm doing for the last year a half. It's just been me flying by the seat of my pants and hoping that it all turns out the way it's supposed to. The thing is; it never turns out the way it's supposed to. Every single decision that I've made, all in an effort to make things right again, seems to go tragically wrong.

Giving myself over to Lucifer in an effort to save Ryan might have been the start of it. Hell, it's probably not the start, I've been taking bonehead chances long before that, but that's the first time I really remember making a choice that had nothing to do with me and everything to do with someone else. I thought that in giving myself over to the devil, I would save Ryan and it did work, just not before almost taking me into the darkness in the process.

Saving Graham came next. I really didn't think that one out at all. All I thought about was making sure that Ryan didn't reach his destiny and get himself taken from me. It was selfish yet sacrificial at the same time because I wanted nothing more than to be the one to save Graham. I saved him because the plan worked the way it was meant to at the start, but everything that came next blew the good deed I did to shit. Lucifer possessed me and Ryan had been forced to stand before me and take my life away.

Lucifer planned for that or at least that's what I believe happened because I didn't die. I ended up in Hell with him the way he wanted from the start. At least Ryan didn't have to live with my death on his conscience. It was still a bonehead move

113

that I rushed too quickly into though. Ryan's right when he said I was doing what he has always done. I am rushing into things without thinking them out and doing that only causes more damage.

I'm here and I'm doing it again, except this time I have no clue how it's all going to turn out and even if I sit back and go over everything, taking the time and planning out my every move from this point on, I still can't plan it entirely. Anything can still happen. I know I'm about to make another stupid choice, but I can only hope that in doing it alone, I'm sparing anyone else the pain of whatever my choices leave behind.

As long as I walk into this way, go to Lucifer and attempt to save Gabriel alone, then everyone else remains safe and I don't have to worry about the fallout. There is always fallout though and it's the kind that will be felt for years to come. I don't want that, but I really don't have any way around it. It's inevitable.

His words haunt me, not because of the way I feel about him, but because everything he said is right. Well mostly everything. The last bit about me feeding off his emotions is wrong. I know that I do that, it's something we're going to have to face in our life together, if there is even a life together anymore, but in this one instance, everything I felt had been me.

I'm blinded by my own feelings and the emotional upheaval I've been through, not only in the last few days, but few months. I need Gabriel and as stupid as that sounds, it doesn't make it any less true. All of this, what's going on right now, he would get it. He might not agree with it because it almost seems like his life's mission had been to hate a lot of my choices, but he would accept it and in some way he would offer me advice that could carry me through what has to happen next.

He always did that, talked to me in a way that made things seem more clear. I need that now. I know going into Hell is not going to turn out well for me, but I can't seem to stop myself.

He might not be able to make me stop, but he would slow me down enough to really think all of this through.

I've been doing everything so far based on pure emotion and I need to stop that. Ryan and I fight and the first thing I do is run off and begin preparing myself for my entrance into Hell. Instead of staying in the room and working through this, I'm choosing the far more dangerous option because I'm blinded by my emotions. My need to know if I can save the angel that at one point I had come to love and respect. The need to do right by Lucifer because I know that deep down he deserves so much more than he's been given or even so much more than he's taken. I am being driven by the things I feel for these two beings and even the most rational thought process can't break through it.

I want someone to break through so badly, it hurts. I don't want to keep doing this for the rest of my life. I want to do what Ryan said and just enjoy the rest of our life together, but I don't think I'm ever going to be able to. I'm always going to be the girl that wants to save the world, make things right and somehow find my own worth in the midst of it all. I will always want to do what I believe is the right thing, even if it's wrong.

That's why I walked away from Ryan. He deserves better than that. He deserves better than someone who can't stop sacrificing themselves for the greater good. I don't care how he was before I met him; he's always been so much more. I don't think I can be that person for him, not anymore.

From my confusion with Graham, to the bond with not only Gabriel, but the one that even now lingers on my heart for Lucifer, I can never truly be his. No matter how hard I try to force it to be otherwise. We might be born of the same light, we may mean the same things and we might even be bonded even tighter together because of what Gabriel did, but he is by far the better person. The part of me that I want so desperately to be, but can't.

I need to move forward, face Lucifer again and let Ryan go.

"Just because you let me go, doesn't mean I'm letting you go."

No, this is not happening right now. This is not the way it's supposed to be.

"Well it's the way it's going to be, so I suggest you get used to it."

Spinning around and being met with the cloudy blue eyes I have come to love so much, the comeback I'd been prepared to give falls flat as I'm rendered speechless. How am I supposed to do the right thing by him, let him go, when he's standing this close to me? At this rate I would never be able to do what I need to do. I would just fail again.

"You know, I'm starting to see why I didn't do relationships before."

If we were going to get into this again, fight with each other because we couldn't see eye to eye about what needed to happen next, I want no part of it. The damage had already been done in his dorm room.

"Serenity, I'm not here to fight with you..." he whispers, his eyes lowering just slightly from my own, which causes my heart to hurt even more than it already was.

"Then stop reading my mind."

"I can't help it! Your thoughts, they're so fucking loud in my head that I can't help but hear them! If you don't want me doing it then stop thinking so much."

"What do you mean by, you see why you didn't do relationships before?"

"Because you're all bat shit crazy. I mean, really. The things I'm hearing you think are beyond crazy and if I could shut off this damn ability, I would. I really don't want to spend another second inside a woman's head, especially when all it's filled with is bullshit."

"So not only am I feeding off you and not feeling things for myself, but now my thoughts are bullshit. Wow Ryan, tell me how you really feel."

"Fine!" he yells before moving toward me, bridging the already tiny gap between us. "That thought you have that you always fail, bullshit. The one you have where you think I deserve better, that one's bullshit too. If you actually think about it, there is no being alive that is better for me than you. Because you're not the only one that is bat shit crazy and leaps before they think. You're not the only one who wants to do the right thing so badly they're willing to give up their own useless life to make sure it happens. Serenity, you are me."

Well shit. Now I really don't know what to say. The anger I had been ready to unleash fades away so fast, that I don't even remember what the hell I was so mad about to begin with.

"It's not bull—shit." I stammer, trying to collect my thoughts and get back to the way I felt before he showed up and blew it apart. "You deserve better and I am not you."

"Pretty girl..." he whispers, the breath from his words now warming my face. "We don't need a bond between us to know that we are one. Deny it all you want, but you know it's the truth."

When he's this close to me, I've never been able to think straight and this time is no different. Everything that I could have planned out to say is just no longer there. All I can focus on is the way my body feels having him this close. How safe and protected I feel. It's exactly what he says it is. We are one because there is no one that I've ever felt this feeling with.

I'm complete.

It still doesn't change what I need to do, which means we're right back where we always seem to be. At a crossroads, neither one of us prepared to back down on what we truly believe to be the right thing.

"It doesn't change the facts, Ryan."

"I know that, it's actually why I'm here."

Now I'm confused. If he knows that nothing changes, why is he here?

"You're doing it again..."

"Doing what?"

117

"Thinking too loud."

"Do it then. Read me. Say whatever you want to say, though I can't see how it's going to change anything."

"I don't entirely understand why you need to do this, I swear I'm trying, but I can't because I didn't experience everything that you went through during your time with Lucifer. I only know what my time with him was like. So I got angry. I felt betrayed, but most of all, I felt disconnected. I haven't felt so far away from you since he took you from me and I don't want to feel it for another minute longer."

"What are you saying?"

"I'm saying that even though I don't understand it, I'm not going to let you go through it alone. I made a promise before and I plan to stick by it now. I will never leave you again Serenity, so if you need to do this, then I need to do it too."

I can't believe what I'm hearing. This is not something I expected to hear from him, despite knowing the way he feels about me. I also don't expect it to be dripping in truth even though that's the only way Ryan has ever been. Where most guys would say whatever the girl wants to hear and I would be able to see right through it, it isn't the case with him He's being completely one hundred percent honest with me.

If he comes with me the way he's saying he wants to then I can't guarantee that something horrible won't happen. I can't guarantee his safety. If I do it alone, I could make sure that no matter what happened he would survive, even if he lost me in the process. This way, nothing is clear and I don't like it.

"If you think for a second that I'm letting you face him alone then you might as well kill me now. If something happens to you and I'm not there to protect you, I'm going to end up dead anyway."

"You don't mean that."

He runs his fingers across my face and rests his forehead against mine, sending an electrified shiver through my body the minute our bodies connect, which causes him to smile before he speaks again.

"I mean every word, Serenity. I will not live without you."

"If something happens to you, I'll never be able to live with myself."

"Well, I guess," he whispers, his breath again, blowing hot on my cheeks. "We make sure nothing happens to me, huh?"

Before I can even process his words, he places his lips to mine and all rational response fades as I succumb to the electricity that runs through me, through us, the same way it always has. The pull between us at an all time high, thanks in part to the very bond we share between us.

Pulling away a few seconds later, leaving me with the tingle that remains on my lips where his had just been, he tips my head up so that my eyes are locked on his again, both of us frozen in place, not even a blink occurring between us.

"You are me, Serenity and if we're going to do this, we're going to do it together. Always."

Chapter Fifteen

Lucifer

With each moment that passes, I am beginning to doubt that Serenity is coming the way she claimed she would. With only the memories of a life long ago lived to keep me company, it is taking everything in me to continue to believe in her and in the plan that I am so desperate to make happen.

It all centers on her. If she does not come the way that I have asked her to then all of this will be worthless and I am going to have to resign myself to a life lived very much in the very hell that I have created, much the way Ryan yelled at me that fateful evening. She must see this through; it is the only way we all get that which we want.

There is more work to be done of course. Once she is here and she learns of the lie at which I told in order to garner her trust, I must take it a step further and make her see the truth behind the lie. I have only taken this step in an effort to finally do what I should have done so long ago.

Go home again.

Having firsthand knowledge of the mess I have made during the time since I have been cast out has been an eye opener for me. I have always known that the method of memory torture was truly horrific, but to have it placed on me the way in which it is now is truly something to behold. With the humans I have used it on, showing them the darkest parts of themselves, or the worst moments of their lives was always pleasurable, but with me the horrible things I have done has no effect. It is the memories of the good times that do damage.

It is made even worse when all of the good memories I can recall all seem to center around one being. The one being that despite all of my attempts otherwise, I cannot feel an ounce of hatred for.

Gabriel.

There are instances in time with my brother that I recall easier than others, a lot of them taking place sometime after I had been cast out. It is not known to many, but Gabriel despite acting otherwise when in the presence of others, has been to see me on more than one occasion, all in a misguided attempt to rectify what had taken place and to try and bring me around to what lies at my very core. He wanted nothing more than for me to come home again, more than prepared to go to our father on my behalf.

I remember the visits fondly even though they never went the way he hoped they would. I envied him more than I think he knew and I envy him now. The light so strong inside of him working side by side with the emotions that Father had given him, one of the most pure and true angels alive.

The hole in my chest where my heart should be aches remembering that much of him, yet I cannot seem to turn away from the pain. Instead, I let them overtake me and allow myself to feel everything that I felt then, but never showed. It is my penance for the things I have not only put everyone through, but also put Gabriel himself through.

*****

"Why do you insist on doing things this way brother? You must realize by now that the last thing I want is to return home again. If anything, you have all done me a great service kicking me out in the manner you did. I am now free to live as I see fit."

"Surely you do not believe that, Lucifer. Even after all of this time and all the animosity that you harbor towards all beings of the light, you must still long for the simplicity of home."

121

"I cannot say that I do. Immersing myself in a life among the humans, as trying as it can be at times, has its advantages. I do not believe it would be wise to give that up even if I had the option afforded to me."

"You know as well as I do that Father has always had one motivation in every single move he makes. There is not a being alive that cannot be redeemed if they are willing to own that which they have done against him. The same can be said for you. If you just go to Father, with me by your side and you own all of what you have done, I have no doubt he will look upon you favorably."

My brother in his true form is such a sight to behold and I do not mean the way he appears before me now. I mean the heart at which is displayed at any given time, regardless of the situation he finds himself in. He has always worn his heart on his sleeve and even now when he should keep it hidden under lock and key, it is paramount in every word he speaks.

He truly wants me to come back home and believes that despite all of the havoc I have created, both in the world and here in Hell that it is achievable. I do not want to be the one to burst his bubble, but there is no beautiful ending for me. When and if the time ever comes, I will not see the light again; I will only see the flames.

"Gabriel, you know how much I love and respect you even with us being on opposite sides, but Father is not the pure one you believe him to be. I assure you, even if I wanted to take this step with you right now, he would look at me any way but favorably."

"I refuse to believe that. He loves each and every one of us equally, even when we go up against him and do things that he does not like. He is a forgiving God and if you would only come home with me, I can prove it to you."

"I will die before entering the gates, brother. I admire the desire inside of you to see me redeemed, not only in fathers eyes, but the eyes of all beings born of the light but it is just not possible. You must leave here now, before they suspect you of *consorting with the enemy, but Gabriel, take these final words with you as you go."*

I pause, giving him the chance to prepare himself for the gravity of what I am about to say next and when I see his light begin to burn even brighter awaiting my words, I know he is more than ready to hear what I've been dying to tell him since the moment I fell.

"I know that we will come across each other in battle as time continues to move forward, but please know that when we do, no harm will come to you by my hand. You are the only remaining piece of the light that I want to keep protected at all costs and I will go to my death doing just that."

*****

I meant every word spoken during that visit and I only hope that as he reached his end he went knowing that I kept my promise. Despite coming up against him as many times as I have, I always kept him separate from the anger I am driven by. Even in death he remains the only being of light that I will always want to protect and do right by, even if it's not possible.

At least that's how I looked at it until I met his beloved. Serenity reminded me a great deal of Gabriel, which might have been the reason I pursued her as hard as I did, even going so far as to visit her father when she was a young child and becoming one with him in an effort to get closer to her. As the years went on, the need to have her became compulsive and more dark in nature, but the minute I learned of the light that resided inside her, how pure and untainted it really is, I gravitated toward it like no other being before other than my brother.

When she spent time with me here, I told her the truth from the very pit of whatever is left of my soul. I wanted to keep her here with me and protect her, spending my life with her because if I could not have Gabriel by my side or even

Ryan, it had to be her. I needed to have that constant reminder of the light, which is why I never stripped her of it once I had her.

I could have done it easily, but it has always been about the light. I have a very complicated relationship with that which I have left behind. I hate it, loathe it even, yet I love it just as deeply and do not want to be without it. Serenity was the key to having it all and being here now as I am, for the first time since the day I fell, I feel broken and in need of fixing. I want the light the way Gabriel described it to me that day and I want it badly.

So bad that I'm willing to wait until she comes so that right before her very eyes I can do the one thing I should done that day he came to me.

I can renounce the darkness that has haunted my soul once and for all.

I want to go home.

Ryan

When she left my room I knew where she would go. It's the only place that despite everything we've been through, both together and apart, she can't seem to let go of. So when I took the detour and went to see Graham, I knew that when the time was right, I would see her again.

Am I naïve enough to think that just because I'm here now, holding her in my arms that we've worked through all of our issues? No, of course I don't, but being here in this moment with her, letting her know I'm coming with her, I'm doing what needs to be done.

Some can say that I don't know her as well as I like to think I do, but they haven't exactly walked a day in my shoes to know just how much I've learned about her and come to love even more. This place, the park in Green Haven where I first experienced the lengths at which she would go to save me, is a treasured location to her. It's the place that she went and looked up at the stars, a place where she prayed for me, even if she didn't realize it. It is the place where all of her issues didn't seem quite so huge anymore. It is the one true place other then with me that I know she feels safe.

I had no idea what I was going to say to her or even if she would be willing to listen to me, but with her final words weighing so heavily on my mind and knowing the true meaning behind all of them, I had to try.

Serenity would never be the girl that did what she was told without question. She wouldn't follow rules and she would most definitely never settle for someone who only wanted that with her. I knew this about her yet despite that, I still tried to force her to do what I knew in her heart she would never be able to. Yes, everything I said is right, but just because it was right didn't make it right for her and somewhere along the way I lost sight of that.

She believes me to be deserving of better than her and the simple truth is, just as I've told her, there is no better because we're the same. She'd known it all along even though it had taken her a long time to share it with me. Right from the beginning she believed me to be her soul mate, the other half of her and even though that's not my title, there is no doubt in my mind that is exactly what we are. She is me and I am her and we are one.

It has always been that way, even before we knew it ourselves.

So I stand here now, with her in my arms about to again venture into something all because this beautiful light can't rest until she knows for sure and for certain that she has done everything in her power to mend what is broken. It's not about Gabriel or even Lucifer anymore, this is about her. My pretty girl is broken and this is the only way she can think of to fix it.

By saving not only an angel that was gone too soon, but also the fallen brother she believes deserves more than he's been given. In doing that she will begin to heal and become the woman that she's always been underneath all of the pain. She will become the woman I fell in love with again and I will stop at nothing, even if I don't entirely agree with it, to make sure that happens.

I will keep my promise to her. She will never go through life alone. Not while there is still breath in my body to fight.

"I'm sorry that I can't give you that perfect life you want, Ryan."

With as much as I was enjoying the comfortable silence that surrounded us here, I'm more than a little grateful she finally spoke though I don't like the words she says.

"You have given it to me."

"So being in constant fight mode, ready to sacrifice everything in a moment's notice, is your idea of perfect then?"

"Well, when you put it that way, no, but what you have given me outweighs all of that."

"I'm not sure what you mean."

I'm not entirely sure how to explain to her everything she's done for me just in the time I've known her, so the only way I can think of to get my point across is to show her. Reaching my hand out and pointing across the park to the swing set that sits cold and abandoned, I see the perfect way to make her see.

"Why are you pointing at the swings, Ry?"

"Because I'm going to explain something and then I'm going to ask you to do something with me and I'm hoping that by the end of it, it might make more sense what I'm trying to say and can't. I suck at this bearing your soul thing."

"You say things like *you are me, we are one* and you think you suck at baring your soul? You really have no clue what actually works on girls do you?"

"Well, since you're the only girl I've ever said and done anything with, I guess you already know the answer to that."

She laughs and it's a sound that stops me in my tracks. I'm fully prepared one second to explain something to her, proceeding to show her what I mean and suddenly, it fades away the minute the sound breaks from her lips. I never want

126

to forget the way she sounds when she laughs and the ability it has to steady my heart, even at the darkest moment.

"Where are all your smooth moves now, McGregor?"

"Pretty girl, you really need a memory refresh. You're the one that said I didn't have any moves remember? So again, you already know the answer."

Again she laughs and this time I waste no time making my move, immediately placing my lips to her forehead.

"Don't ever stop laughing...promise me."

"I promise." She says, her voice coming out far more breathless than expected. "Didn't you have something you wanted to explain to me?"

"Yeah, I do. You see that swing over there, the one I pointed to? I want you to think of that swing as me." When she smiles, I laugh, knowing how silly it sounds. "Trust me; just imagine me as that swing. You see how there are no others around it? That was me before you. I was cold just like the swing is and more importantly I was alone."

"Is it supposed to sound this depressing Ry? Cause I swear if you're trying to make me cry, it's working."

"No, that's not what I'm trying to do at all." I answer as I lock my hand in hers. "It's time for the show portion of the program. Come on."

Making our way over to the swing that's barely moving with the force of the wind, I again point and watch as she looks back at me confused.

"Sit."

"Ryan, it's like twenty below out here, I'm not sitting on the swing. I don't want to know what it feels like to literally freeze your ass off."

"Please just sit for me; I swear it's only going to be for a few seconds."

She does as I ask and I immediately walk around until I'm directly behind her. As I pull the swing backwards, preparing to propel her forward, I again go over what my intent is in wanting to do this and I wonder if this is the best way to get my point across. I want her to know in some small way how she's affected my life and this is the only way available to do it. I only hope it works.

As I push her forward and stand back, I listen to her shriek as she flies into the air and then the laughter as it comes pouring out as she continues what I started by pumping her legs and pushing herself even higher. It's in the moment that her laughter spills out that it's proven to me. This is the best way to show her what she does to me. It couldn't be more perfect.

Waiting until she slows to a crawl, I wrap my hands around the bars and come around to face her, bending down and looking straight into her eyes, the same way she does with me when she looks into my soul.

"You wanted to know how you've made my life perfect, well now you know."

"You're still not making sense."

"That cold lonely swing, the moment you sat on it and I pushed you into the air, you brought it to life, Serenity. It's exactly what you've done to me since the moment I met you. You reached out to the cold, lonely part of me and with your laughter, smile and the beautiful way you are inside, you brought me to life."

Before she has a chance to say another word, I hold my finger up to her lip and speak again. With what we're about to face, I want to make sure every single card is out on the table. She needs to know it all, whether we're completely healed or not.

"You've already made my life perfect just by bringing the light back into it and I don't mean the light that you saw in me before anyone else. I'm talking about the actual light. Do you feel the bars under your hands? How do they feel right now?"

"Well honestly, they're a little wet from me warming them up."

"Okay that's not what I was going for..." I say, unable to hide the grin threatening to break through.

"I know, but I wanted to see your smirk. Mission accomplished. I win. He reacts to the word wet."

She doesn't even realize she's doing it, but this is exactly what I've been craving from her for months. Just like the night of our date when she made light of the things I did and said, she's doing it again and reminding me again just how lucky I am. This is my Serenity, the one that fights even when everything in her wants to be consumed by the grief. I have never been more thankful then I am now. I've got my girl back, even if it is only for a little while.

"Okay focus, pretty girl. How do the bars feel, besides the wetness?"

"Warm."

"That's what you do for me, Serenity. You seem to think that everything has to be a certain way in order to be perfect, but I swear to you, my version of perfect is far less complicated. You're like the sunshine to me. You broke out through the darkness and you did exactly what your hands did to the swing. You brought me into the light and warmed my heart. That's perfection to me."

"Even after everything I've put you through with all the stupid choices I've made?"

"Because of the choices you've made. You're imperfectly perfect, Serenity and that's exactly what makes this, us, my version of perfection."

"I'm your version of perfection?"

"You're not my version, pretty girl. You are my perfection."

Caught up in the sight of her as my words register not only across her face, but in her heart, I lean in, fully prepared to do what I've been dying to since the second I stopped the swing, but before my lips can reach hers, I hear it, clear as day, ruining the moment just like always.

"It is time."

Chapter Sixteen

Michael

It is quite obvious by the looks on their faces that I had once again popped in on them at the wrong moment. After speaking with Father and learning as much as I had, I wanted to get a jumpstart on what was due to happen next. Using the power afforded to me, I located Ryan and was surprised to find him again with his beloved, especially after the fight I witnessed earlier in the day.

Whether they have worked through their problems or not is the least of my concerns. The only problem I have is where is the Hudson boy?

"As usual Michael, you have *the best* timing."

"Just be thankful that I have respected your wishes and have not shown up at your dorm room when you are in various stages of undress."

Serenity laughs as Ryan rolls his eyes in my direction, but before I can question the whereabouts of Graham, she speaks first.

"You've seen my husband naked? Before or after I did?"

"After." Both Ryan and I say simultaneously.

"I don't know what's worse," Serenity says as she tries to choke down her laughter. "The fact that you're speaking at the same time or that Michael even knows what I'm talking about."

"Serenity, between me and Gabriel, we have been sworn to protect you at all costs, so it should not come as a surprise that I am aware of all that goes on as it pertains to you. More than that, the two of you are some of the loudest beings I have ever heard, including the animals."

"Go loud or go home." Ryan whispers under his breath as Serenity's cheeks go pink as she giggles.

Yes, it appears as though the two of them have gotten past their issues, at least the more pressing ones. A fact that pleases me as it means we will have a much easier time moving forward.

"After a very informative talk with Father I do believe that Serenity doing this is the right step. I may not entirely understand why everything is taking place in this way, but I'm confident moving ahead. There is only one thing that disturbs me."

"You say what you just said and there's only one thing that disturbs you?" Serenity asks, the smile still locked firmly in place on her face.

Choosing to ignore her statement in favor of getting some much needed answers, I turn to Ryan. Before leaving to visit Father I was of the impression that he would be making his way to the Hudson boy and now more than ever I need to know where he is. After what happened to him the last time we left him alone, there is validity in my concerns.

"Did you speak to Graham as I suggested?"

"I did."

"Then why is he not standing here with us now? It was my understanding he would want to be a part of this as it does concern him."

"Michael, there's been some shit going down since you cut communication with us. Actually, it's been going on before that, at least according to him. It's because of it that he's not here right now."

"What is this shit that you speak of?"

"He's been getting headaches. Nightmares of what Lucifer put him through. Mike, it's bad. He can't put himself through it again and honestly I can't say I blame him."

This upsets me greatly. Graham Hudson had been a warrior I could only compare as equal to me during our time in Hell. He was strong willed, filled with the right levels of need for justice and overall, a great companion to have at my side for the fight we had endured. To hear that he was experiencing horrors now of which I couldn't even begin to imagine, pains me.

I know I am not made of the same things as my brother despite the both of us being born of the same light, but I would have hoped he knew he could bring anything to me and I would help in any manner I am able. The fact that he hasn't done that speaks volumes about just how hard he is taking my brothers passing.

"Did he tell you why he did not bring this to our attention?"

"Well, since it started back when Serenity was missing, I figure he kept it silent because he wanted us focused on her. After Hell though, I can't tell you. All I know is he's self medicating and if he's not careful it's gonna take him down a bad road."

"Why didn't you tell me?" Serenity interrupts, the pain she feels at hearing of Graham's plight clearly evident as she frowns.

"I just found out, Ser and honestly you were pretty pissed at me. I'm not sure you would have believed me."

"When have I ever doubted you that way? Oh whatever, it doesn't even matter because even if he was okay, I still wouldn't want him there with me. I don't even want you two there, but I don't seem to have a choice. Looks like Gabriel was right."

The minute my brother's name fell from her lips I found myself desiring more information. Just what had he been right about and if it was before or after his passing? Even though I know the latter is impossible, I can't help but wonder what if it isn't?

"What was Gabriel right about, Serenity?"

Her eyes look at me warily, almost as if she is afraid of what the answer she gives might do to me.

"The night before we went to save Graham, he said something to me about the two of you and he was right."

"What was it?" I ask a little more eagerly then I am intending.

132

"I asked him if there was some other way around what Ryan had to do and he said no, unless I wanted to go my own way, something that he knew I wouldn't get very far with given your power level and Ryan's feelings. This reminds me of that. He was right. You're never going to let me face anything alone."

"We are family, Serenity so of course we won't. That is what family does, is it not?"

I am most unfamiliar with the ways in which human families operate, but I do know a thing or two about the way it works above and Serenity is a part of that whether she wants to acknowledge it or not. I would go to my death to protect her.

"You must accept that you are no longer alone in any of this. Ryan and I will be there with you every step of the way. I am aware of your fears for our safety as well as Graham's, but I assure you, we were built for this very thing."

"I can't expect you to always ride to the rescue when I make stupid choices." She answers back almost immediately.

I spent a lot of time with her during Ryan's recovery in Heaven and I feel that I have gotten to know her quite well because of it. In the moment, with the words she just uttered, she is being at her most open and honest. This is the girl I remember from all of those months ago and I could only hope that as we move forward, both now and in the future, I would see more of this from her.

"The choices you have made in the past are only stupid to you. You have had reasons for each choice you made and despite what may have happened because of them, it does not change the fact that they were decisions made purely because of the way that you are. They are based solely in the light because at your most basic, that is who you are. You are a pure being of light and you will always want to do right by everyone."

I can tell that my words make her uncomfortable and while I do understand the human condition much better than I did in the beginning, I am at a loss as to why she has such a hard time believing them even though she knows it to be the truth.

"You don't think wanting to fix things for Lucifer is wrong? Is that what I'm hearing?"

"Despite my past with my brother, no I do not. Father made the choice to have me be the one to cast him out and that is between me and him. It is not something you need to concern yourself with. You wanting to do right by him is not wrong nor will I ever tell you such a thing. You saw a side of him that he has not shown many and it is because of that and the branding he placed on your heart that drives you now. It is pure Serenity."

"Looks like I'm the only one that doesn't get it then." Ryan spoke up causing me to turn away from Serenity and again put my focus on the other being of light before me.

"There is actually an answer for that as well Ryan, though because of how close you are, both to the situation and to Serenity, you are unable to see it as easily as I can."

"All ears, man."

"You spent a great deal of your human lifetime by the side of Lucifer that he deemed worthy to show. You did not experience him the way your beloved did and because of that you are unable to see past all of the darkness that he created and that you helped with. She is not wrong in her want to do this and you are not wrong in your need to want to keep her from it."

"Are we going to be able to do this without Graham?" Ryan asks, not even bothering to acknowledge my words which irritates me to no end. I am more than willing to get them both on the same page again, but not if they aren't willing to accept it. Their mistaken belief would be the very thing that ended them and the sooner they realize that and come together, realizing that they are both right, they would never be able to move on with the life they want with each other.

"Lucifer told me that he is going to keep everything away from me so that I can make it to him in one piece. Not sure if you showing up with me is going to change that though."

"He has to assume that even with the brand, you will not be going through this alone. Whether or not he realizes that I will be coming along with the both of you is something I cannot say, but I do know at the very least he will be expecting Ryan. We should be able to get through with minimal issues."

"So I guess that settles it. We're going to Hell." Serenity states, her voice barely an octave above a whisper.

"That is exactly what it means. So are we ready?"

I watch as Serenity nods her head and turning to Ryan I see a man conflicted. An understandable reaction given that again, he is about to come face to face with the man he believed he put an end to. He may not have the darkness in him any longer, but it is obvious that the history between the two men still ran thick.

Before I can ask him again if he is ready, he seems to shake off the place he allowed his mind to take him, leveling me with his gaze, the blue of his eyes almost brighter in comparison to times past.

"Let's get this over with."

Lucifer

For the first time in months I can feel her energy and while I am weak from everything that I have been through, I can feel what is left of my strength rise slowly to the surface inside of me.

She has always given me this reaction. Just being in her presence during the short time I had her with me, she always seemed to give me strength to go on, especially with the damage that had been done to me during battles past. This is another one of the reasons that she had been the one chosen. I enjoyed the way I felt when in her company and for as long as possible I wanted to surround myself with it.

It is not dark in nature, though I am sure that my brother would not feel the same. It appears as though she has not come alone. I can feel Ryan easily, but I can also feel the power of the light though it is not shining at its strongest given the location it finds itself in. Beggars cannot be choosers when communicating with someone in the outside world and even though I do not like that she did not come alone, the fact that she is here at all and I can feel her so powerfully is more than enough.

In just a short period of time she would be standing before me and I would be able to do and say all of the things that I had never gotten the chance to before my existence had been ripped from me. This is my one and only shot to do this right. The way Gabriel would want. I only hope that in some small way, he can feel the changes inside of me and believe in them because I know that if he can, maybe Serenity can as well.

With nothing but time on my hands, I have been going over exactly what needs to be said to her in order for me to move forward from one step to the other. I want to remove the brand from her heart before going any further. Call it what you will, but I know now that I should have never done it to begin with. I am no better than the practicing witches that live above me with their silly love potions. In fact, I am much worse because even though we both share the ability to do it and have the subject be unsuspecting, theirs will eventually wear off where this brand will not. Unless I remove it, it will remain with her forever and that is something that in my new way of thinking, I cannot live with.

If Gabriel were still alive then the brand I placed on her could be used to keep her from him and the bond that they share. The brother that I love so much and have tried to do right by even at my darkest point would be kept from the woman his very soul calls to and it would be my fault. Yes, he is no longer with us so that bond no longer matters, but it is the overall principle of it that bothers me the most. I could never do that to Gabriel and even in death, I will not do it now. No matter how badly I want to have her with me.

It really is like the humans assume. You cannot make someone love you, it will never work out and in the end you will lose them anyway. Graham Hudson had learned that lesson during the time when Serenity had been taken from me and he is paying for it dearly now, if what I sense is any indication. I could not be like him no matter how badly I wanted to keep her mine. She needs to be the one to make the decision to stay with me, the same way she did before and forcing her hand would only burn me in the end.

Getting her to the point where she trusts in me enough to remove the brand from her, is not a task I am looking forward to. There is far too much history between us to expect it to go easily, but I want to give her what she deserves moving forward, even if in the end I am stuck here forever.

"I'm here, but I'm not alone. Before I take another step further you must promise me that you will not harm Michael and Ryan as they are my only way to get to you."

Her voice warms me. It reminds me of times past, not only with her, but also of happier moments in my life before everything had turned so wrong. The warming of one's heart in instances such as this is a sensation I am familiar with, but one that I have not felt in millennia. I am more than a little thankful for it now. It means that at least in some small way, I still have the light inside of me pushing me toward a much different ending.

"You have my word Serenity; no harm will come to you or either of them. I do believe you know my feelings toward my brother, but I will not do anything that risks you reaching me or Gabriel."

Now that she is here, I can stop the lie that I used in an effort to get her to this point, but I do not. There is still nothing stopping her from turning around the way she came and walking away again and that is something I cannot afford. This must work the way I envision it. I cannot fail as I have done countless times before. Those failures were deserved, this one is not.

"Thank you. We will see you shortly."

Her response is curt and hard to get a read on. I can only hope that the two beings with her now do not talk her out of what she is about to do. In doing so, they would be doing more damage than I had and I am responsible for a lot of bloodshed and evil during my time both above and below ground.

I am reminded again of times past, this time with both Michael and Gabriel. Reminded of just how different from all of them I am yet despite it all, at least one of them had never given up on me.

*****

"What part of 'ease up on the power' did you not get the first time it was spoken, Lucifer? You know how Father feels about overkill. He is going to be most angry with the way this was handled."

"Father will understand when I explain my reasoning. He always does."

"Just because he seems to respect you more than the rest of us, does not mean that you are exempt from his wrath. There will come a day when you will not be able to talk yourself out of situations such as these."

Michael has always been this way toward me. I do not believe he likes how close to Father I have gotten over the years. I know that he feels he should be the one standing beside the Almighty and I do not begrudge him that. I cannot help that Father trusts me more and has put his faith in me for events such as the one we now face. I just wish I was able to make him see that. It seems though that as usual, it has to be Gabriel to get through to him.

"Michael, you know that I do not agree with the use of excessive force in any manner. It causes me great deals of discomfort, but the being of light that Lucifer just did away with

was a traitor of the worst kind and as such deserved the worst kind of punishment. Surely Father will see it the same way."

"You are naïve, little brother. You follow Lucifer without question, all because he deems a small part of his day to you and one day it will come back to bite you. Mark my words."

"The only way Father is going to be upset in this case, is with the way the two of you are behaving toward one another. We are family, whether you believe it or not. Your lack of faith in Lucifer is what will do the damage in the long run. It has nothing at all to do with the time I spend with him."

Gabriel has always been the emotionally driven brother, but now as Michael levels me with his icy gaze, he speaks nothing but the truth. I have no ill will toward Michael, in fact I understand him and what drives him more than any other, but it is impossible to make him see that. Even Gabriel cannot seem to break through the wall he has constructed.

"We may be family Gabriel, but it does not mean I have to bend to his every whim. I do not agree with the way this was handled and if Father asks me, I will tell him much the same. The more time that passes, the more it appears as though Lucifer is becoming lost in the power that is afforded him and that way of being will only bring about disaster."

"We'll see little brother. Until then, I'm the one in charge and as such, you will follow my command. Now collect the remains, it is time we made our way back home."

*****

Even when put in a position where he would have to choose, Gabriel stood his ground. He had chosen of course because he walked beside me while Michael trailed behind as we made the long and winding trek back home, but he did it in such a way where the choice was never obvious. He still managed to include Michael in discussions, going so far as to ask his opinion on things and involve him in his own way of thinking.

It only made me respect my brother more.

Knowing that very same angel that doubted me is now on his way to stand in front of me does nothing good. Anytime that I have come into contact with Michael, the need to end his very existence rises in me. The very thing he had spoken off that day, I did become and nothing could be done to change it now.

The hatred I feel for Michael needs to be pushed down and I have to move forward in mending the fences I have broken between us. If I can get Michael to believe in me, then maybe I can get Serenity to as well.

My very existence from this point depends on it.

Chapter Seventeen

Ryan

This is so fucking weird.

You spend your entire life in and out of this place, going through it both with the creator by your side and then alone. Feeling the burning in your chest, the hunger eating its way through you with each passing second, the need to feed so unbelievably strong that you feel like you're going to break and then all of a sudden you come here and it's all gone.

Every single sensation, the overwhelming need, all just gone, as if the way it had all been in times before is a figment of your imagination.

That is exactly how I feel as I walk hand in hand with Serenity, Michael two steps ahead of us, going through the same levels I almost cracked under the last time I was here. Weird isn't even the right word for the way this feels for me right now. It feels wrong. Like at any given moment I'm gonna wake up, drenched in sweat in my dorm room, finding out this is all some really elaborate nightmare of my minds design.

I'm not the only one feeling it. Michael keeps turning around every few seconds, almost as if he's expecting me to demon out and attack him. If it wasn't such a serious situation I would laugh my ass off at the way we're all acting right now. Serenity has no idea what we went through because even though we told her some of it, we never really went into much detail, so she's just moving along as if nothing is up. Me and Mike, we're both losing our shit at how strange all of this is.

"I wasn't going to say anything, but Ry, if you hold my hand any tighter you're gonna crush it."

The minute she speaks, I immediately ease up the pressure I've been putting on her, completely unaware I've even been doing it at all. See, this is why it's so strange to me. I keep expecting something to pop out from around the corner so my body is reacting, even though she's right with what she said earlier, he really did clear the way for us.

"Sorry...I'm just," I stop myself, trying to find the right word, but when nothing comes, I just let the words linger.

"He is behaving in the manner he is, Serenity because this is nothing like what we experienced the last time we came through these same areas. He's on the defensive just as I am."

Thank Christ. At least Michael gets it.

"Oh..." She answers, as we continue on, all of moving as quickly as possible.

We're almost past the area where we faced down the blood suckers and the very place where I cut myself in an effort to make sure the others were able to get through. As the memory plays its way through my brain, I feel Serenity's hand squeeze mine and as I turn to look at her, I realize what's happened.

She's seen inside my head. Shit.

"You sacrificed yourself here?"

I don't know how to answer her. I mean I'm going to tell her the truth, but I'm not entirely sure how much of it I want to share. She already hates when I put myself in danger or do anything she thinks is reckless. If I let her know everything that I did, I'm pretty sure she's going to want to kill me herself.

"I did what I had to do in order to get through this part, yeah."

"What does that mean, Ryan? I mean I saw what you did, but why did you have to do it?"

"The hunger was too strong here. It's always been that way and Lucifer told me once that the only way to really make it through, especially with the way my blood is, was to go full demon."

"So you had to do that in order to get through here?"

142

I nod and she looks away. I can only imagine what she's thinking, but for once, I'm not privy to it and I'm actually kind of surprised. Whenever she is deep in thought it seems I can see right into her mind as if I'm the one experiencing it, but now there's nothing.

"Pretty girl, what are you thinking?"

"You can't tell?" she asks, the same surprised feeling I have evident on her face as she asks me.

"No, I can't and even if I could, I don't think I want to. So just tell me please."

"Something happened that day and now that I see what you did, it actually makes sense, but doesn't make sense at the same time."

"Care to elaborate? I'm not following."

"When you cut yourself, I woke up from a rest Lucifer insisted I have and I had slashes on my wrists. No matter what I did, I couldn't stop the blood. I thought maybe it had something to do with what happened the day we got married, but then just as quickly as it happened, they were healed."

"Gabriel healed him shortly after we made our way through this part." Michael chimes in before I can answer her and I just nod my approval.

I'm beginning to see what she meant by it making sense yet not making sense because hearing that she had experienced what happened to me even though we were nowhere near each other, is confusing to me too. Just what the hell does it mean?

"Michael, you wanna weigh in here?"

"I am not entirely sure that I have anything that I can add. Your relationship continues to confuse me and I am not sure I like it. I have never seen anything like it."

Well that was a whole lot of nothing.

"We've always been weird Ryan, right from the beginning. Just blame it on that because honestly, I don't think anyone has the answers that we want about us."

Now that is something I could get behind. As we continued walking, I braced myself for what was waiting me for around the next corner. We were closer to Lucifer now and I'm not entirely sure how I feel about it. When I drove the weapon down into him multiple times in the church, I thought it would be the end of it. Now that I know it's not and I'm only minutes away from seeing him again, everything inside my head is one big jumble and I hate every second of it.

Slowing my body down to a crawl and watching as Serenity fell into step evenly with me, I lifted up her arm until I had a full view of her wrist. Staring back at me is the faint scarring that I can only assume was from our time in the church as I had seen the very same lines before, though now they appear even lighter. With what she told me, I was hoping I would be able to see some form of proof that she had experienced what I went through.

I see her look at me out of the corner of my eye and not wasting any time, I slide the sleeve up on my hoodie and hold it up so she can get a closer view. Same as the markings on her wrist, I had ones of my own and as her eyes go wide, I can tell she's as amazed by it as I am.

Just another way we're connected.

Before I know it, she untangles her fingers from mine and lifts my wrist to her lips. The minute her lips make contact with my skin, I feel my entire body go warm. I've felt the same way before when she's touched me, but this time, I felt almost drunk off of it and its new to me.

"I'm sorry that you had to go through that for me."

"I'm not." I manage to choke out, meaning every word of it. I felt a lot of conflicting things about everything I've been through coming for her the way I did, but sorry is not one of them. I do not regret it for a second, the reaction I'm having proof of that. It was just something I had to do and I would do it again in a heartbeat.

"Promise me something." She says as she lowers my hand, lacing her fingers with mine again.

"Anything."

"Don't ever do something stupid like that again."

Before I can answer her, Michael chooses to enter his two cents into the equation.

"Good luck getting him to agree to that. He's even more stubborn then you are."

"Don't listen to him, pretty girl. I swear to you, I won't do it again."

"Of course you're promising it to her now. You no longer have the demon inside of you that would cause you to do it. Nicely played, angel."

"Shut up Mike, it's got nothing to do with that."

As Michael and I continue to go back and forth at each other, I see Serenity out of the corner of my eye and my heart does flips at the sight. She's laughing at us, even though she's covering her mouth in order to hide it.

Yes, this is definitely the strangest experience of my life, but damn, she does look perfect when she's laughing like that.

"Sorry to interrupt your sappy thoughts Ryan, but prepare yourself accordingly."

There is only one reason Michael would want me to prepare myself, especially knowing that I no longer had to prepare myself in the way I would have in the past. We were finally here.

It's time to face down Lucifer—again.

Serenity

It actually feels really good having answers to something that until now I hadn't been able to explain.

I remember everything about my time here now, Lucifer having given me back that part of my memories before everything happened later and that is the one thing that despite all of the brain wracking I've done, I could never quite understand.

I have no idea why it happened or even what causes it, but I don't really need to. I'm content knowing that what I experienced that day, as supernatural as it is, was actually because of something happening to the person I love and not an actual sign of me losing my mind. For months I honestly thought that I might have imagined it because it was too unbelievable. I can accept it once and for all now.

Michael letting us know that we're about to reach Lucifer put an end to the rush of goodness I've felt since coming here. Somehow, even though I reached out to him the minute we got here, I put him out of my mind, instead focusing on how Ryan was coping and also the way Michael was acting. I put a lot of my attention into the way Ryan's hand felt holding my own and the security that I got from the simple gesture. As prepared as I had been to do this alone, I'm really glad that I'm not.

I don't think I could actually face what happens next without at least one of these people by my side. I'm lucky that I've got both. It means that no matter what Lucifer tries, he won't succeed because neither one of these men, these angels, will let him.

"Did he ever take you into the chambers, Ser?" Ryan asks, squeezing my hand, bringing me back out of my thoughts. As I look up at him he beams a smile back at me, almost as if he's letting me know that no matter what, everything is okay.

"No. I'm pretty sure what he had me doing and where was torture for the people going through it, but I've never actually seen the chambers."

"I know he said he would have this place cleared out to allow us entrance, but the minute we go in there, you need to be prepared for what's there. It's not going to be pretty."

"There's nothing in Hell that's pretty Ry, but thank you for the warning. I'm alright though. I just want to get this over with."

Even though I feel an awkwardness in the pit of my stomach at what I'm about to come face to face with, I mean every word I'm saying. I can handle this. No matter what I see

146

when I walk into the room, whether it's Gabriel caught and strung up or just Lucifer on his own with a trail of dead bodies in his wake, I can handle it. I'm not sure how I know it, but I do. Nothing can shock me anymore, especially after everything I've seen and done.

"He made you do all of those things Serenity. I want you to remember that. No matter what he says to you or tries to get you to believe. You may have done them, but you wouldn't have if he hadn't done things to you first."

There he is. My husband. The man I walked through hell and back for. The man that no matter what dark and evil things I've done, still refuses to let me blame myself. The one that despite everything we've been through always has my back because he loves me that damn much.

"Ry, I love you, but I have to take ownership for the things I do. He didn't have me under a spell and the brand didn't even take effect until the day you came for me. I did what I had to do in an effort to survive and then even after that, for the pleasure that it seemed to bring not only him, but me too. As much as you want to take the blame off me, you can't this time and that's okay."

This is why I love him so much because even after what I just said, he still seems to struggle with me taking the blame. He has no problem owning his own stuff, but when it comes to me, he always wants to believe that I am untainted and pure and I'm not. Sure, I've got the light inside of me, but just because I have it doesn't mean that I'm pure. Lucifer sure wasn't and even God himself is not without some fault.

We are all flawed in some way and that's okay. I'm honestly starting to believe that's exactly how God wanted it. It makes it more real somehow.

"I love you, pretty girl." He whispers as we round the bend that will take us to Lucifer. Looking up at the words, the smile that crosses my face unable to deny, I bend in, kiss his nose before giving him an Eskimo kiss and saying the words back to him. The words I never get tired of saying.

"I love you more, McGregor. Now let's get this over with."

As we make our way forward, I see it. The blood along the walls and the chains and other torture necessities and it takes everything in me not to turn around and throw up again, much the same way I did when Gabriel showed me the hell Graham had gone through. Shifting my eyes away from the carnage laid out before me, just the way Ryan warned me, I look up and come face to face with the man of the hour. The very reason we are even here to begin with.

It's only when he opens his eyes and looks into mine that I release the breath I didn't even know I'd been holding.

"Serenity, my belle. Welcome home."

Chapter Eighteen

Michael

There has only been one instance before the one I find myself in that I truly felt the art of loathing. Both incidents revolved around the man I am standing before now, though in the earlier instance, it had gone down much differently than the one I am presented with.

The day Father tasked me with casting Lucifer out of Heaven has always been the one day I have loathed more than any other. Standing before the brother that deep inside I love so much and casting him out of the only home he had ever known, all because Father did not like his belief system, will forever go down as the worst moment in my own personal history.

It is true that over time I had come to lose a great deal of respect for him, but I never believed for a second the way that he was then, was cause to eradicate him from his home. To treat him like a leper and send him down into a life he surely would not be able to handle.

No one ever wants to become one of the Fallen. It is not a life that many beings of light can handle. It is evident now with the way Lucifer has lived his very existence since the moment I kicked him out that he hadn't been able to handle it either, even though he had most definitely tried in his own unique way.

Contrary to common belief, I do not hate my fallen brother. In fact I still have a great deal of love inside of me for him though all respect is gone. I may not have seen him the way that Gabriel did or even as Raphael and Uriel had seen him right up until they lost hope in him, but I did love him.

Standing before him now and seeing just how broken he is, experiencing the true death the way Father intended, does strange things to me because of the way that I feel. This is a day that just like the casting out day before it, threatens to break me. I am saddened because deep down I always hoped that Lucifer would find a way back home and not to this fate. It is hard to come to terms with.

If he had only followed the rules and done things the way Father wanted, we would not be standing where we are now and facing each other this way. We would not be on opposite sides, instead on the same one, fighting the same things we had been made to fight so long ago. Serenity would not be what she is to him, she would instead be a sister, much the way she is to me and we would be able to delight in the fact that a being such as her was born of the very same thing as us.

Everything had turned out so wrong and despite the anger I still hold on to, I find myself sympathetic to him as well. I am sure that is the way Father designed it when he tasked me with coming here and seeing Serenity's destiny through to its end, even not knowing exactly what that entailed.

It comes as no surprise as I take in my surroundings that he had indeed lied about Gabriel. I had known that it was too good to be true and judging from the way Serenity is looking more through him then at him, I can tell that she also shares the same belief. Somewhere deep inside of her I do believe she knew he was lying, but it did not mean she hadn't grasped on to the lifeline Lucifer had thrown her. To look at her though, her face betrayed none of it.

She, much like me, had expected it, as Ryan did as well. In comparison though it appears as though Ryan is the more affected of the two of them and it actually makes me wonder why that is. I would have expected Serenity to be the one affected given that she had come here partially because of Gabriel.

"As you can see, I lied in order to get you here, but if you would just give me a moment to explain, I hope to make you understand why."

"Why should I stick around and listen to anything you have to say?" Serenity answers and I marvel at the strength she's displaying even though there has to be a part of her deep inside that is threatening to break.

"I want to remove the brand I have put on your heart. I believe that you want that very same thing so that is why you will hear what I have to say."

He is in no position to barter anything at this stage and I am not going to let him think otherwise. Serenity will not fall under his spell again, not while I am standing here.

"Even as you state your need to do something that is right, you are still bathed in darkness as you are making the choice of whether she stays or goes, for her. You are attempting to barter some sort of trade and I will not stand for it Lucifer. Your time for having control is long past."

"Michael, I mean no disrespect. You misunderstand me. She can still choose to turn around and walk out of here and I will not stop her, nor will I let any harm come to her. I only want to do right, but in order to do that; she needs to hear what I have to say and open up to it."

Before I have a chance to respond, I watch as Ryan takes a few steps forward. Virtually silent since the moment we entered the space, it is apparent now that the time has come for him to break it.

"Just what the hell is your game? You lie to get her here, with claims of Gabriel being trapped here, so you can do what exactly? Whisper a few sweet words you think she wants to hear and have her free you from the place you're supposed to spend eternity rotting in?"

"That was not my intent, Ryan and if you would only open your mind the way I have taught, you would be able to see that. As Michael said, I have nothing to barter with and I do not wish to do that anyway. I just wish to speak to Serenity honestly, as I have always been with her and from there, let her make the choice of whether she wishes the brand removed or not."

"You don't do anything for free. You want me to think the way that you taught me? Then how's this? You taught me to take from people, to take without asking and you taught me to enjoy it. So why the fuck should I believe that you want to do something completely different from that now?"

I can sense the anger building in the boy and even though I no longer have the concern of the demonic side of him breaking free, I still feel the need to warn him to contain it. Knowing how Serenity can still tap into his emotional state, the last thing I believe he wants is to have something happen to her because of what she felt from him.

Think of your beloved now Ryan, you must remain in control of your emotions. She will be able to see through him just as easily as we can.

As if controlled by something other than himself, he seems to heed my words as he takes a step back and again closes his mouth tightly. In doing as he does, it gives Serenity again the opportunity to speak.

"He brings up a good point. If that's the way he remembers you, why should I believe anything you have to say to me? How is this time any different than any other time we have been in each other's company? "

"We were not always this way with one another, Serenity. Deep down you know that I was different with you than any other being I have ever come into contact with, including the very brother that stands beside you now."

He is speaking the truth and I have no doubt that Serenity is aware of it, which only makes this entire situation that much harder. I want to tell her not to believe him and that we would be better served leaving, but he is truthful when he speaks of wanting to take the brand from her. It is the one thing that all of us in this room want more than anything moving forward.

Lucifer does indeed want to do the right thing.

"Serenity, he is speaking the truth. I cannot believe that I am saying it, but much like the last time I stood in his presence, he seems to be doing the right thing."

I can tell from the scowl on Ryan's face that he does not like the words I have spoken, but I cannot afford to care about that now. I am here to support Serenity. If we can get the brand removed from her heart than it will do nothing but strengthen what has been slowly falling apart since Lucifer's death.

It is something that Ryan should want, though to look at him it appears as though it is the last thing he wants or at least is opening himself up to believe in.

"You said he spoke the truth the last time we were here too and you see how well that turned out. We're a brother short because of his lies."

The pain that presents itself on Lucifer's face at the mention of Gabriel shocks me. I have always known them to have a connection unlike any other, but for as long as I can recall I have never seen Lucifer react this way in any of our later meetings. There has only ever been hatred, yet it is not hatred I am witnessing now.

It is sadness, regret and pain. All of the things I feel so deeply inside of me as it pertains to that very same brother. It appears as though we have something in common after all.

The way Ryan mentions Gabriel is not lost on me either. Whether he is doing it in an attempt to get at the man he used to follow so religiously or if he truly means it, I cannot say, but hearing Gabriel referred to so reverently warms a place within me that for months has been cold and shut off. Ryan's usage of the word brother warms my very soul.

"I must know, now that you have brought him up, no matter how inadvertently. What did you mean when you said you were not killing me for Heaven, but for my brother?"

"You know Gabriel is dead and if you really think about it, I'm sure you can figure out why he's dead. Who is at fault."

"I am aware that you believe me to be the reason that Gabriel perished and you would not be wrong. That is precisely

153

the reason I have brought you all here now. At least it is the reason that Serenity stands before me."

The truth in Lucifer's words, the way he reacts to the mention of Gabriel and the way he almost seems defeated suddenly starts to make sense as he speaks. It also brings to light Father's earlier words to me and it is in that moment that I believe I have figured out exactly why it is that we are all standing here.

Lucifer is finally ready to come home.

Lucifer

It is no surprise to me that Ryan is so confrontational. He is a demon after all. One of the strongest ones I have ever had the pleasure of having in my company. I do find it odd though that his eyes do not seem to display the darkness they once did whenever he would let the anger grow. I want to ask about it, but considering what else has been taking place in the few minutes since we have all come face to face again, I feel it best to wait and deal with the more pressing issue at hand.

Michael.

Even though I am able to see his hesitation clear as day, it would appear as though he sees the truthfulness behind the words I speak. The goal of course, is to get Serenity to believe in me once more in order to gain the one thing that can make everything right again, at least as far as me and my deceased brother are concerned.

If the knowing look I am now receiving from Michael is any indication it appears as though he is starting to see the real reason I wanted Serenity here so badly. He may not be on my side yet, but I am hoping that when everything is said and done, he will see just as he has already that I am telling the truth and do want to go about things in a much different manner than before.

It is not completely unheard of for one that has fallen from grace to be redeemed in the eyes of our father, but it is unheard of for that someone to be me. I have done things far worse than any other being before me and because of that, every move I make from this moment on has to be the right one. I cannot afford even the slightest slip up because that very thing could stand between me and the reason behind everything I have ever done.

Attention and Redemption.

I did not lie to Serenity when I told her that I acted like a petulant child before being cast out and remained that way for quite some time afterward. In fact I do believe if I am completely honest, I have always been that way, but it is only because I cherished my father's attention and love so much that being without it, even in the smallest of ways, was wrong to me. I am not naïve enough to believe that Father will welcome me back with open arms, but to be able to have the chance to stand before him and repent for every dark and twisted deed I have ever done would be enough.

"What exactly do you want from me, Lucifer?"

"Is it her blood you want this time because you know how *exquisite* it is or do you want to rip the very soul from her, turning her into an even darker version then yourself?"

Again I am forced to forgo answering Serenity in favor of focusing my attention on my protégé. I am certain that until I ask the question, I am going to continue going in this cycle the way that I have been since they arrived. I need to know why the darkness does not seem to be taking him over and it is not only for the basic knowledge of it, but also for a selfish reason. If he is able to control the urges within him this well, maybe I can too.

"You must tell me. How did you come to lose the dark ring around your eyes that I have come to recognize so easily and more importantly, how is the anger boiling over inside of you not changing you?"

Ryan smiles at me in a way that I have only seen him do on two previous occasions, both of which were when he thought he was getting his way or knew something that I did not. As it turned out, I had only let him believe he had achieved those things, but it still did not change the fact that now, he did seem to know something that I did not and I was in no way controlling it.

"Gabriel."

The pain at hearing his name again strikes me in the chest much the same way the blade Ryan used on me months before did. Would it ever become easier hearing his name spoken now that he was no longer here with us or am I destined to always feel the sting and ache of a lost brother I had not been able to protect the way I wanted?

"Gabriel, doing the selfless act that he did that night in the church separated the darkness from Ryan once and for all. In doing so it has allowed him to take his rightful place in Heaven once the time is right."

"I do not understand. What do you mean by rightful place?"

"Since it is of no consequence any longer, I do believe I can tell you, but I do believe that it might be better coming from the horse's mouth so to speak." Michael replies before turning and motioning for Ryan to again speak.

"Did you never wonder why it was always me, Lucifer? Why no matter what you did, I was always the one that you faced in the end?"

"You fancy yourself in love with Serenity, there is nothing more to know."

"That's where you're wrong."

As hard as I am trying to maintain my composure given my current predicament and also what I am attempting to prove to each person standing before me, the boy is trying my patience. If there is something that needs to be said, I just wish he could get on with already. He is wasting precious time.

"As entertaining as I am sure you find this, time really is of the essence here, as I can only hold back the full force of Hell

156

for so long these days. So why don't you just get on with it already."

"Lucifer, the boy is made of Heaven. There was a mistake made years ago and instead of becoming what he should have, he instead landed in the arms of the demon loving harlot."

Oh yes, the woman that as soon as they got me out of here, I would be personally handling as it is still a promise I had yet to fulfill. Not only did my most trusted confidante lay down with her, but they had also made the man now standing before me and proceeded to treat him in such a manner that it was a miracle he even survived it. Yes, wanting to be back in the light or not, I would be dealing with that woman.

"He's an angel, Lucifer." Serenity says easily before rubbing her temples. "He is one of the purest ones ever created. He was never meant to be what you turned him into."

I watch as both Michael and Ryan turn to face her, stunned as they are that she had been the one to tell me what they had been holding out on. It is only when she fixes her steely gaze on both of them that I find myself laughing. It would appear as though they didn't have her as under control as they thought. She still bent to me when push came to shove.

"You two were taking too long and honestly, it needed to be said." Is her only reply, which only caused the smile across my features to grow. Maybe getting through to her would be easier than I thought. Though made of the light, it would still appear as though Serenity followed her own path.

"A pure angel? That explains why it had to be you that finished me off, but I'm afraid that any other reaction you were looking for, you will not find because it means little to me what you actually are; only what you became."

"What I was. I'm not that person anymore, no thanks to you."

"You can continue to tell that to anyone that will listen Ryan, but you forget how well I know you. The demonic side of you may be gone, but you are still the same person at your very core and that will never change. I am intrigued by one thing

157

that you said though so I would appreciate one of you elaborating for me."

"What do you want to know?" Serenity asks first, before either of the men with her can respond.

"How was Gabriel able to remove the darkness inside of him?"

"He sacrificed himself as Michael said. In an effort to save Ryan from the fate that you afforded him, he did the unimaginable and stripped himself of the light."

"He placed the light within Ryan?"

Serenity nods, no longer able to speak and it is a reaction I understand. Just as it is hard for me to even hear his name spoken, given what they had once meant to each other, it must be even harder for her. We are again on the same page.

"I would have thought that when the time came for something of that nature to happen, it would have been the Hudson boy that received the gift. The light inside of him was unmatched by any other living human. He would have been the perfect home for Gabriel's power."

"Well it was Ryan, not Graham so it doesn't really matter what you think about it. It happened and it's done."

There has never been a moment, even when I have been at my most powerful that I have ever wanted to lay a hand on her in any way other then loving, but the minute the words fall from her lips it takes every ounce of energy in me not to reach through the cage and rip her eyes out. The cavalier way she speaks of what Gabriel did for the man standing beside her makes me angry in a way that I cannot even describe.

I may have wanted to take her life a year ago when we first came face to face, but it was only a means to an end. It was never about hatred I had for her. This though, I could easily hate her for.

"You watch your tongue! You do not speak of Gabriel and the sacrifice he made in that regard. Not in front of me."

She takes a few steps back and I know my change in attitude has been well received. She is now afraid of me. It may go against what I want, but I cannot sit idly by as she trivializes things the way she has just done.

"I'm—sorry, I didn't mean it that way." she stammers and despite the anger inside of me, I begin to soften, again the effect that only she can have on me.

"It is alright Serenity. I apologize for snapping at you. Gabriel is a tough subject."

"This is a joke right? Where's the King of Hell when you need him? Why are we left with this wannabe? Where's the guy that almost got off while he was taking souls and the light from helpless victims?"

"Ryan, it would be best right now if you remained silent." Michael spoke up, taking me by surprise.

"What do you want from me Lucifer? You said that Gabriel is the reason you wanted me here, well here I am. What do you really want?"

"I wanted you here so that I can apologize to you for everything that I have put you through. All of you," I say, making sure that I look at each and every one of them before continuing. "More than that, I want the chance to make things right again and the first way I know of to do that is to remove the brand that I so selfishly put on your heart."

Serenity looks to Michael and it is only when my brother nods back in her direction, almost as if they are speaking silently to one another that I realize just what it means. She is turning to him and his expertise now to make sure that what she senses from me is accurate.

"I assure you, I am telling you the truth. I no longer have anything to lose, as you can easily see. I want to do right by you. It is the only way that I can make up for all of the horrendous things I have done."

"And then what?" she asks me, either ignoring my words all together or hearing them and pressing forward because of my earlier statement about holding off the demons.

"I want to see my Father."

"Jesus Christ."

"Serenity..."

"Michael, I'm sorry, but come on, really? I can buy into him wanting to say sorry for what he did to me, Ryan, hell, every single person he's ever come into contact with, but wanting to stand before God? That just proves what Ryan said is right."

"How does anything I have said prove Ryan right?" I ask, genuinely wanting to know how she has reached this conclusion so easily.

"You never do the right thing for free. You want to remove the brand that *you* put on me, but in return you want me to use whatever pull I have with the man upstairs to get you a meeting with him. Again, you're trying to barter and I'm sorry, I won't have any part of it."

As she turns from me, her point made, I immediately begin to feel the separation between us and realize that even though she is wrong in her assumption, she does have a point. The steps she takes toward Ryan show me that I am watching my one chance at real and true redemption walking away from me for the final time.

Before it can completely settle in around me, pulling me down with it, I hear the clearing of a throat and the words that follow immediately bring something forth inside of me that I haven't felt in centuries.

Hope.

"Take the brand from her and I'll make sure you get your meeting with Father."

Chapter Nineteen

Ryan

I gotta say, there was a minute there where I thought my girl was lost to me. That she was actually buying into everything he was telling her and leaning toward going along with it.

I'm so damn glad I was wrong.

It just goes to show just how far she's come since the day I met her. She was so unsure of herself back then, almost as if every step she took had to be planned out far in advance because there had to be no doubt that it was the right one. She was timid, shy and for the first couple of days we spent together, I wondered if I would ever see the strong person that I knew lived inside her.

The girl in front of me now is not the same person she was then. She is someone different, yet still the same in all of the ways that make her the pretty girl I love so much. Even with a brand on her heart that should bend her to him easily, she is still side by side with me, going so far as to agree with me when even his own brother is falling victim to the ultimate lie.

I can tell Michael's words are eating at her even though she remains stoic as ever. There is no way that they can't be. The very angel that had cast out Lucifer is basically giving him everything he wants. I hate to even think it, but it looks like Michael and Serenity have switched places in this whole thing. It's like the angel is the one with the brand on his heart and is powerless to fight against it.

"Excuse me?" Serenity speaks up, never moving from her position by my side. "Don't you think since you're talking about the brand on my heart, I should have some say in this?"

"Serenity, there is much that you do not know. I need to speak with you, but for now I am asking that you do as you have done before and trust me."

"Not good enough Michael. What you're suggesting is bringing God here or freeing him and bringing him to Heaven. I think you need to talk to your father before you do it."

"She's got a point Mike. You don't wanna go down this road. If you free him, you have no idea what he'll do."

"The both of you do not understand everything that is at play and it is because of that lack of knowledge, that you say what you are now. I know far more than you, as Father informed me before leaving home. I understand your feelings on this matter, but this is exactly what Father wants me to do."

"I don't believe that."

"You do not need to believe it. You have spent a great deal of time with me Serenity. Have you ever known me to lie, especially to you and about something of this magnitude?"

I know for a fact that Michael has never lied to either of us. It was another reason why I gravitated more in his direction and not Gabriel's whenever we had to work together. Michael seemed to operate the same way I did and that made him reliable. Right now though, I wasn't entirely sure he was thinking clearly considering what he's readily agreeing to.

"Michael is asking that you trust in him, but I am also asking the same thing of you, Serenity. This cannot happen with your acceptance."

Every single time that he speaks I want to go to him, wrap my arms around his throat and choke him until he dies, despite knowing that he's being completely honest with every word he says and it's turning me inside out. I've spent my entire life being guarded and groomed by this guy to do the very opposite of what he's asking to do now and I can't reconcile the way he is, with the man I knew. They're like two completely different people.

"Alright fine," I say, bridging the gap between all of us by moving forward, Serenity falling into step easily beside me the minute my feet begin moving. "Do this, free him, but the minute he's free, he has to do whatever it takes to get that brand off her heart, right away. No waiting. If this blows up in our faces Michael, I don't care if we're brothers or not, I will kill you where you stand."

"I swear it's like I'm not even in the room anymore. Would you all rather I leave and let you hash it out? Because last I checked, I'm the one with the brand on her heart to begin with! As much as I want it removed, I'm not entirely sure this is the way to do it."

"Ser..."

"No Ryan. I don't want to hear it. Yes, I trust Michael, but there's a reason God wanted Lucifer here to begin with, so I'd rather live with this brand on my heart for the rest of my life, along with everything it brings than go against that. Gabriel died because of his sick plan to end you or did you all forget that?"

"You really think I could forget that?" I yell back at her. "It's with me every freaking second!"

"The two of you need to stop this before it leads to a place neither one of you can come back from. It is time I told the both of you what happened during my stay in Heaven and once that is done, we can make the decisions that need to be made. Together."

I have never been more thankful for Michael then I am right now. I don't want to yell at her, I don't want to yell at anyone, but hearing what she said and the way it seems to be directed more at me than anyone else in the room just pisses me off. She may have been the one to rip the light from the angel and put it into me, killing him in the process, but I'm the one that has to live with it. Not even the love of my life is going to tell me that I've forgotten what happened to me.

I don't even realize it, but as Serenity moves toward Michael, I see our hands are no longer locked together the way they were before and it's the first time that she's ever separated from me where I didn't feel it. There is no loss this time. It's like I don't even miss her at all.

"You son of a bitch—you're doing this aren't you?" I scream, turning all of the rage inside of me directly at the angel responsible for everything that's happened. "You and that god damned brand are screwing with me!"

I don't know why I think it's him, but I swear, for the last year and a half, there has never been a second where we've been separated from each other that I didn't feel it. Even during her time in Hell, I still felt connected even though we weren't near each other. I still felt the loss of her, but right now, I don't feel it and I can tell by the look on her face as she watches me losing my shit that she's wondering the same thing.

"It is not something I am aware of doing. Is it possible, of course, but I am not actively trying to create distance between the two of you."

"Ry..." Serenity calls as she makes her way toward me, her face a mixture of sadness and fear, her gaze never once leaving me and the anger that is now so strong inside of me that I'm shaking. "Baby, you need to relax. Ignore whatever he's doing and come talk to Michael. We need to get answers right now, not fight."

Just in times past, my breathing immediately begins to even out as she speaks and I can feel the anger breaking away. It's as I feel it fading away that I realize exactly what's going on.

I'm feeding off her emotions.

"Son of a bitch..."

"Yes Ryan, you are, now come on." She says with a smirk, one that the minute I see it, I'm able to return. If she's calming herself this easily and it's true what I believe then it will be just as easy for me to do the same.

God, this bond is a pain in the ass.

164

"It's not the bond baby. It's just us. We're weird remember?"

"Cheater."

"Maybe so, but it's not like you haven't done it to me a bunch since you figured out you could."

Locking her fingers in mine again and leaning in quickly, I place the softest kiss I can on her forehead before whispering the words we both so desperately need to hear.

"I'm sorry."

"Me too, angel."

As I finally turn away from Lucifer and again place my attention on the other angel in the room, I see his face is a mask of stone. Whatever it is that he needs to say to us, I know it's not going to be good. In fact I'm pretty damn sure I'm going to hate every second of it.

"So Mike, what the hell is going on?"

There were a million different things he could have said in that moment that wouldn't have shocked me, but when he does finally open his mouth, he says the one thing that almost brings me to my knees with the weight of it.

"This is Serenity's destiny."

Chapter Twenty

Serenity

Stop me if you've heard this one.

A demon walks up to a seemingly regular girl, who may or may not be a little on the shy side and he says *hey baby, you're actually this really bright light thingy from heaven and the devil wants to use you against them.* The girl is all shell shocked yet somehow understanding, at least until an angel comes to her telling her the same thing. They go through hell and back and suddenly the whole destiny thing has been repeated like six times and it's lost its appeal.

Yeah, that one. I've heard that, hell, I've lived that, for the past year and a half and quite frankly I'm tired of it.

It's mind blowing when I think about it. Everything that's happened to me and it's all taken place in the last year and a half. Things that should span lifetimes, all neat and put together in this crazy ass bubble of a little over a year. It doesn't change the fact that I've heard what seems like this exact line out of about four different people's mouths in that span of time too, yet it never seems like I'm reaching it. This so called destiny stuff is garbage if you ask me.

As strongly as I feel about Michael and trust me, it's pretty damn strong considering we're family and all, he says the words and they fall flat. As least they do to me. I haven't really looked at Ryan in the past two minutes, but I have to figure he's feeling the same way considering he hasn't said anything either.

When you're reaching your destiny, it's supposed to mean something and you know, there is a point in all of this death, destruction and complete catastrophe that it actually did have meaning. When I walked into the church in Green Haven and agreed to marry Ryan, all in an effort to save him from the path he'd been thrown on, that's when all of this meant something. I had the blood drained from me until I completely passed out and I did all of that because that was my destiny. I don't care who says what now, but I reached my true calling that day and no one is going to convince me otherwise.

All they can do now is say things that because of the light inside of me, I'm supposed to do. Save Graham from Lucifer's possession. Check, did that. Wasn't my destiny, but they said it was and I did it. Going to Hell was just a really backwards accident in the process. Then we have the undertaking, again in Green Haven, with the same players where the angel that I was bonded to gave his life all in an effort to make sure I reached my destiny. Ryan killed Lucifer and I helped by faking him out with my own death. Check, did that one too.

It makes hearing anything Michael has to say, pointless to me. Why couldn't he just say 'Serenity, hey, this is your life and right now you've gotta free Lucifer so we can take the branding off your heart'? That would have gone over a whole lot better. Okay, so I'm lying, it wouldn't have gone over well at all, but I'm sure you get the idea. I get the idea anyway and I'm the only one other then Ryan that really matters in all of this.

Case and point, I'm so far in my head right now thinking about all of this and exactly what it means that I don't even realize their lips are moving. Shit. They're talking about me and this so called destiny and I'm not even paying attention.

"You mind repeating what you just said?" I ask, turning to the angel and laying on the sweetest smile I can come up with, praying it works.

"Was there some part of that which you did not understand?"

"Actually, yeah. I didn't understand any of it because I sort of wasn't paying attention."

I blush and immediately feel the squeeze of Ryan's hand in mine. It's only when I look up and meet his eyes that I see my own painted on smile reflected right back at me, except his isn't painted on, it's completely, one hundred percent real.

God, I love this man.

"You are standing in the middle of Hell itself and you choose now to stop paying attention?"

"Seems that way. Look Michael, we wouldn't be standing here at all if you had just left me alone from the beginning. He asked for me to come here alone and honestly, with everything I'm finding out that you've been keeping from us, I'm sort of thinking I should have done what he said."

"You do not mean that. I understand that you feel betrayed, but I assure you, I didn't keep anything from you. It is only here and now that I have realized exactly what it was that my father, our father, was getting at."

"Okay, well I'm listening now, so why don't you explain it to me, but leave the whole destiny thing out of it. I'm sick of hearing that today is the day the undertaking comes to pass, or that I am about to do what I was made to do. I already did it; even Gabriel believed that, so just tell me what you need me to do."

"Answer me something before I explain all that I know."

"Of course."

"When you made the decision to come here, what was the real motivation behind it?"

Naturally this would be what he asks me. The very thing that caused Ryan and me to fight earlier is now being thrown out there again. The last thing I'm in the mood for right now, considering where we are and who we're surrounded by, is another fight. I think it's pretty obvious the real motivation behind why I came here, so spelling it out seems pointless.

"You already know the answer to that, as does Ryan, so why even bother asking?" I snap, knowing the minute the words come out that I'm being defensive, but too stuck in my ways to care.

"Because I want to hear you say it. It may have been spearheaded by the mistaken belief about Gabriel, but it was Lucifer and the way that you have come to feel about him that drove you to want to go through with it, is it not?"

"Yes Michael, are you happy now? I came here because of some loyalty I feel to him."

I don't even bother looking at Ryan. He already knows this though I didn't come right out and say as much to him when we got into it earlier. I couldn't say this to him. I seem to have no problem letting him assume it, but to actually let the words come out of my mouth, I can't. Who wants to hear that their wife feels connected to another being, man, or whatever? No one. It's heartbreaking and I don't want to do that to him.

"It's okay, Ser. I already knew it. It's the brand he put on you, that's all."

"No, it's not Ryan. It's more than the bond and I know saying that is going to hurt you, but I don't want to lie and hide things anymore. That's half the reason we keep fighting and it needs to stop. Michael, there was a small part of me that believed him about Gabriel, but mostly I just wanted to fix what I started three months ago."

"Explain what you mean by fix, Serenity. I am not entirely sure I understand."

"He's right with everything he says you know. I did see a different side of him when I was here and it was a side that I willingly embraced even with the light still inside me. I respected him for telling me the truth when no one else around me seemed to want to, at least until the last minute. So when he came back to me that day when Ryan left with Graham and Emma, I wanted to do right by him. I just had no idea what he was going to ask of me once he had me back. That's when everything went to shit."

"Went to shit how Ser?" Ryan asked, his hand never leaving mine yet his body turning into me more.

"I wanted to save you both, Ry. I knew one of you would walk into that room and come for me. I was torn between who

169

I wanted it to be. Gabriel told me that a lot of it had to do with Lucifer's desires being thrown onto me because of the brand and that may have been true, but it didn't change the fact that I had two things I wanted to do and I failed at both."

"Serenity, I must stop you. You did not fail in the church that night. In fact you succeeded because what was meant to happen, did take place. It just wasn't your time. What I mean is, it wasn't the thing that Father needed you to do." Michael answers, catching himself near the end and rectifying the situation before I could level him with the eye roll he deserved for again bringing my so called destiny into it.

"I did fail, don't you see? I couldn't save Ryan from the fate that Lucifer damned him to, instead Gabriel had to do it and well, we all know how well that turned out. I hoped that somehow I could make Lucifer come around to my way of thinking and save him since even now I can sense light inside him. He is better than the things he's done and I wanted to give him a chance to prove that. I just wasn't strong or brave enough to make it happen."

Both men have gone completely silent now and I have to admit it's kind of scary. I want one of them to say something, even if its them getting mad at me for the way I think or the decisions I made that brought us to where we are now, anything that could erase this ugly feeling of uselessness from my system.

"Are you ready to hear now what Father has told me?" Michael says after a few more seconds of silence. "I do believe with everything you have just told us that you may be more understanding of it now."

I nod my head to let him know I want to hear it all, but I turn away from him in an effort to check on Ryan. I can't imagine any of this being easy for him to hear and the last thing I want from him now is silence because I know what it means. He will pull away. He cannot shut down on me. Not now.

"I'm fine pretty girl, I promise you. It's just a lot to hear." He whispers, motioning with his hand for me to turn my attention back to Michael, who just seems to be getting more impatient by the second.

"Father told me some things earlier and they have everything to do with what you are experiencing now. You are right when you say that the urge to want something better for him is not the brands fault. It is most definitely not the brand he placed on you causing that reaction. It is your inherent goodness and the true reason for you even existing that is doing it."

"Here we go again..." I mumble, preparing myself for yet another destiny speech.

"Serenity, you can close yourself off from it as much as you like, but it doesn't change the facts. So please just open your mind and be willing to listen."

"I am." I answer with a pout. I'm acting childish and I know it, but I honestly don't care anymore. I sort of want to hear him say it was the brand so then I wouldn't feel as horrible as I do now. It's just another reminder of what I told Ryan earlier. He deserves so much better.

"Do you remember what Gabriel told you about your true calling? What you are actually meant to mean to the world?"

"Yeah, like any of you would ever let me forget it."

"Well then you know that you are to bring about true peace in the world. Now think about how that can be reached. Killing Lucifer should have done it, I will grant you that, but in the end, it still means a lot of work on our part to eradicate the rest of what remains here in Hell. So it has to be something much larger that does it. This is the something larger."

"Freeing the very person God wanted you to put away?"

"Yes, but not in the way you mean. Lucifer is telling you the truth in that he wants to make things right with you. He wants to remove the brand and I have no doubt despite his previous actions that he will see it through. At the same time, the only thing he wants in return is the very thing that only you can truly grant him. With your forgiveness we can move forward

171

and do the right thing. The very thing you've wanted to do since he took you from us."

Can what Michael says be true? More than that, can I forgive him for all of the things he's done to me, to us, since he came barreling into our lives what feels like forever ago?

"You are the only one that can answer that question, Serenity and I understand that it is not an easy answer even when it does come."

"There is no guarantee that even in doing this that God will listen to him or even to me. How can you be so sure that I'm the answer here Michael? Why isn't it you?"

"I was not created for this purpose. You were."

I don't want this to actually appeal to me, but it does. It's the very thing I wanted in the church that night and despite every attempt I've made at not trying to acknowledge it, I don't think I can force it away anymore. There is truth in Michael's words, just like there is in Lucifer's. They both want this to happen and Michael even believes that it's supposed to happen.

There's only one problem with it and of course it's such a big problem that I can't move forward until I know the answer for sure.

How the hell am I going to make God believe that this is the right thing?

Chapter Twenty-One

Michael

I am not sure how I feel about this. I know what I have told Serenity and I stand by it, as I believe it to be exactly what Father had been getting at. I am just not sure this is the way it's all supposed to end.

There was a reason he had been cast out from home and considering all of the evil things he's managed to do since, it hardly showed him to be the angel of old. In fact it showed him to be exactly what he believed Ryan to be. A demon of the worst kind and that didn't exactly speak highly for his chances at redemption.

This is Serenity's destiny though, of that I have no doubt, even if she is finding it hard to believe. It is no secret to any of us that she believes Ryan's redemption to be her moment as she did succeed in setting things right, only she is not meant to save only one, she is meant to save them all and this proves it.

What I cannot wrap my mind around quite yet is how Gregory Richards plays into this. Father stated that he has a greater role to play and it would all make sense when the time is right, but as far as I can see, that time is now. All should be revealed and make sense, yet it doesn't. It is only made worse by the fact that Serenity has no clue.

She is aware of her father, but in the time since I've made my way back she hasn't mentioned him, which makes bringing him up to her now much more difficult. How do I even begin to explain that not only is freeing Lucifer part of her destiny but so is the father that disappeared from her life years before? I can only see it making everything worse.

"There is more that you need to know, Serenity."

"No, Michael, I got it all thanks."

"As much as I would love to say that is the case, it is not. There is even more that I have not told you, but to move forward you must be made aware."

Not only am I going to drop the bomb of visiting her father on her, I'm also about to tell her that in order to achieve her true purpose, he's going to have to be involved in it. The amount of prayers alone that I receive from children moving through life minus a parent makes what I am about to say that much harder. She was one of those kids before she finally let go and telling her this now is only going to make her go back to that place.

"It is regarding your father."

I have her attention now, her focus entirely on me. It's apparent that even though she's moved on with her life over the years, there is still a soft spot for the man that left her behind.

"What about him?"

"I have been to sit with him in an effort to discern exactly what causes the abilities within him."

"So you've been chilling with my dad and you're choosing now to tell me?"

"I only learned of him as you did. I have been to see him once. Despite claims made by others, he seems to be in control of all of his faculties, mental and otherwise. He is being treated much the same as you were during your time in the center."

"Well, considering my mom had him labeled crazy, it's not all that surprising. What does my dad have to do with this?"

"Father believes him to have been another being that slipped through the heavenly cracks. It matters to the current situation because the state your father is in is because of the very man you went against everything to save."

There, the truth is out now. At least the part of it that is most important. Everything else can come later. The information I learned from not only Serenity's father, but my own is now out. We can now deal with it and move forward.

"Lucifer put my father in the hospital?"

"He played a part in it, yes. Your mother is the one that had him check himself in due to the voices he was hearing, but none of that would have happened had it not been for my fallen brother."

She spins around and in seconds finds herself in front of the chamber where Lucifer is barely hanging on, though still able to take in every word that's been spoken. I have no doubt he expected this reaction.

"What the hell did you do to my father?"

"I used him."

"Used him how, and better yet, why?"

"He was my way to be close to you. I needed to be near you and Gregory gave me the chance to do that. When I was done with him, I explained that soon I would be back for you and he accepted it."

"You possessed my Dad?" She chokes out, the emotional upheaval coursing through her finally getting to me.

"Yes."

"Serenity, there is more. Father believes Gregory to be involved in this final act in some way. He did not share all of the details, but in some way he plays a part in how all of this happens."

"Of course he does!" She exclaims before turning away from Lucifer, making her way to Ryan who immediately brings her into his arms, showing just how close to the edge she really is. A gesture I'm more then thankful for.

He's going to be needed in this way even more with what comes next.

"What did he ever do to deserve this? All he did was get stuck with a kid that had issues."

"He got stuck with a gift from God, more like." I answer, not allowing her one second more believing she is anything other than treasured. As much as I know that Lucifer is to stand before Father in an attempt to be redeemed, it doesn't change the fact that he was the reason behind all of this.

His obsession had caused this now, which made me only want to turn my back on this plan despite my earlier statement to the contrary.

"So he's the reason my dad left—great. Are you sure freeing him is the right thing, Michael?"

"I wouldn't be here if I didn't believe in that very thing."

"Well, I guess there's nothing else left to talk about. I mean everything's been decided. The only thing to do now is free him and get on with it."

I'm not content with her answer. Even though she knows everything she needs to, I can still see the struggle she's facing moving ahead with this plan, despite my knowledge that it is the path Father has chosen.

Before I have the chance to make mention of it , Ryan clears his throat and speaks, again reminding me of why he is the best person to be by my side in this situation. It's almost as if because of his feelings for the ball of light, we are on the same page, always.

"Not yet. We're not letting that son of a bitch out until I talk to her—alone."

Ryan

Call me crazy, but with the amount of information I've sat and listened to, there is no way I'm just going to let her move forward without talking about it. No way in hell.

As much as I don't want to admit it, I can see this being her true calling. Knowing Serenity the way I do, this seems like the kind of thing I would expect from her. She has always been so innately good that having the most hated being alive redeemed by her hand is the best way to reach her destiny. If there is anyone that can make it happen it's her. No one knows that better than me seeing as she's done the same thing with me and I still have a hard time believing I should have been.

I was right there alongside Lucifer doing the very things that God loathed and worked so hard to prevent, whether it happened because of a mistake on Heaven's part or not. I still did them and I did it with a smile on my face. Redemption should never have been in the cards for me, at least from where I sit. I might not have been the one to make the choice and had it forced on me, but it didn't stop me. I could have turned around and stopped at any point and I didn't.

So yeah, I don't really think I'm due the redemption I received, it's not exactly a secret. Everyone knows how I feel about what happened and what I believe I truly deserve. The thing is, she changed all of that. The goodness in her, the way that she just sees past all of the crap and gets straight to the heart, made it possible for me to eventually reach my place in the light. I have no doubt that she's the reason I'm even standing here now. It could just as easily be me in the chambers with Lucifer, yet I'm not.

That's why I know that if anyone can do this, stand before God himself and plead the case of the fallen angel, it's her. Even though it still bothers me that she feels connected to that evil sadistic son of a bitch, I know that in the end it will be that connection that will determine exactly where Lucifer ends up. Really, it will determine where we all end up.

She doesn't want to do this. I can feel it even though she's not really thinking it strong enough for me to pick up on. She's weighing everything that's happened to all of us against what she believes is the right thing. She admitted to wanting to save Lucifer and bring him back into the light, the same light that she'd been able to see burning inside of him, despite the darkness that overshadowed it. That is the right thing for her, but reconciling it against the horrendous events she's been through is leaving her conflicted.

That's where I come in. I want to talk to her alone so I can find out exactly where her head is and what she wants to do. I want to make sure that once she makes the decision, she is secure in it because there is no going back once you put something in motion. She has to be completely at peace with it. Maybe it's selfish or even a bit egotistic, but I know that I can get her to the right place and it has nothing to do with our bond and everything to do with the trust we have in each other. I will never lead Serenity down a path that could in the end do more harm to her then good and she knows it.

At least I sure hope she knows it because it's crystal clear to me.

I want the brand off her more than anyone, but I will not make that the only reason we release him. There has to be more to it than that, despite what I want and feel is the right way to go. This is why it isn't my choice, because even now, with all of this light inside of me and the power of Heaven backing me, I want nothing more than to watch him burn for the rest of eternity.

I meant every word I said to him months ago. I want to see him rot and burn in the hell he created because for me, there is no more fitting end to the evil that he spent millennia creating. This is why I can never be the one that makes the choice. I can never be the person that brings about true world peace. It's also the very reason why Serenity and I are so damn good together. She is the heart that I lack. She is the light; she is everything pure and good that even now, I can't be.

"Pretty girl, talk to me. Tell me what you're thinking."

"You really don't want to know, Ry, trust me. You'll just get mad at me and I really don't need that right now."

If she believes that I'm going to get mad at her than she must be doing the very thing I hate her doing most, blaming herself. I want to tell her that I won't get mad at her, but that would be telling her a lie and I can't do it. I may not be able to promise that it won't make me mad, but I can give her something else. Acceptance and an ear and right now, those are what she needs most despite how upset it might make me.

"Just say it. I know what you're doing and yeah, I don't like it, but I'm going to accept it because you need to get it out."

178

"I brought this on my father, because of what I am. My father had to pay the price and you wanna know the worst part? Even knowing that Lucifer did that to him, I still want to do the right thing and help him. It makes me sick."

Just as I suspected, she's conflicted. We might not have the same situations with our fathers, especially given who mine really is, but there are some similarities. My father didn't give a shit about me other than using me as a means to an end and for years she believed hers to have walked out on her, not giving a shit either. I can sympathize more than ever with that though what she faced now, I can't help her with.

Even if my father came back now, I don't think I could ever let him in. Not because of what he is, but because of everything that's happened since. I can't let it go. Serenity faces a much harder decision because she has the choice to bring her father back into her life because he'd been ripped from it. He wasn't a deadbeat and learning about that now put her at a crossroads.

Lucifer had done this and she's supposed to overlook it in an effort to make sure she reaches her true purpose. It's one hell of a decision and even though I want to be supportive, I can't help but be thankful that it isn't me that has to make it. I'm not even sure I could.

"I know how it looks Ser, but maybe it's not the way it appears."

"What do you mean? How can it be anything other than the way it looks? I mean I can keep Lucifer where he is, turning my back on whatever Heaven thinks is my actual destiny, forging some kind of relationship with my father or I can do what Michael wants me to do and turn my back on my father and everything that happened to him."

"Michael said that your father is involved in this some way and sure, we don't know what that is yet, but maybe we're not supposed to know. Maybe we're supposed to decide."

"So I'm supposed to seal my own father's fate?"

When she puts it that way, I want to tell her that's not what I mean, but the more I think about it, it's exactly what I mean.

Sure, it looks bad, but if Serenity chooses the path that her father takes then maybe she can work out a better ending then the man would have gotten if he remains where he is.

"You can't think of it as sealing his fate, that's wrong. If you think about it, you can decide how he ends up. I mean, if Michael hadn't found out about him and your mother didn't come clean, none of us would know he's even here. He would have been stuck in that hospital forever."

"Yeah, you're right. He would have gone on for the rest of his life sitting in that place, same as I did eight years ago. The only difference is, I got out because I knew how to act in order for people to believe that I was cured. He doesn't have that option, which means anything I choose for him has to be better than the alternative. I just don't think I can play with people's lives that way, especially my own father."

She understands what I'm trying to say which makes me happy, but her final point I understand more. Having the fate of someone else's life in your hands is not something anyone longs for, especially when they're still trying to figure out their own complicated path.

"There's a way here that you can do the right thing by both people. You just need to figure out exactly what that is and how to go about making it happen. I wish I could give you the answers and tell you step by step what you need to do, but I can't. Not because I know and don't want to tell you, but because I've never faced anything like this and I don't know what the right answer is."

She nods in understanding and as I watch her head moving back and forth, I see something in her eyes that wasn't there before. It's a look I haven't seen since the night I looked into her eyes in the church and told her to trust me before I drained the very light from her. I want to say she looks at peace, though it doesn't seem like the right word. There is no way she can feel even remotely at peace with any of this, but the look in her eyes now, is a determination like I've never seen. It's acceptance.

180

She's figured it out.

"You're doing it again, pretty girl. Talk to me, something seems off."

"Nothing's off. In fact, I think what you just said is exactly what makes everything alright."

"What does that mean?"

"I know what I have to do."

She turns from me and makes her way back over to Michael and as thankful as I am that she seems to have come up with a plan of action, I can't help the confusion lingering in me at exactly what I said that somehow helped her reach that point.

"Michael, call your father. It's time we did what we've been sent here to do."

Serenity has made her decision. Lucifer is about to be free.

Chapter Twenty-Two

Serenity

I haven't processed everything my mom told me about what happened to my dad. I mean I have, at least in the sense that I know what happened to him and why it happened, but other than those small things, I haven't actually sat down and given myself time to think about what I'm going to do with the information.

When Michael said that Lucifer was the reason my dad ended up where he is, all I could see is red. I actually had to stop myself from ripping him to bits. I guess it's actually worse than the time in Heaven, but it still brings out the same feelings inside of me. I really don't want to hear that Lucifer played a part in every single thing that's happened to me in my life. Just thinking about it now makes me sick.

It's strange, but I'm really glad Ryan pulled me away from the others in order to talk to me before I made a decision that could potentially end us all. If I had just gone ahead in the moment then I wouldn't have felt right about it and I would have spent all my time doubting, but now, after everything he said, I know what I need to do and what the right thing is.

He has no idea what he said that helped me and I could easily tell him, but there's something different about this and I want him to find out what I'm about to do at the same time as everyone else. Once he sees where I'm going with this, he'll remember what he said that turned everything around and not only will I be able to do right by my father and Lucifer, I will also be able to do right by him.

This is the both of us doing what we did that night all over again. We're working together to reach a better ending. He was right that night when he said it wasn't just about one of us seeing things through. It was supposed to be us as a team. Michael can believe that it's me that will fix everything, but I know better. Ryan may not have to do anything physical this time, but he is just as much a part of it because of the advice he gave me.

"Michael, call your Father. It's time we did what we've been sent here to do."

"Are you sure?"

"I've never been more sure. You want me to accept that this is what I'm meant to do; well I'm standing here telling you that I believe you now. We need to do this, so it's time."

"As you wish."

"You have no idea how much this means to me, Serenity. I swear to you that I will not make you regret taking this step."

There was a time when hearing him speak to me this way would have caused one of two reactions in me. I would have been filled with a chill that not even the weather could bring about inside me or I would melt at the truth in his words. Now, it's not happening and I'm surprised by it. I'm completely indifferent to his words and I know what's causing it.

I no longer fear Lucifer and what he may have waiting for me around the bend. I'm completely secure in my position. Lucifer would always be a wild card, but I'm finding it hard in the moment to concern myself with it.

I'm the one holding all of the cards this time, even if he thinks he still has some he can play. I only hope that God doesn't keep us waiting much longer. The only concern I still have, is just how much longer Lucifer's control of Hell would remain intact. The last thing I need to happen is for him to break and the weight of hell to come down on us with a force that we're unable to control and stop.

"Just be ready to do what you said you would do."

"The minute I am given my freedom, I will do just that. You can trust me."

If I didn't know he's being serious I would laugh. Time has already proven that trusting him is the last thing I should do, but if he wants to believe that he can be trusted, I'm not going to stop him. Nothing can go wrong now, not when it seems so right.

"What exactly are you planning to do, Ser?" Ryan asks as he makes his way over, placing himself between me and the view I have of Lucifer.

"You'll see soon enough, but I'm doing exactly what you told me to do."

"I thought we said no more keeping things from each other?"

"We did, but this; I need to do this part on my own. It's all going to make sense really soon Ryan and I only hope that when it does, you don't hate me for keeping it from you."

"All this time and you still don't get it, do you?"

There are a whole lot of things that I admit I don't get but right now, I really have no idea what he's talking about. I know it has something to do with us but exactly what, I'm lost on.

"I guess I don't, but you're gonna tell me right?" I ask, batting my eyelashes in his direction before cracking up at how weird it feels doing it.

"I could never hate you. I know why you're doing it this way and I'm alright with it. I just wish you would tell me what I said so I can inflate my ego a bit."

"You said I had to do the right thing by everyone and well, that's exactly what I'm doing."

"Wow, I'm pretty awesome."

"Yes, you are." I grin. "So is that a big enough stroke to your ego?"

The minute the words come out of my mouth I know they've had the desired effect, as his eyes fill with what I can only assume is desire and the smirk I've come to love so much appears. Yes, making this decision has definitely made me feel

184

lighter than I've ever been. It also seems to help me finally embrace the art of flirting; something that until now, I utterly failed at every single time it came up.

"You enjoyed stroking it, did you?" he whispers in my ear as he pulls me to him, bringing us as close as we can get to each other.

"Oh, you have no idea."

Just as he's about to lean in to kiss me, sensing it and closing my eyes in anticipation, Michael speaks and we're both immediately slammed back into the reality of what is going on around us.

"Serenity, it is time."

"What did he say?" I ask, turning just slightly from my position in Ryan's arms.

"We need to free Lucifer."

"So do it."

"It cannot be me. It has to come from you."

Well shit. I guess there are still some surprises after all.

"How am I supposed to get him out of there? I mean, I know I've got some power, but I don't think it's enough to do what you need here. He seems locked in pretty tight there."

"It is not something that is based in power, Serenity, at least not the way that you assume. Hell works much the same way as Heaven as it pertains to what you see during your time here. You see Lucifer as being locked in a chamber correct? Metal hangings and things of that nature?"

I nod slowly. It seems the more time I spend here; the more I continue to learn though this is not something I'm all that enthused about. It was one thing imagining Ryan in a hospital bed in Heaven, it's another to be imagining what I'm actually seeing right now. I don't even wanna know how he really appears if this is the vision my mind conjures.

"That is not how he actually appears. It's of little consequence, so just know that the way in which you have to do this in order for him to be freed is a method that I know for a fact you will not enjoy."

"What do I have to do?"

"He's got to possess her, doesn't he?" Ryan throws out, his expression much the same as it's been since the minute he pulled me into his arms, not giving anything away about how he really feels. He can't enjoy being the one to drop it on me, yet he never deviates from his stance. He continues rubbing his hands slowly up and down my back, the smirk still across his face even though it's a little less now than it had been minutes before.

It's actually strange seeing him this in control considering what he just said.

"That is exactly what must happen. I know that it is most unpleasant, but it is the only way this can happen."

As much as I appreciate Michael's understanding attitude, he seems to forget this is not my first rodeo in terms of being possessed. Not only has Lucifer himself done it before, but Michael had also spent a little time in my skin. So summoning every ounce of strength I know I have, I think of Graham and everything he endured and pull myself slowly out of Ryan's arms.

The chill in the air the minute I distance myself from him made me feel better. It meant that whatever happened earlier between us is long past and the bond and all of the trimmings that come along with it are back in full effect again.

"Let's get this over with."

Lucifer

I am dealing with a different Serenity and it is delightful.

When I possessed her before, she had been most unwilling to do so and fought against me as hard as she could. Having her standing before me now and opening up willingly, knowing that at any point I could turn her against the other two people in the room, using her for my own selfish gain, it brought forth a much different reaction in me.

186

This is not one born of pleasure the way it had been the first time, at least not the devious pleasure I garnered from it. It warmed me inside because having her trust me in this way meant everything to me. This is the woman that is bonded to my brother. Out of all of the beings of light both above and below, this had been the one that Gabriel's heart called to and in being trusted with her now, especially with him no longer here, it made it that much more powerful in comparison to the last time we had been this way.

I am going to do exactly as I said and remove the brand on her heart the minute the binding process is complete, but I would be lying if I said I wouldn't enjoy the few minutes I'm going to have being connected to her this way.

"Don't get any ideas about making this a permanent home." She states as I feel myself being drawn into her light. Her words only prove again why she had been the perfect choice, not only for me, but also for my brother. There could be no other being alive that could stand next to either one of us and still hold her own the way Serenity does.

"I would not dream of it, my belle. I will make this as quick and painless as I can."

We are speaking to one another yet there is no other being around that can hear us. This is the true art of possession. I have no doubt that anything said would be passed along the minute the process is over, but for the time being, we are truly alone with each other and I am enjoying every second of it.

"Removing the brand, is it going to hurt?"

"It will bring no harm to you; I can assure you of that. It only affects those that you are bonded with, but because neither Graham nor Gabriel is in the room to witness it, they will remain unscathed by the process, as will you."

I feel a shift within her as the process completes and I want to ask her about it, but before I have the chance, I hear my brother speaking loud and clear in our minds. Given the power that still resides inside of me, it appears as though I have taken

Serenity completely over, something that at one time would have made me happy, but now only causes tinges of pain.

Remove yourself brother, before I am forced to do it for you.

"Of course, Michael, as you wish."

Joining with a vessel is always the hardest part, so breaking apart from Serenity is a most tolerable experience, other than the emptiness I feel when I am again free from her. She will never experience that part of it, which I am thankful for. I can already feel the conflict on her heart because of the brand I placed there, the last thing I want to do is have her feel just how affected I am with the whole process.

"You know what you must do now, brother."

As always, Michael is all business. While I am still acclimating to the way that it feels to be free of the binds that have held me, he is pushing to move ahead. For all of the feeling he claims to have for the ball of heavenly light that he again stands beside, his insistence on rushing demonstrates the opposite. I am not the only one that will need a moment to acclimate back to normal, she will as well and he should remember that.

"Give her a moment Michael, you know as well as I do how possession affects the human condition."

"I remember quite well, Lucifer."

"So removing the brand...what exactly does he have to do?" Serenity asks, her voice still labored from what we went through, yet her mind focused as always on what comes next.

"It is similar to what Gabriel had to do with you that day in your dorm. It will be uncomfortable, but not in the same way it was then."

"Lucifer told me that it won't affect me."

"That is true."

"As I told her, it will only affect those that are bonded with her. Due to the fact that Graham is not here, I do believe we are safe moving forward."

"Yes, I am in agreement brother; I do believe everything will go smoothly. So if you wouldn't mind, I believe we should get started. The sooner that we complete this process, the sooner we can meet with Father."

There is one thing that needs to be handled before I take my next step. I am aware that I will not be received in the fondest light, but I cannot move forward without doing it. So turning away from both Serenity and my brother I make my way over to where Ryan now stands alone, a sullen expression across his face.

"What is about to take place is not going to be easy to take, and for that, I am truly sorry. I am aware that you will not believe a word of what I'm saying, but I want you to know that I am only doing this now because it needs to be done. It is the right thing to do and any pain that comes from what you see, I am eternally sorry for."

I mean every word of it. I am to embrace the woman he loves and bring her as close as two people can get, reaching first into her mind, the very mind that I corrupted and then into her heart, all in an effort to remove what I placed there. None of it would be pleasurable to him and despite what he believes, it causes me pain.

I'm not sure when it happened, but somewhere along the way I have realized just how far I strayed, not only from what my father wanted, but also what Heaven expected and needed of me. I know it may not make any difference moving forward, but I have to take the chance to make up for all of it. It may have started out with me wanting it because it is what Gabriel wanted but the more I sit back and focus on it, I realize it's all I've ever wanted and this is my final shot at achieving it.

"Thank you..."

Words I never expected have stunned me as I turn to make my way back to Serenity and what has to happen now. It may not be much, but that simple thank you means a lot to me. That thank you would carry us through.

"You are most welcome."

"Now that we have gotten that out of the way," Michael speaks, looking between both me and Serenity, his eyes filled with question. "It is time to right this wrong."

Chapter Twenty-Three

Ryan

I want to believe that he's getting off on this. That he doesn't want to do the right thing and this is just another ploy to somehow get Serenity under his control. He knows what she means to me, so doing the right thing or at least making her and Michael believe that's what he wants to do, would work perfectly in any plan he has to bring me to my knees.

Trusting him again is something that will never happen. I had fallen for his tricks and his false truths one too many times and I'll be damned if I let myself fall victim to it again. No matter how honest he seems.

Something happened when he walked over to me this time. He looked me directly in the eye and the hatred I had come to know so well with him is no longer there. That alone wouldn't have been enough to make me change my mind, but there was more to it. He's telling me the truth or at least his version of it and for the first time, he seems sincere. I can feel it dripping off his every word. He might not like me, hell, I know he doesn't like me, but he did want to do the right thing by Serenity and in turn me.

That's why I said thank you though no one was more shocked to hear those two words come out, then me. He has done so much over the years that honestly, thank you is something he should never hear, but hear it he did because I realized as I said it that I meant it.

There was a moment, where I could almost see why Serenity wanted to save him so badly. If he had been this way with me during my time with him, I can't say I wouldn't have wanted to save him too. It's extremely easy to see why he had been part of the highest order of angels, something that has never been noticeable before.

As much as I hate to admit it, he earned his one shot with me. I only hope that as I prepare to watch my wife again have her soul breached by someone other than me, that I don't live to regret it.

"Ryan, before this begins there is something that I must warn you about."

Whenever an angel comes up to you and says the word 'warn' and 'you' in the same sentence, it is never going to be good. The minute he says them, I wonder if the olive branch I'm willing to extend Lucifer is about to come back and bite me in the ass.

"It is about the beloved bond and what is about to take place. You must listen very carefully and protect yourself as much as possible."

What the hell is he going on about? Why is he bringing up our bond now? I know I'm not going to handle this well and I'm sure he's concerned about me, but the way I would have reacted before is no longer an issue now, so his concern is misplaced.

"Michael, it's seriously going to be fine. That part of me is gone remember?"

"I am not referring to the demonic, Ryan. It is something far worse than that."

I'm about to ask him just what he means, but before I can get the words out, I feel it. The pull in my chest, almost as if someone is punching a hole into it, ripping out my insides. Before I can even get a handle on exactly what the hell could possibly be causing it, hearing Michael's voice growing faint in the distance, I again feel another sensation I can't place.

There is a squeezing sensation on my heart and with each passing second it gets tighter and tighter and unable to control myself, I allow my body to fall to my knees, all the while gripping onto my chest with both hands and pounding my own hole into it, in an effort to stop the choke hold that seems to be placed there.

The pain is so strong that I can barely keep my eyes open. I turn and look to where I saw Michael standing seconds before. Whatever is happening to me, he has to have the answers to, if only I can keep my eyes open long enough to see him say it, as the pounding in my eardrums as the hold grows tighter is blocking my ability to hear.

If I can only read his lips, maybe I can find out what the hell is happening to me.

"Michael."

I can just barely make him out as I slide my eyes open one more time and as hard as I try to make out what I can see his lips trying to say, I'm unable to. The pain unbearable, I let my body fall to the floor finally, using what little strength I have left to curl myself into a ball and try as hard as I can to push the pain away.

The minute my eyes shut, the world seems to go completely dark around me and it's as if the weight has been lifted off my shoulders. I'm finally able to breathe again, yet try as I might to open my eyes and get back to my feet, I find myself frozen. It's only when the memories begin to take form like a movie in my head that I realize what's going on.

Whatever Lucifer is doing to Serenity in an effort to fix her—I'm living it.

Clear as day I'm thrown into Serenity's dorm room and from where I sit, I can see Emma's bed and all of the posters she insists need to be covering every free space of the wall. I know with certainty that I'm either laying or sitting on Serenity's bed as there is no other vantage point in the room that would give me this view.

*****

"You do not see it Serenity, but you are very special. That is why I want to protect you and why I come to you every night. I'm taking a tremendous risk being around you this way, but for some reason I cannot ascertain, I need to be here."

"I know you have many questions for me and I promise you, when the time is right, I will answer every one of them, but right now is not that time. I have said as much as I can without going against the very reason I'm here. I'm very sorry."

"Please don't leave. I have so much I want to say..."

"I will never leave you, Serenity. I am always with you."

*****

As I begin to get a handle on exactly what I'm seeing, I realize I'm reliving a private moment between her and Gabriel, one that no matter how much I've learned about the two of them, I know nothing about. I'm not sure why I can see it this vividly, almost as if I'm living it through their eyes, but however it's possible, I just want it to end.

The ache in her tone as she asks to him to stay feels like a million knives being shoved into my chest and it takes everything in me not to scream out in terror. Whatever's happening to me right now just needs to stop. I don't want to see this.

As soon as I think I've got a handle on it, I feel myself being dragged from my spot and being placed in another scene, one even worse than the last because I'm not only reliving yet another moment between the angel and the woman I love, but I'm witnessing her pain at having Gabriel not be there for her. Something I knew about, but could never understand.

*****

"Where have you been? What happened to always being with me? Or were you just lying when you said that?"

"I want to tell you everything, but right now isn't the time."

"You know what? Spare me, Gabriel. You're just saying the same stupid line you always do. I'm starting to think it's the only words you know how to say."

"I am sorry that you feel that way, but that is not the case."

"I waited for you for three days; I missed you, but did that matter to you? Does it matter to you now? No, because if it did, then you'd tell me the truth. So how about you just do us both a favor and continue doing exactly what you've been doing. Leave me the hell alone."

*****

I know this moment. This is the day that I first met her, but when it happened, I'm not entirely sure. It's either what happened before she walked into the class that day or something that happened after we'd gotten out. Serenity talked about it with me, but she hadn't given me all the details.

Now I understand why.

My Serenity, the woman I love, in these memories is falling in love with her beloved and the thought makes me sick to my stomach. Curling my body into itself as much as possible, I do everything in my power to force the visions away. I can only imagine what comes next if this is what I'm being shown now and I don't wanna see it.

I can't see it. It will kill me.

When nothing I do seems to work, I finally try one last tactic in hopes that it will stop the random shuffle of memories being thrown my way. The stabbing pain in my chest is back and it's stronger than ever now. I can hear the beating of my heart, its consistent pounding drowning out the voices as much as possible, but not nearly as much as I need them too.

"Michael! Please make it stop!" I scream, praying that the angel hears me and can finally put a stop to it. Before I can focus on a response, the scene in front of me shifts again and this time, I'm back in Serenity's dorm room and I'm not alone. Sitting on the bed beside her is none other than the other keeper of her heart.

It's her soul mate.

Graham Hudson.

*****

"Do you remember the night of the party, the one you got drunk at?"

"What about it?"

"I was an idiot that night, but in my defense I really believed I was doing the right thing. Turns out, I've been bothered by it ever since and I'm not sure that what I did was the right thing after all. I think I fucked things up. We were never the same after that."

"What are you talking about?"

"That night, when you kissed me, I thought you'd done it because you'd been drinking. All I could see was that I needed to get you home before you did anything else you'd regret. I didn't want to be your regret, Serenity. I don't think my heart could handle it. Hell, it's been years and my heart still can't handle the fact that we don't even talk on the phone anymore."

"I'm an idiot for never telling you that when you kissed me, it was like you read my mind. That you were doing the one thing I'd been dying to do for months. I lost my best friend because I couldn't handle the fact that she might have done what she did because she liked me too."

"Okay..."

"Come on, princess. You can't hear all that and not respond. You're driving me crazy here."

"Say something Ser, please."

"What am I supposed to say to that, Graham? It's been two years..."

"You say what you feel. You yell or scream at me. You can punch me. Anything you want to. Just don't keep giving me the silent treatment. I need to know what you're thinking."

"I was drunk that night, you're right. I'd never done anything like that before, but I liked the way it made me feel. It gave me courage that I didn't have normally. I may have been out of it, but I knew exactly what I was doing."

"So wait. You're saying you really did want to kiss me?"

"I thought I was the one that stammered. Since when do you do it?"

"What can I say, you inspire me."

"Yeah, okay smart ass. To answer your question, yes Graham. I wanted to kiss you that night and for weeks beforehand. You were..."

"I was what?"

"You were different. You've always been different."

*****

Fuck. I can't take any more of this. It's bad enough seeing her emotional reaction to Gabriel before she even knew what he was to her, but to watch her with Graham, knowing exactly what they would mean to each other, is too much to take. Before I can get a handle on the scene though, I'm pulled again and this time, it's to the other side of the room and it's the vision I know in graphic detail. A scene that I thought I would never have to relive again.

The day Serenity truly bonded with Graham the way they were meant to.

The day my heart was ripped out.

*****

"Serenity I need to make this up to you. Please let me make this up to you!"

"Graham..."

"No, don't say anything yet. I've got something else I need to say."

"Fine. Say whatever you want."

"Every one of the girls I was with, they didn't mean anything."

"Graham, if you want me to forgive you, telling me about sex with other girls is not going to get you anywhere."

"Every time I was with a girl, it wasn't them I was with. I know that makes no sense, but you have to believe me. Yes I wanted to get laid and yes I didn't give a shit who it was with, but every single time I closed my eyes it wasn't them I saw. All I could see was you."

"You saw me while you were screwing other girls?"

"No—Yes—I don't know. You are all I ever see, Serenity. God, I can't even take a step without thinking about you, seeing you in my head and wanting nothing more than to find you and—

"And what, Graham?"

"Do this."

*****

Why won't this stop? Why do I need to sit here and take this right now after everything I've already had to endure?

I see the way his hands move over her body and the way she leans into his, accepting it and even wanting more of him. The way their lips seem to move together in unison, neither one of them wanting to break away from whatever is ignited between them. It doesn't matter that I've already seen this exact moment a million times after reliving it on my own, being tortured with it now just makes it that much worse.

It's starting to make sense to me, as I prepare my body for yet another shifted scene. Lucifer is attempting to break the brand he placed on her heart and because of what I mean to her, or even because of the bond that now exists between us,

198

I'm getting a front row seat to the moments that most impacted her heart. It's the very last thing I want to see.

*****

This is the happiest day of my existence to date. The way she is looking at me now could never be taken from me, even if she was. I would treasure it always.

"It would appear as though someone is enjoying themselves."

"Enjoying it doesn't seem right." She replies, her smile growing bigger. "I am overdosing on it. Even now, knowing that the blood is finished, I still crave more. Please tell me that we get to do this often."

"As often as you would like, my queen. You do seem to have taken quite a liking to it and I would like nothing more than for you to enjoy your time here with me."

"I can think of only one other thing that could happen now that would make me enjoy my time here. The question is—are you eagerly awaiting it as I am or do we need to continue on with the rest of the tour?"

*****

I'm aware that I'm doing it, but I can't feel it or even smell it. I'm finally succumbing to the bile that's been growing in my throat with each vision and I'm finally throwing up. There was a moment after watching her and Graham where I knew it would come, but I prayed for control. The last thing I need to do is lose control of myself, but now that I've seen exactly what happened to her during her stay with Lucifer and just how close the two of them had gotten, there's no going back. I can't keep it inside anymore. I'm losing it.

Just in time for another time shift, this time back in her room and another moment in time that I've been told about, but never gotten to experience through her eyes. It appears that now, I'm special enough to do that and as badly as the last memory hurt me, this one makes it even worse.

*****

"You..."

"What about me, Serenity? What is it that you are remembering?"

"You must realize that I have seen that reaction many times before. You have remembered something that has changed something deep within you. Where before you were unwilling to accept everything I wanted to show you, now you seem to ache for more knowledge."

"I do remember. I remember a lot, but it is one thing in particular I seem to recall more than anything else you have shown me."

"What is it?"

"You love me."

"In the way that a being such as myself can love, yes I do, very much so."

"I never wanted to leave you, so why did you let me go?"

"Oh, my sweet belle, I never wanted to let you go. I know that as you recall it now, it is also filled with other times where you have been left behind by those that have claimed to love you, but you must remember that I am not them. I am only me and I never let you go."

*****

As the last memory takes hold, I feel a rush of blood rise into my head and everything begins to fade out. There is still a tightening in my chest and an ache in my heart, but I'm finally able to breathe again. As I'm able to open my eyes, I see Michael crouched over me and it's the last thing I want.

I don't want to see anymore. I've seen more than enough to last me a lifetime. No matter where we go from here and how fixed she is, all I'm going to see every single time I close my eyes is how easily her heart had been taken from me. If it had been that easy before, what's to stop it from happening now? Every single event but one happened before the brand was even on her heart and even though they could all be talked away with words like soul mate and beloved, it didn't change the fact that they happened.

"Ryan, if you can hear me, you must answer me now."

I can hear the words and I want to answer him, but I can't. So I do the only thing I can. I close my eyes, this time allowing everything to go black and knowing what to expect. As the world closes in around me, the aching in my chest growing by the minute, I finally let myself go, letting something that I haven't experienced for months take form inside of me.

I embrace the darkness.

Michael

It had been my hope that in reaching out to Ryan the way I did before Lucifer prepared to remove the brand from Serenity, I would be able to prepare him for what he was about to experience. Watching the man fall right in front of my eyes had been extremely hard to take.

I'm familiar with the beloved bond and what one can experience in moments like the one we find ourselves in, but the way in which Ryan reacted throughout and even now as he lies still before me, is not something I had been prepared for. The human part of him is melding with the angelic and what he is being forced to endure took a toll in both ways. Judging by the mess that surrounds us now, it had been more powerful than a being of his caliber could handle.

Remnants of the very human reaction were strewn around him and as much as I want to erase all trace of what happened here from both Serenity and Ryan when he does awaken from wherever he finds himself, I know I cannot. The both of them need to be made aware of exactly what the bond between them means and this is the only way possible to get the point across, no matter how hard it may be to actually see.

There is one thing that I can do in the moment though and that is to heal the damage that he managed to do to himself while he had been under the influence of the bond. He ripped through his shirt, almost as if he was a rabid animal. It is shredded in the spot right above his heart and is now seeping blood as he cut clean through his own skin.

The bond we share with the one that is meant for us is a powerful thing. Though Ryan knew of it and had taken it on easily after Gabriel's passing, I do not believe he thought about the long term affect it would have on him. I know for a fact that Serenity hadn't even begun to give it the focus it deserved, despite having had the time to get used to it when it had been a part of my brother.

Placing my hand over his heart, I channel every peaceful reminder of Heaven I can manage and I force it forward in an effort to heal him as only I can. Where Gabriel had the power of healing at his disposal, able to do it easily, it did not come quite so simply for me. I am most definitely the warrior of the family and that is always where my focus has been. I can heal, but it takes much more focus then it does with Gabriel.

It is only when he opens his eyes again, that I notice the change and I'm struck again with an experience I have no real knowledge of. Unsure if what I am even witnessing is real, I do as I have seen the humans do in situations such as this and I blink, going so far as to clear my eyes in an effort to be positive that what I am actually seeing is reality.

As he stares up at me, looking much the same, despite everything I have done, I realize that there is no mistaking it. Just on the outer portion of his blue eyes, much like in times past is the faintest line of black.

The darkness has returned.

Chapter Twenty-Four

Serenity

The minute Lucifer's finished with me, he rises and backs away, his focus no longer on me but on something on the other side of the room. The minute he turns, I know something's wrong. Rising up from my position on the ground, slowly reclaiming the use of my body again after the ordeal it's been through, I make my way over to where the fallen angel now stands and see exactly what it is that got his attention.

What I see stops my heart. Ryan is curled in around himself, his face hidden but the area around him is splattered with what I can only assume is what he'd eaten before coming to meet me. Michael is bent over him and I can barely make out what looks to be blood stains on the angels hands.

It doesn't make any sense. I know that Lucifer said my beloved would feel what happened with me, but how is it possible that it got to him this bad? Is the connection between us really this powerful that it can cause the scene I'm seeing now? Just what kind of bond is this if all it seems to cause is agony?

"I should have known." Lucifer whispers before turning and catching my eyes. "He is your beloved, is he not?"

I nod, not trusting my voice to say anything more. If I had known it would break Ryan this way, I would have made Michael take him away from it like Graham is. He didn't need to experience everything that came along with what Lucifer just had to do.

"This is not going to be good, Serenity."

He didn't have to tell me that. It already wasn't good if Ryan's motionless body is any indication.

"I should have warned him."

"I believe that goes without saying. What he is experiencing right now I would not wish on anyone and I've spent a great deal of time torturing people for pleasure. Why did you keep it from me?"

"Because it wasn't any of your business and it's not just up to me. It's Ryan's decision too."

"One I am sure he is regretting now."

I want to snap at him, but before I can come up with a comeback Michael stands and turns to face us, the expression on his face turning my blood cold. It looks like it's even worse then I imagined.

"Has it been completed?"

"Yes brother, it has been handled. I'm to assume that the boy didn't take the experience well?" Lucifer answers making me wanna slap him again. Obviously Ryan didn't handle it well.

"That is an understatement. I do not mean to be cold about this, but I need to get him out of here."

"Michael," I beg pushing forward. "Can I see him?"

"In his current state, I do not believe that is wise. I know that you are concerned for him, but he is not right at the moment. What took place between you and Lucifer seems to have created a response in him that even I was not prepared for. If you come any closer, you are in danger."

He obviously has no idea what he's talking about. Even after all the time he's spent with us, he has no idea the affect we have on each other. There's no way in hell I'm in danger from Ryan, especially now that the light had been restored in him and the darkness taken away. I wasn't going to let him tell me no. I need to see Ryan. End of story.

"Serenity, it is that very darkness that is behind my attempt to keep you away. I need to take him far from the both of you before he awakens or I fear something far more tragic will take place. You must trust me."

"How is that even possible, Michael? You saw what happened in the church. The light changed him."

He nods in understanding, but I can tell that he's as confused by all of this as I am. He isn't lying when he said that what happened hadn't been expected. Even knowing about the bond, we wouldn't have seen it coming.

"I have no idea, but I plan on finding out. In the meantime, I have informed Father of all that has happened. Proceed back home Serenity. He plans to meet you upon arrival. I know you're worried about Ryan, but I solemnly swear to you that I will fix him to the best of my ability and you will see him again soon."

If only it was that easy for me to do. Just put one foot in front of the other and walk away from the man I love when he needs me. The guilt I feel in the pit of my stomach doesn't exactly help either. I mean, if I had just done this alone like I wanted to, none of this would be happening now. He would be safe in his dorm room the way he's meant to.

"Do not think that way, you did not cause this."

I turn to Michael, fully prepared to give him the speech about letting me take the blame when I realize it wasn't him that said it, but the fallen angel beside me.

"Not intentionally, but you can't say that I'm not partially to blame."

"The bond is to blame and your lack of knowledge of its true power, but that is all."

I don't agree with him, but I can't deny that there is one thing he says that gets to me. My lack of knowledge. He's right about that, which only makes the guilt that much worse. I should have talked to Gabriel about this when it was us. Maybe if I did then Ryan would be spared now or we could have faced it together and beaten it.

"Are all of you exactly the same as my brother? I swear, just when I think I have dealt with this once and for all, it rears its ugly head again."

"What's that supposed to mean?" I snap.

"Gabriel let the doubt eat him alive and then during our time here Ryan went through much the same thing. Now it

205

appears as though I need to tell you the same thing I told the both of them."

"And what's that?"

"You cannot move forward with what comes next when you are locked so deeply in your own doubts and fears. You must not let it consume you; instead, you need to rise above it."

"Yeah, that's easier to say then to do, Michael."

"You're correct, but you can still try."

"Serenity, I know that it is not what you want to hear but Michael is right. If this is indeed what your purpose is, you must not give in because of what is happening now. You must stand your ground, accept that it's not perfect and forge forward."

Shit. Now even the fallen angel is telling me what to do. There is something seriously messed up about this entire thing, but with no other options I would do what they need me to do. I would move forward despite the way that everything has blown up in my face.

"You'll come get me the minute you know anything?" I ask, again putting my attention back on Michael.

"Yes of course. We will figure all of this out Serenity. He will be back with you where he belongs in no time at all. That I promise you."

I don't want to hold much stock in his promises, but there is no mistaking that those few words help in making me move forward. Whether or not the evil is back for good or is just a response to what he had gone through while Lucifer removed my brand didn't matter. He would come back to me and we would get through this together, just like we have every other time.

"Go now so I can remove Ryan from here with minimal distractions. Lucifer, despite my lack of trust in you after everything that has happened, I trust you now. Go with her and do not even think of trying anything. You might be getting another shot to do the right thing, but I have no issue making sure you end up right back where you started."

"Michael, I can't leave yet…"

"Serenity, I understand your trepidation, but you must do as I have said. Time is of the essence, not only for you and Lucifer, but for Ryan. I have no idea how he will react when he opens his eyes again and that is something you do not need to be present for. The Ryan that wakes now will not be the Ryan you have come to know and love."

Does he really think I care about that?

I know the risks, but I will not leave here without at least saying goodbye to him. It doesn't matter what package he comes in, human, angel or demon. He will always be my Ryan regardless. I didn't care about any of that before and I definitely don't care about it now. Even if he can't hear me, see me or even sense my presence, I can't leave here without seeing and touching him one more time.

"I can handle myself, but I'm not leaving without saying goodbye Michael, so you're just going to have to deal with it." I explain as I start moving toward the crumpled form in front of me.

The keeper of my heart and the strongest person I have ever known, now at his weakest right in front of me. It takes all of the strength I have inside to keep my feet moving forward, scared at what I am going to find when I finally come face to face with him. He might not be awake, but if the way the area around him looks is any indication, I'm pretty sure the way he looks is going to rip my heart out.

"Be careful." Michael warns as he stands guard above me. I hear him and even as I lower my body down to the ground, I heed the warning, but I do not let it deter me from what needs to be done.

Stroking his face ever so gently, I see what remains of what looks to be Michael's healing and as I expect, my heart instantly feels heavy. As much as I cherish the bond that we share, the fact that it could cause destruction like this makes me sick. A bond that is so beautiful in nature looks anything but in the moment. As I bend down and place my lips on his cheek, noticing the grayish tint to his skin as I do, I realize that if I had my way, I'd strip us of this bond all together. Anything that would take what he is going through away. He didn't deserve this because of his love for me. No one did.

"It's almost over baby, I swear. When you wake up, I won't be with you, but know that the minute I finish what I started, I'm coming back for you and we're going to get married, just the way you picture it. I swear to you. We will get our happy ending."

With one last stroke of my fingers on his cheek, I get to my feet again and my eyes lock with Michael's. Even though I believe he knows what I'm thinking and no words need to be said, I say them anyway because I don't think I can move forward and do what everyone wants of me until I do.

"Bring him back to me, Michael because none of this means anything without him."

Lucifer

It does not surprise me now that I have learned the truth that the darkest parts of Ryan had been awakened going through what we all experienced. There is no way with the magnitude of what just happened that it couldn't have touched him in that way.

There was a time that seeing him this broken would have pleased me to no end, but seeing him now, it breaks what remains of my heart. This is not the end I wanted for the boy that I had come to envision as my own. Sure, the anger I felt towards him had driven me to some dark scenarios, but never this.

Though I am familiar with the beloved bond, it is the one thing that I never got to experience before I was cast out. I had heard of it of course, but never felt that there was one out there meant for me in that manner. With the way I questioned everything, never content with the way anything seemed to be destined to go, I couldn't put my faith and hope in something like the bond that each one of my brothers has experienced.

I suppose that makes me lucky because I cannot even begin to imagine the torture that he endured physically and mentally over what I had just done with the woman he loves. Not even Michael, who has connected with his can truly understand the places that the mind will take you when faced with something of this magnitude. It is my hope that he never does. I want what Ryan is going through to be a lesson to him in that regard.

It raises the question, especially with Ryan's reaction, of whether or not I can be redeemed. It may be written that it needs to happen, but it doesn't mean that I am deserving of it in any capacity. Maybe what Gabriel wanted for me is just not possible. Maybe it is as Father always wanted and I am to remain here in the hell I created for eternity. It would be a fitting end with all of the pain I've caused. I ruined what Father had taken so much pride in by corrupting them right from the moment of their creation and enjoyed it despite my recent change of heart. If I were in my father's shoes, I do not believe I would be so willing to let this happen now.

I did the unforgiveable, despite any other claims or belief otherwise.

"There will never be a way for me to make up for everything I have done. Ryan was right. I am due to spend the rest of my existence in the very darkness I created. It is what I deserve."

"Lucifer, I want to agree with you, but it would be only selfishness on my part. As you know, Father is a forgiving God, despite the way he has been depicted in recent years."

"There is a level to the amount of forgiveness one can give and receive brother. Selfish or not, your agreement is not wrong."

"Didn't you both just tell me a few minutes ago that the doubt needs to stop? Well, listen to your own advice here. I'm not exactly your father's biggest fan, but there is one thing I know about him. What Michael says is right. If he is willing to come to you at all, it speaks volumes about exactly what kind of God he really is."

She is right. In granting me a chance to stand before him and beg for his mercy and forgiveness means something. I may not believe myself to be worthy of true redemption, but it is obvious that in some small way, Father does, otherwise he wouldn't want to meet with me at all.

As I watch Ryan's body begin to stir, I am again brought back to the reality of the situation. It is time to move ahead.

"Serenity, I believe it's time we do as Michael has requested and move on, but before we go, I just want to say one final thing."

"As we move forward, I want the both of you and even Ryan when he is up to it, to know that no matter what way this turns out for me, I am humbled by the trust you have all placed in me today and I swear, I will do nothing to break it again. It may have taken a lot longer then he wanted it to, but I believe I have finally seen what Gabriel has been trying to get me to see for a lifetime. Even when it doesn't seem like it, it is never too late to do the right thing. Thank you for allowing me the chance to do that."

I expect no response from either of them, but am surprised when Michael moves away from Ryan and closer to me. Before I am able to question exactly what his intent is, I feel the embrace and I feel something that only Serenity has been able to give me since the day I was cast out.

Acceptance.

Chapter Twenty-Five

God

There have only been a handful of occasions that I have appeared in this way. As ever present as I am for those that believe in me, I tend to not reach out in this manner often, preferring instead to remain at home and handle things from there. It is easier because of the magnitude of my power. Appearing before a human is out of the question. It is true when they say that humans cannot handle the sight of me. It is not me that they cannot handle; it is the light and power that reside within me.

Today is a day like none other before it, so there has to be exceptions made. When I put this undertaking into motion, I always knew it would reach this point and I would have to make the choice of whether to allow my fallen son entrance to Heaven or appear before him on the planet that up until recently he had been set to destroy. As much faith as I have in what happens next, I still cannot bring myself to take the risk of allowing him entrance to what had once been his home. So a meeting on the planet it has to be.

Contrary to what has been written and said about me, I do not harbor hate in my heart for Lucifer. In fact, it is the opposite. I believe that the problems between us were caused because I loved him too much. He was unable to handle the sheer magnitude of it. With that and the free will I instilled within him, he made choices that in the end tore us apart, bringing us to where we are now.

I love all of my children, celestial or human and despite what they may do; I am always willing to listen when they are ready to speak to me. Lucifer may say that I am not that way, but it is only because any time that I felt him wanting to stand

211

before me, he had not been where he needed to be within his own heart and mind. I would never have turned him away had he been ready.

This is where Serenity plays such a large part. When I made her, I knew that she would be the one being in all of creation to bring my fallen son back to me. She would be the link that would bring us together in the same space and time, finally giving us what we have been craving since the day I let my love get the better of me and had Michael cast him out. It was always meant to be her and as I stand here now before her, I am forever thankful that she turned out even better than I originally made her to be.

In Serenity's case, it appears as though the light within her mixed with the very human that she has become and it created something that even in my infinite wisdom, I didn't realize was possible. It is no surprise that not one, but two of my sons have managed to find themselves at one time or another in love with her. She truly is perfection personified.

Judging by the look on her face, I can tell that when Michael told her I wanted to meet with her, in the place that it all began, she had been expecting me much the way she has witnessed both Michael and Gabriel since learning of them. In my true form. For the first time in what seems like forever, I am able to stand before her now, in a vessel of my choosing and enjoy the complete look of shock that envelopes her features, reminding me again why everyone that comes into contact with her becomes taken with her.

It's almost enchanting how pure it is.

"You seem surprised to find me in this form Serenity; may I ask you why that is?"

Seeing into her mind in this way brings me immeasurable amounts of joy. For all of the light inside her, she is still distinctly human, as her reaction proves.

What am I supposed to say here? It's not like I can admit that he actually looks pretty hot, I mean that seems wrong considering he's pretty much like my Heavenly father and all. Oh crap, he can probably hear every single thing I'm thinking. He's smiling. Crap! That means he can hear it. Ugh, he probably thinks I'm such a loser. Ball of light my ass.

"Serenity, please free your mind of all concerns as it pertains to your reaction to my chosen vessel. It is actually one I have been meaning to use for some time now, but the situation I desired never seemed to arise. Pay no mind to your bodily reaction; I do believe it is quite normal under the circumstances."

"Human women never cease to amaze me." Lucifer replies with a laugh, one that I want to share. His statement is very true; even though I am quite sure Serenity would not agree.

"What's that supposed to mean?" she asks as she angles her body in his direction and away from my own.

"It means, you all act the same as it pertains to a body that looks the way that Father appears to you now. There is something about the muscular form of a man when added to the long blonde locks and crystal blue eyes that seems to drive you all mad."

"That is so—not true."

She hesitates in her answer which only makes both Lucifer and I smile. She may not agree with the statement, but in her own reaction, she is proving us correct. A fact I am sure does not sit well with her.

"Serenity, it matters little. As I said, ignore the vessel. We have much that we need to discuss. Michael said that in following along with the undertaking, you have come up with a suitable solution that will please everyone involved. I would love to hear more about it."

"If she can stop drooling, she may be able to get it out."

"Lucifer this is not the time for jokes. I do believe she is what stands between your true death and what you wish to accomplish here, so it would be wise not to make her turn against you now."

"I'm not exactly sure how I feel about this being put on me. I know what you all think I am, but do you really think I'm the one that should be making the decisions here?"

Even after all of this time, hearing her doubt herself pains me. She is made from the purest part of Heaven, which is why she is so strongly bonded to the pure angel himself. She is stronger and more powerful than most other beings of light and I want nothing more than for her to accept it as fact and move forward with the knowledge because it will change her life and the way she views the world forever.

"This is what you have been made to do, Serenity. I know that you cannot wrap your human mind around it, but it has always been you that is to decide what step we take next and I trust you to make the right one."

The conflict within her is strong. Even with the brand removed, she still has a soft spot for my fallen son and wants to do right by him, yet at the same time does not want to give into it. It is exactly what I expect of her given the magnitude of the situation and just who and what she holds in her hands making it. It is not only Lucifer that she has to concern herself with. It is all of Heaven and Earth, as well as what will happen in regards to the Hell which Lucifer created. It is a daunting task, but one I know she will do right.

"You told Michael that my father plays a part in all of this. What did you mean by that?"

"This is something that you already know the answer to."

"Okay fine, tell me this then because it's definitely something I don't know and I need to know it before I can decide on anything."

"I will answer any and all questions you have, as long as they are ones you do not already have the answers to."

"Will my Dad get out of the hospital or is that his fate in all of this if I don't choose the right thing?"

"The only way he can exit the place where he finds himself is through heavenly intervention. He would need to be possessed, either by me or another being of light. I can assure you though that there are no plans as of right now for that to happen."

"So he's trapped there. Great."

"I am sure you aware by now that every single thought process you have is visible to me, but I am blocking you because I want you to be the one to tell me what it is you believe we need to do. So, please tell me what you decided during your time in Hell."

Her thoughts are scattered as I expect them to be and as easy as it would be for me to sit here and sort them, I mean the words that I spoke to her. I want her to be the one to tell me, just as Gabriel wanted to do before me. It is much easier for a human to come to terms with any decisions they make when they know they are not being violated in a manner that is uncomfortable to them. This is how I want to go ahead. Letting her be free to speak and not hide away because of any invasion on her mind and heart.

"I don't think Lucifer should be redeemed."

The minute the words fall from her lips, I see the agony cross Lucifer's face and I know it is not the answer he expected to hear.

"Serenity, I thought that—

"You didn't let me finish. He wants to know what I think should happen so I'm going to tell him and honestly, after everything you've done, do you really think you get a say in what happens anyway?"

There can be no doubt of her heritage. In this moment as she puts Lucifer in his place, she is realizing her true place in the plan I so intricately put together. She is exercising her power and I couldn't be more pleased.

"My father is where he is right now because of you and the choices you made twenty years ago. It is on you, all of it. I know you want to be redeemed, that you want to go home again and on some level, I want to give you that, but you need to earn it. With as much as you've done, not only to me, but to the world as a whole, you shouldn't just be given what you want on a silver platter. Humans learn the art of earning their keep real quickly growing up. I think you need to learn it too."

"How am I supposed to learn that lesson?"

"You heard your father. The only way my dad can ever get out of the place you put him is for a being of light to possess him. You are that being of light. You want to go home again; well first you need to start fixing the things that you broke."

She had indeed known the answer to her earlier question as is apparent by the very idea that is now being spoken. This is the undertaking in its purest form. This is the way it has been written to be and even though I still have to level my decision in the matter, it also has been written. In this regard, what Serenity has decided is exactly what will come to pass.

"You're damning me to life as a human? How is that doing the right thing by Gabriel?"

Serenity will not have the answer to this question or at least not the answer that he needs to hear. This is something that needs to come from me and come from me it shall.

"Lucifer, even now, as you stand before me, you question the chance you are being given. Just as before when you were cast out, you doubt it and that is unacceptable. I stand before you now because of my infinite amount of love for you and the desire to fix all that we have broken. You are not the only one at fault, for I am as well. What Serenity is proposing is the best possible outcome for all involved and if you only open your heart to it, you will see it as easily as I do."

"My decision, it's selfish in nature too." Serenity cuts in, pulling out attention away from each other and putting it back on the very reason we are here.

"What does that mean?"

"How can you not see what is so clearly placed in front of you, my son? It does not even involve me yet I can see it. Serenity is being selfish because this is her way of keeping you close to her, at least for the time she has remaining of her life on the planet."

The dawn of understanding, is such a powerful moment, whether it happens with an angel or a human. It really does appear as though a light bulb goes off above ones head and everything seems to make sense and it is clear as day with Lucifer now. He is beginning to see what I have been able to see right from the start.

"She has taught you how to love again, has she not?"

"Yes Father, she has. It is something I did not believe myself capable of experiencing again."

"That was her purpose. It was through her and the emotional tie that you have always had with Gabriel that brings us to this moment now. I believe you see why she was created and why she is revered so highly by me."

"You wanted to bring me back?"

"Yes, I never wanted you gone in the first place. You were cast out because I felt you needed to learn a lesson. I do believe my love for you changed you in some way and in an effort to fix that, not only for you, but for me as well, I moved forward in a way that cost us both dearly."

"I don't even know what to say..."

"What needs to be said is that you see this chance for what it is and you will follow through with it. It is only on this path that Serenity has come to map out for you that you will find your way back home."

"No Father, you misunderstand me. I am not at a loss for words because of everything you have said, it is more a combination of everything that has been said since the moment you arrived before us. It is almost too much to take."

"The choice now lies with you. What Serenity is offering and the reason she is offering it, is exactly how it has been written to occur, but every decision that is made has the power to change the course of events that is written, as I do believe Gabriel's passing has taught us all. So now, as we all stand here together, despite everything you have heard and still need to process, I have to ask you the question."

Serenity moves as I am about to ask him what path he wants to take and I take a step back, letting her do whatever it is that she feels moved to do. This ball of light before me now has given me the one thing I have waited so very long to find and it is because of it, that I am more than willing to step back and give her the space she needs to do what comes next.

"Before he asks you the question, I need to say something. I don't want anything I say to be the reason for your answer, but I want you to hear me out."

"I will always hear you out, my belle."

"I want you to choose to do this because I don't think I can live with it going back to the way it was. When Ryan did what he did to you that night, as much as I wanted it to happen, I also wanted to be taken with you. It was like a part of me died when you did. I can't imagine what it's going to feel like if you choose to not do things this way and end up back where we found you. He's right you know, I want you to do this so I can keep you close to me."

"Even after everything you have endured at my hand, you still wish to have me near you?"

"What we shared in Hell, it will never be recreated Lucifer and I think you know that and have accepted it, but there is still something that we can share and it means just as much if not more than what we shared during my time with you."

"I do not understand."

"You have the chance to give my father his life back and also be given the one thing that you want most, besides the chance to return home. You get to remain with me."

"Are you sure that is what you want? You know that when Ryan is healed, he will want nothing to do with this plan. Can you really stand before me and say with unwavering certainty that this is what you want to do? That it is the right thing to do?"

"Yes. I want you in my life and even though it may not be the way you want, it's a way that works out well for both of us. I need you to do this; not only for me, but for the one person

218

that moving forward won't be here with me the way I desperately want him to be. I want this for Gabriel too."

It is in the moment that Gabriel's name is spoken, the love she feels for him ever present just in the softness of her tone that I know what Lucifer's choice is going to be. Again, right before my eyes she has reached into the very heart of the fallen angel and given him the one thing he had been missing all along.

His way back home.

Chapter Twenty-Six

Serenity

It's hard doing this right now.

It isn't hard because I have reservations about what I think needs to happen because honestly, I have never felt so sure about a decision in my life. It's hard because the person that pushed me to this point isn't here with me to see it taking form. I told him before Lucifer was released that he would see how he helped me and now that we're here and doing this, he is nowhere to be seen.

Never in a million years did I think I would be standing here, much less standing between two of the most powerful beings in existence only seconds away from possibly ending the world's problems forever. The girl everyone thought was strange, weird and downright crazy is the very person that decides their fate. If it wasn't actually happening to me right now I swear it would be laughable.

There is no doubt in my mind what path Lucifer is going to choose. I can see it in his eyes. He might want access to Heaven again, but deep down I think he realizes that it is exactly how I said. It will have to be something that he earns. If there is any being alive aside from Ryan that can do this, it's him. There's no doubt about it. He can make it happen and with the light that seems to be growing around him, it won't be long now until I get to see it firsthand.

All of this makes me ache for Ryan more. He needs to be here to see this happening. He's a lot like me in that he never saw it reaching this point and because of that, I want him here so bad I can taste it. If everything goes the way it has been, it won't be very long until we get to have the happy ending he describes to me so much. A life together where we aren't constantly looking over our shoulder, waiting for the next big bad to come out of hiding and drag us down with it.

I want that more than anything. We are due a long life of happiness after all we've endured. I know now that everything we've gone through has been to lead us to this moment here and going it alone doesn't seem right.

If I'm honest, I'm actually kind of worried we might not get what we want so badly and it isn't because of any lingering doubt about what Lucifer wants. It's because of what happened during our time in Hell. What he endured down there, I saw it, at least what was left of it and now I have to wonder, when everything is said and done, if he's going to want the same things he did before it happened.

It's pretty obvious that whether he's got the demon in him or just the light, I'm going to love him and stand by him. He was a half demon when I met him and even finding out about it couldn't keep me away. Add to that the day we found out what he was truly meant to be, the purest form of angel imaginable and again, I stayed right by his side and no matter what happens this time around, that's where I'm going to remain.

You can take away saving the world, all talk of true destinies and everything else that comes along with it and what's left is all that I want. Me and Ryan, side by side, taking on what comes next and doing it together. Building each other up when we don't feel our best, and bringing each other back down when we get a little too big for our britches. Never wavering, no matter how hard things get.

The fun's in the fixin'.

It all comes back to that very simple statement from my father so long ago. Even at our most broken, I always want to experience what it feels like to fix it and the only person that I want to do that with is Ryan.

"It is time, Lucifer. Serenity has said all that she can say; it is now up to you which road you choose. Will you take the path that will award you the true redemption you seek or will you choose the path of the darkness once more?"

There's actually another reason I wish Ryan was here. I think having my husband by my side might make it easier to look away from the man standing across from me now. I sort of expected that when God chose a vessel, it would be beautiful beyond measure, but to have a virtual Adonis right in front of my eyes is a distraction I didn't need but find extremely hard to look away from.

Yes, this is definitely where a husband would come in handy.

"You already know my answer do you not? Just as I am sure Serenity does. There can be no other one for me. There is only one issue that I want to address before saying the words you wish to hear."

"What concerns you, Lucifer?"

"Gregory Richards. I may have taken control of him in the past, but this time around it will not be done in the same manner as I am sure you agree with. We need to gain his acceptance before this plan of Serenity's can come to fruition."

Silly Lucifer. Doesn't he realize that I've thought about all of that too? There is no way I would move forward using my dad as a vessel without thinking it all the way through. It's actually the next step in the process that I can see so clearly in my mind. I've put it off long enough as it is since learning the truth from my mom. It's time that I finally went to see him. Most importantly, it's time for me to tell him that I love him and despite what I may have grown up believing, that I never stopped. I would never stop.

It is true what Lucifer said. We aren't so different after all.

"Where do you think we're going as soon as you say the words we all know you're desperate to say? It's way past time for me to see my father again." I answer before immediately covering my mouth, realizing the impact of my statement. "My human father."

It's the strangest thing, but for the first time since all of this began; I'm actually getting to see what God looks like when he laughs. It hits me that if I wasn't one hundred percent positive this was my life, I'd think I was stuck in a dream, or at least the strangest movie. God is actually standing in front of me and laughing and since he can see straight into my mind, I have no doubt he's only going to laugh more with the way my thoughts are going.

"Serenity, he is your only father. I may have been the one to create you, but that is all. The man, even though he was taken from you before you could develop a long lasting relationship with him, is very much your father in every way. I do appreciate the sentiment though."

"You really have thought all of this through." Lucifer states, almost as if he's surprised by it.

"Of course. I mean it's not like I had much choice."

"You always have a choice."

I could easily turn his own words back around on him given everything he put me through, but I won't. That's one of the things I learned during the time alone with him. It's how I knew that I couldn't just accept him dying and being stuck for eternity. He had the light in him, even then and just like I did with Ryan, I wanted it to be seen, even if it took a life and death battle to do it.

"I made the right choice I think."

"You did as you have always done, Serenity. You let the light inside guide you, even when to most around you, it seemed wrong."

I always thought that every choice I made lead to disaster and even though God is telling me it's not the case, it doesn't change the fact that deep down, I still sort of believe that to be true. What seems right at the time isn't always the right thing to do and looking back, I swear that's the story of my life. I must have done something right in all of my wrong turns though because we're standing here now and not one drop of blood has been shed.

There won't be another drop of blood shed again. It's that realization that hits me as Lucifer says the words that will carry us forward to the end.

"I'm ready to earn my redemption."

Michael

I have never encountered anything like this before and I am unsure what to do in order to put everything back to normal the way that Serenity asked of me.

He has been like this since I removed him from the chambers and brought him here. I thought that tapping into the returned darkness inside would heal him of this, much the way it had the first time we attempted it. It hadn't been an easy process, but he had come around and become much more than his old self. That is what I need him to do now, but every avenue I try, he fights and he is so strong that he is winning.

I am aware that pain mixed with jealousy and rage can turn even the softest person into something uncontrollable, but there is always a way to combat that and bring them back to the level headed person they were. In Ryan's case that doesn't seem to work. His eyes have long since gone completely black in color; the smile that I have come to recognize so easily is now turned downward into a snarl. The only thing missing from this transformation is the primal yell, though at the speed we seem to be moving, it is not far off.

The very place I healed in Hell is again broken open and blood is spilling out, though not at the rate it had earlier when the incident first took place. The agony of what he has experienced had made him want to rip his own heart out of his chest and I want to heal it, but I cannot get within two feet of him or he begins to act even more like a caged animal.

Could I easily take care of that problem? I could, but it would not be without its own set of repercussions. I do not wish to damage the man in any way and any step I take using the power at my disposal, would do that and more. I cannot allow that to happen. After everything that he has endured all in an effort to see us reach this true ending, the last thing he deserves is to be taken down like a dog.

He's clawing at his chest again and it pains me to no end every single time his nails dig in. Whether he is aware of it or not, we are brothers and any pain that he brings onto himself, I can sense and feel. It is not to the same degree as what he feels, but still most unpleasant.

I want to damn Lucifer for this despite what I know is taking place below me now. He deserves to feel this same level of agony. It is the only way he can truly understand all of the horrible things he's done. Gabriel may have seen the best in him and even I could see the truth in his words during my earlier dealings with him, but it didn't change the fact that deep down he needed to pay for this.

My only experience with the beloved bond has been a positive one. I have never seen the way it works at its hardest point. It is no secret that it is a powerful bond, even more so than the soul mate, but I have no experience with what is happening because of it now.

I have felt pain from my beloved as she has experienced it and it was not pretty, but it never caused quite this kind of reaction and I have never been so powerless against something of its nature before. I am an archangel, one trained to be able to handle any situation thrown my way, especially as it pertains to the warrior within me, but other than using the full weight of my power on this man right now; I am at a loss as to what to do.

"Use your power Michael. I know what you are afraid of, but the longer he remains this way, the more damage long term it will do to the very light that burns inside of him."

Raphael is right. The effects of this in the long term will not be kind to him and if he wants to have some semblance of a normal life moving forward, I need to do whatever is needed now.

"Are you able to heal him?"

"When you have done what is needed I have no problem healing him, but I see no point in doing so before that point. He will only continue to rip at himself in this manner."

"What is causing this?"

"Gabriel never explained to you exactly how it feels to reach into your beloved's soul during the time he did it?"

"No. I tried to get him to speak of it, but he would have no part of it. It actually started an argument between the two of us."

It's strange, but for some reason speaking of my brother does not seem to hurt in the way I have become accustomed to. This is the point I hoped to reach during my moments of solitude here and it had been just out of my reach. I am not sure if I am thankful that I am healing or troubled by it. The last thing I want to do is move on and forget about him entirely.

"Michael, I do believe I can give you the information you seek. Not because I have experienced it as Ryan is, but because I am always on the hunt for answers as it pertains to the bond we share with our other halves. I have seen both the good and bad sides of this bond and what Ryan is experiencing now is the worst of it. It is something that we will never experience."

"What can you tell me, Raphael? I do not want to use my power on him if there is another way around this that will result in a more tolerable ending."

"I am not sure there is a tolerable ending here brother, but what Ryan is experiencing is all of the worst human emotions rolled around the memories of the times that Serenity's heart has been impacted most."

"I do not follow."

"He is experiencing what Serenity has felt for Gabriel, at its most pure, as well as the soul mate bond with the Hudson boy. I have not been made aware of what happened during her time with Lucifer, but considering the brand he put on her heart and what needs to take place for that to happen at all, I am sure he is experiencing their moments together as well. Anyone that has impacted her heart in some way, he will be deeply haunted by. It will appear like a movie on a constant loop."

"What is the off switch?"

"There isn't one, which is why I said you need to use your power on him. Incapacitate him to the point where we can begin to heal the damage. You are going to need to step into his mind as well. It is the only way to untangle the mess that has been left there."

"I cannot enter without his permission, you know this."

"When he has begun to heal, appeal to the part of him that adores Serenity. You may have to lie, but do whatever it takes to appeal to that part of him so that you can get him to allow you entrance. It is the only way that all of this can be rectified."

"What if it doesn't work?"

I did not want to think that way, but I need to know what I would have to deal with should what Raphael suggests not work. I want to know everything there is to know, so that I can prepare Serenity in case I am unable to bring him back to her. She said she would love him regardless of what he held deep inside, but the way he is acting now, I am unsure she will even be able to witness, let alone accept.

After everything the two of them have been through the last thing I want to happen is for them to be torn apart forever. I do not want to be the one that has to explain to her that the man she loves is gone, that he is lost inside of himself because of the brand that Lucifer put on her heart. Nor did I want to be the one that finally put Ryan, or at least the very real human parts of him, out of his misery.

"I believe you already know what happens if nothing that we try works. It is something that we cannot afford to think about."

If this did not work, Ryan would be lost to us forever.

Chapter Twenty-Seven

Lucifer

This is a risk for any being, demon or celestial in nature when they take a human vessel. There is always the chance that when finished with them, they will go through changes that are not at all pleasant and will in certain circumstances end up in places such as this, completely broken down.

It is no surprise that this is where we find Serenity's father. Not only had I possessed him during the earlier parts of her childhood, but I had also visited him on more than one occasion. All in preparation for the plan I thought would make everything right again. I believed in it so strongly that I had done everything possible to make sure that it reached its end. It began with this man and standing before him now, I am experiencing things that I never thought I would.

I am ashamed of myself. In my own defense, at the time, I only knew that I wanted Serenity for the light and power that lived within her. I wanted to use her, harness it, eventually using all of it and her to take over the world and bring everything burning to the ground. I truly believed that it was the right thing to do and in the long run I wanted Father to feel it.

The older she became and the closer we got to what I believed to be the perfect ending, I had become manic in my pursuit of her, not only stalking her myself but having my most trusted companions doing it as well. It was then I brought Ryan into the fold and had him continue where I could not. He had been the perfect object to put in her path, just another casualty like her father before him.

Joining with this man, while the right thing to do, would not fix everything I had done to him. As Serenity said, it is a start to earning back what she believes I deserve to have, but I cannot help but wonder if what we both seem to believe is achievable, really is at all.

The first step for me would have to be not only earning this man's forgiveness, but also forgiving myself. As I stand here now and look back on every step I took in the wrong direction, all of the twists and turns and true darkness I embraced, I am not sure I can forgive myself or even accept his forgiveness if it is given. I do not believe I am deserving of it. Gabriel was wrong all along. I am too far gone to even reach the smallest form of redemption.

"Lucifer, you must not think in that way or every step we are taking in an effort to make things better will be for naught. You, despite your misgivings about it, are destined for this, just as Serenity is in getting you to this very place now."

"I know that you believe that Father, but I am having a hard time reconciling it. I did horrible things to the man and left him scarred in a way that I am unsure I can ever fix, despite what you believe."

"All wounds can be healed in time, Lucifer, even the ones that seem to last the longest."

"The fun is in the fixin'; at least that's what he used to tell me. So if you can't believe what your own father is telling you, believe in that."

I am still at a loss as to how this woman standing with me can be so forgiving. Father was right in how he described her; she is definitely pure of heart, mind and soul and unique to the rest of the occupants of Heaven. I am unsure as to how she can stand here, as strong as she is and not want to throttle me for not only what I did to the man she knows as her father, but for taking him away from her all of these years.

"We all screw up, that's how."

"You sound so sure."

"Of course I do. I'm not going to tell you that I think you're completely innocent and I understand why you did the things you did, because I don't, but I do know that everyone deserves a second chance. Even the devil."

"Let us waste no more time on this method of thinking. The man has waited far too long as it is to see you again, Serenity. We must focus on that and leave the rest of the stuff in the background where it belongs."

She has not made her way around us so she cannot yet see what we see, but the more I take in of the broken man before me, I see Serenity in him. If there are features she has that belong to her mother, I would be hard pressed to find them. All I can see as I look at him directly is his daughter looking back at me.

Not only do they share the same shading of hair, but I now see where Serenity gained the hazel of her eyes. The soul that you can see when you look at her the way I have so many times over the last year, I can also see in Gregory Richards. It is something that during my earlier visits to the man I had not paid the right amount of attention to, but now could not ignore.

There is no doubt of the biological makeup of the two of them. They are most definitely a part of each other. Two sides of a coin. A coin I melted down and ripped apart for the fun of it.

"I know you..."

At the sound of the man's voice, all other thought processes fade and I am forced to again face everything I've done.

"Yes Gregory, you do know me. We have spoken on more than one occasion."

There is so much more that I want to say to the man, but I know that something much more important needs to happen first. I need to right the wrongs I have done by giving him back the one thing I never should have taken away in the first place.

"I do believe I have someone here with me that you have been dying to see for quite some time."

It is then that Serenity moves out from behind me and Father, sliding her way through the bare crack of space that we left between us. His eyes go wide in surprise and speak to the fact that he had not seen this visit coming. There is softness in them and with that I know that even though I do not believe myself worthy of redemption, I have taken the first step in doing the right thing.

"Serenity—is it really you? Please tell me this is not an illusion..."

"It's me, Daddy. It's really me."

"Oh, my peaceful princess! I never thought I would see you again even though the angel gave me hope."

"The angel?"

"Michael. He visited with me, but I'm not exactly sure how long ago it was now. He told me about you and spoke of bringing us together again when the time was right."

"Well, that's why I'm here now. The time is right."

She is affected by this more than she wants to let on. Her tone of voice rises and falls and I can tell that even with as strong as she is attempting to be, she is very close to giving into the emotion of it all. It is exactly as I expected. She would not come out of this unscathed. This would affect her from this point on and if I had my way now I would make sure it was only in the most positive ways.

I also have a lot of fixing to do with her and I would spend the rest of my eternity, joined with this man or not, doing just that. I would see to it that she has nothing but happiness from this moment on.

"You're even more beautiful then I imagined."

"Thank—you." She stutters, a sound that in all of my confrontations with her, I do not recall her ever displaying. My earlier assessment of how affected she is by this meeting seems to be true. I am not sure how Father feels in this moment, but I am eager to help end the awkwardness by moving things along. There is a reason for us being here after all.

"There is a reason we are all here Gregory and a lot of that has to do with the choices I have made in the past. It is time I rectify that which I have done. In order to do that, we must have your acceptance moving forward."

"Lucifer…"

"Did you just call him Lucifer?" Gregory speaks up as realization dawns, which pains me. He is aware of who I am.

"Yeah, I did, but he's right Greg—Dad. There is a reason we're here and we can't do it without you."

"Does this have something to do with the visit from Michael?"

"It has everything to do with that. Lucifer, he did things to you when I was little and even though it took a really long time to make him see it, he wants to fix it. Dad, we want to get you out of here. I know it's about twenty years too late, but it's the best I can do."

"What did he do to me?"

"I possessed you and not in the kind way my brothers would have. It is the very reason you ended up in this place."

"The voices, the pain, the weird dreams, all of that was you? Is that what you're telling me?"

"Yes. I do not expect you to believe in me as I have given you no reason to, but I want to fix that which I have broken even though as Serenity says, it is twenty years too late. I cannot do that without your agreement and acceptance though."

"What is it ya'll want me to accept?"

I am about to tell the man exactly what it is that we need from him, but Serenity holds her hand up, moving even closer to her father. I understand immediately what it is she wants to do and nodding my head in acceptance, I move back to where Father stands in silence.

"The only way you can get out of here is if an angel possesses you. I'm sure a demon could do it too, but that isn't going to happen. Not anymore."

Her last statement is dripping with the anger I have been waiting for since the moment she found out the part I played in where her father ended up. I have known that she wasn't completely in agreement with this part of her destiny, but now I am getting to witness it firsthand.

"You want an angel to possess me to get me out of here?"

"Yeah Dad, that's exactly what I want. You've spent the last twenty years in this place and you don't deserve to be here. Mom did the same thing to me when I turned twelve. I know what places like this can do to a person and well I don't want it happening to you."

"You know the reason I'm here?"

"You hear voices. I know all about that as I'm sure Michael already told you. I can't let you stay here, not for the rest of your life, not when there isn't a damn thing wrong with you."

The way Gregory smiles at her leads me to believe that he is seeing a part of him inside of her and is proud of it. I have to admit that even as I watch her, the determination towards reaching the end goal she's displaying, I am also proud of her. She may have started out being quiet and complacent, but the time for that is over. This is the Serenity that was meant to change the world. There is no doubt about it.

"Well we're in agreement there darlin'. I don't want to spend another minute in this place either."

"There's more, Dad. Things you need to know—about me."

"I know everything that I need to. Michael was very forthcoming with the information, but if there's more that you think I don't know, then feel free to tell me anything you want."

"You know what I am?"

"Yes Serenity, I know what you are and what you're supposed to mean to the world. So you don't need to explain anything to me, other than telling me exactly what it is that I need to do in order to help you do it."

Serenity

The first thing I think about the minute I see my Dad is just how right my Mom was all of these years. She spent a great deal of time being upset with me for what she called 'turning out like my father' and there's no doubt about it looking at him now. We are similar in every way imaginable, from the way our foreheads crinkle when deep in thought, to the color of our hair and eyes, and even the shape of our lips. There is no doubt this man is my Dad.

I wasn't expecting him to know so much but I'm thankful for it. It means that I don't have to go into half as much detail about the turn my life had taken a year and a half ago the way I'd been prepared to. Michael had taken care of all of that for me and was definitely going to get a massive thank you when all of this is said and done. He spared me from having to drop the world's biggest bombshell.

"Lucifer is finally on the road to true redemption, but he has a lot of work ahead of him. That's where you come in. He's agreed to do what God wants of him, but it can't happen without you."

"He's the one that you want to possess me?"

"Yes. Not only can he get you out of here this way but he can start fixing what he broke years ago. I want you out of here Dad. I might have dealt with you being gone this long because of the lie Mom made me believe, but it doesn't mean that I have to continue on for the rest of my life believing it."

"What are you saying?"

"I'm saying I want you out of this place and back in my life where you belong. You should never have been taken from me. I want you to say yes to Lucifer so that we can fix this, fix everything."

"This is your destiny—saving me?"

"Saving you—redeeming Lucifer and bringing the world back to the way that God imagined it, yes."

"Then, I'll do it."

The weight that is lifted off my shoulders as he says the words I've been praying to hear, I can't even begin to describe. Even with as sure as I was that this would work out in the end, I still had the nagging doubt in the back of my mind that even though Lucifer agreed, my Dad wouldn't. If there's anyone on the planet that deserves to say no to this, it was him, but it wasn't the case. He wants to do this, even if it's only for me.

"There is something that I want to say before you do whatever needs to be done."

His eyes move from their locked position on me until they land squarely on the fallen angel beside me. It's obvious that whatever he's about to say, it's for Lucifer alone. Considering all of my own conflicting thoughts where he's concerned, I have no doubt that what my dad is about to say is something he is most definitely not going to like. It only made me that much more eager to hear it.

"I want you to be aware that me saying yes to this does not mean that I in any way forgive you for the position you put me in all of those years ago, nor will it earn you forgiveness for everything that you did to the ball of light that is my daughter. You may have been able to worm your back into her good graces, at least enough for this chance you're getting but it won't be that easy with me at all. It's going to take a lot more work."

As Lucifer opens his mouth to speak, he speaks again, cutting him off.

"Don't you think for one second of somehow pulling a stunt with this either. You won't get another shot at doing the right thing. Not with her, me or even your father who stands before me now."

How he knew just who God was is beyond me but I couldn't help but find it kind of cool that he did. It meant that we were even more alike then I previously thought. It extended past just the physical. I really am my father's daughter after all.

"Yes sir."

Lucifer has never been one to remain silent in any situation but now, with just those two words uttered, it appears as if he's more human than angel. He had just been put in his place by a girl's father, the same way it happened all over the world daily. It was actually kind of funny. Lucifer bending to anyone's will is just something I never thought I'd ever see.

"Good, now that I've said my piece, let's get this show on the road already."

Even though he seemed to be eager to get started, I'm not quite sure I am. There is still so much that he doesn't know and that I want to tell him first. He needs to know the other reason that I want him out of here so badly.

He needs to know about Ryan.

Michael

He has been contained, though with the way he appears now, I'm unsure of just how much of him is left. The light is within him of course, I can feel the pull of it as I look him over, but the human parts of him that made him who he really is, I'm not so sure about anymore.

It hadn't been easy gaining control of him, but take control we did and within minutes and a lot of power later, he is now safely situated where he could do no harm to himself or others and bound so that he could not get away from what needed to happen next.

I do not enjoy taking vessels. I much prefer doing things in my true form and just as in any other time that I had to take one, this one would not be enjoyable for me either. Of course this one was different in comparison with other times because I was only going to join to him in an effort to fix the broken parts of his mind but it is still most unpleasant.

"I think I know why Lucifer wanted him so badly. That is one strong son of a bitch."

"Just be thankful that he is on our side brother and that Lucifer has finally seen the light."

Raphael knew without any further explanation the true meaning of what I am saying. There is no doubt in my mind just witnessing the strength he displayed in his most damaged moments that Ryan could have very well been the end of Heaven and everything that I hold dear if he had followed through with the path that Lucifer had set him on originally. If we had never found out what he really is, then we might be looking at a completely different ending right now.

I do not want to focus on it but it is hard not to. Serenity had been the reason for Ryan's change of heart at the last second and for the way everything is playing out now. She is living up to what is expected of her, exactly what Father set forth when he set up the undertaking. Not only is she bringing about the first bit of peace to the world since Lucifer had been cast out, but she was also fulfilling her other obligation without even realizing it. She truly is Ryan's answered prayer and is the one person in all of creation that would keep this man level and on the right path.

The path that he is destined for. The one that would lead him back home when his time on Earth is done.

I believe that even though Father says all of this is meant to happen in this way, it was actually supposed to turn out differently. That all of the ways we had failed in Heaven actually had worked out in our favor to make this come to pass now. It is common knowledge that both Ryan and Serenity had both sent up different prayers for the same thing at multiple times during their childhood and that we had placed them on each other's path without knowing all of the details. I do not doubt that Father knew what he was doing in that regard, but I do not think he knew it all.

I believe the pull between them, that up until the point Gabriel gave his light to Ryan, made them so inherently wrong for each other is actually a very clear message of what was to come. We hadn't paid enough attention to it when it happened and because of that we had lost one of Heaven's most beloved warriors in the process. Gabriel in some way had known what we did not and in sacrificing himself had gotten us here now. Ryan and Serenity are very much bound together and not because of the beloved bond they share between them. They are bound together because neither one can survive without the other. Just as she saved Ryan and forced us to see what really resides inside of him, he also saved her, bringing her to the very point she stands at now, about to change the world.

With as all knowing as Father is, I do believe he could not have known all of this. I think that these two imperfect humans took the script they were given and changed it in order to make everything that happens in the end, uniquely theirs. This is not Father's undertaking at work anymore, it's theirs.

It has always been theirs.

"Are you ready to do this, Michael?"

"One is never ready for something such as this. I did not enjoy doing it when I had to with Serenity and I enjoy it even less now, but it must be done. I am as ready as I will ever be. I just hope that I am able to fix this."

"Michael, even if you cannot, you must not blame yourself. She will handle whatever the outcome is. It is just her way."

I agree with Raphael's words but it doesn't mean I want to accept them. Yes, Serenity is strong and with what she held inside of her alone, she would rise above whatever happened next, I have no doubt about that. She just wouldn't be the same after it, no matter how strong we all know her to be. Ryan isn't just her beloved or the keeper of her heart and soul, he is the very air she needs to breathe and without it, she would only be half the person she was meant to be.

"She asked me to bring him back to her and even if I have to go to my own death making it happen, Raphael, I will do just that."

"Let's pray that it does not come to that brother."

It is time to wake him up now. If I want to proceed in joining with him in an effort to fix that which Lucifer broke, I must garner his acceptance but before I can make my way to him to begin, I hear the voice of my Father, loud and clear around me, bringing with it, a level of peace that I have never experienced.

With his words, I realize that it has happened. That which I had been so close to giving up on has finally been achieved, despite every event leading up to it, taking such a toll that it appeared as though it would never happen.

"It is done."

Serenity has done it. She has reached her true destiny. Lucifer has begun the road to true redemption and with it has brought something the likes of which the world and even those of us remaining in Heaven has never seen.

True peace for everyone.

Chapter Twenty-Eight

Serenity

There are some things you see that no matter how much you try, you are never entirely able to un-see.

Then there are the moments in time where you see something so beyond amazing that you never want to forget the sight of it. You want it to stay with you forever because it's probably something that's as close to perfect as it gets. The day you get married to the person you love, the birth of your child, things of that nature.

No one but the people around me now is ever going to experience what I just did and for that I feel horrible. I want the world and the people in it to be able to see what just happened here because I swear, they would be forever changed, just the way I am. The light that appears in my dad's eyes the minute Lucifer joins with him and then the glow that seems to just radiate off of them afterward is just so heavy that there are no words to even describe it.

It is true beauty.

There's more. Not only do I get to witness what happens when an angel joins with a human, finally getting to see exactly what it must have been like for Graham during his time with Gabriel, but I also get to experience the changes in me. At first I don't even realize that anything has changed, but the minute I turn away from the brightness of the light and look directly into God's eyes, or at least the vessels eyes, noticing how they dance with happiness, matching the smile that is now so large it seems to encompass his entire face, I know something is different.

He isn't looking at Lucifer or my dad this way; it's directed at me.

"Serenity…"

If the look in his eyes and the expression on his face hadn't been enough for me to tell that things have most definitely changed, the whispered way he says my name is a dead giveaway. There is such reverence in the way he says my name now unlike times before that I crave a reason for it.

"Do you feel it?"

I feel a lot of different things in the moment, but I'm pretty sure none of them are what he means. It only makes the questions I have as to why he is looking at me in the way he is that much more prominent in my mind.

"Serenity, my magnificent ball of light, in following through with the task that I have set out before you, not only have you managed to create a peace unlike any that has been experienced before, but you have also earned your place in Heaven."

Now I'm confused. I thought I already had a place in Heaven. I'm the ball of light after all, he just said as much. So what in the world does he mean by earning my place?

"You have not yet connected with the part of yourself that is inherently made of light, my dear girl. Once you do that you will see what I am witnessing right now."

"How do I do that?" I ask, genuinely wanting to know what I need to do so that I can understand his expression.

"Close your eyes and do as Gabriel has taught you before. Focus on the power inside of you, tap into the light and then let it become one with you."

I do as he says; following the exact way Gabriel explained it to me and when nothing happens right away, I begin to wonder if maybe I'm faulty in some way. That whatever he's talking about is visible to everyone, but me because I'm not strong enough to be able to see it.

"As pure and white as the driven snow, you have now been marked by Heaven. Serenity, surely you can feel the changes."

I don't feel anything. I mean I feel healthy and strong, but I'd been expecting that the minute Lucifer and my dad joined together. If there's something else I'm supposed to feel, it's just not happening.

"You are experiencing all that you are meant to, so now it appears as though I need to show you."

He moved toward me, his expression remaining locked in the brightest smile and before I know it, he is creating in front of my very eyes, a real way for me to see what he sees. I am standing before what appears to be a mirror, in that I can see my reflection, but it's only as I turn around that I finally see what it is he has been trying to tell me all along.

Where there had been nothing but the shirt on my back, there is now the lightest set of white wings and as I move my arms, they seem to move with me effortlessly. If I wasn't completely sure I was awake in the moment, I would have thought I stepped into the world's most beautiful dream. Nothing could ever be this perfect and be real.

"Does this mean it's time for me to go home?" I ask my voice unsteady, assuming that now that I had reached what he had always said was to be my true calling, I'm no longer needed on the planet.

"You have a very long life ahead of you Serenity, but in doing that which you have done here today; you have gained access to Heaven and all that is contained within it. You are no longer just the ball of light I created in an effort to make things right. You are an angel of the purest form, much like your beloved before you."

I'm an angel.

I let the words run over in my mind, attempting to come to terms with the reality of them and failing. Again, all of this just feels like a dream, something that can't happen in the cold light of day. This is not something that happens to normal people; it's not something that happens at all.

"You are right, it does not happen to normal people, but you have never been normal. You have always been you. It is because of who and what you are that you have been given this gift now. Embrace the changes within you Serenity for they will be with you for the remainder of your existence, both here and in Heaven."

"I want to, but I don't think I can."

"There is a part of you missing that is preventing you from achieving the true bliss that comes in situations such as this, am I right?"

"Yeah, that's it exactly. It doesn't feel right because he's not here and as much as I want to achieve true bliss like you say, I can't do it, not without him."

"Then I do believe it is time we make our way back home, so that you can finally allow yourself to experience all that I am. He is there and if what Michael has told me is correct, he is in need of you almost as much as you are him."

Ryan is in Heaven. My heart is finally able to calm with the peace those words bring. When Michael had spoken of removing him from Hell, I couldn't be sure where he would have taken him. I am calmed with the knowledge that he had taken him home because there was nothing that couldn't be fixed there.

"Is he alright?"e

"I do believe the answer to that question needs to be answered when we get there. Serenity, though there is nothing now that can ruin the true beauty of this moment, not only because of what you have done in bringing Lucifer back to me, but also for the gift I have received in witnessing you become one with the light, I feel I need to warn you. You must prepare yourself going home again because what you see when you get there may not be the perfect picture you imagine it to be."

"What do you mean? What's going on with Ryan?"

"Nothing that cannot be fixed in time, but he needs you Serenity, now more than ever."

Michael

I have done all that I can do. I have exhausted every available option to me and now it is up to the man before me to choose what happens next.

Much the way Raphael had predicted, tapping into his love for Serenity had been the opening I needed in order for him to agree to be possessed by me. He was defeated, his body even after being healed by my brother, still very much feeling the effects of the trial he had been through. The mention of Serenity had brought about a light I hadn't been privy to in our time here and after some time spent reminding him of their times alone together, he gave me the access I needed in order to do what came next.

I untangled not only the mess inside of his brain, but the burden that it placed on his heart though to what degree I had been able to fix it, I cannot know until he awakens. It had been hard for me seeing the visions that had been torturing his pure soul and it had taken every bit of strength and power in me to rid him of them.

He is indeed being driven into the pits of despair by a constant stream of about twenty different memories, surrounding not only Graham and Gabriel, but Lucifer as well. I believe it to be the visions of my fallen brother that caused the darkness shift within him. In some way he had attached himself to the way Lucifer had been during those experiences and become like the man himself. It is only my hope that in removing the memories from him all together the way that I have, he will heal back to the way he is meant to be.

Serenity is the only missing piece now. He is resting comfortably for the first time since I brought him here and it is my hope that in seeing her again, he will come out of this relatively unscathed. When I had taken him under and become one with him, I had seen the things that he wants most and they all revolve around her, even after everything that he had been privy to during the attack of the bond.

It is through her now that all of his dreams and hopes will become reality. She again will be the very thing that breaks or saves him and knowing the ball of light the way that I do, she will not settle for being the thing that causes him to break once more. She will do everything in her power to save him, which is exactly what I want her to do.

The light rains down around me and I am struck by just how different everything is. It is not only Father's light that greets me, but that of Serenity and for the first time, I am able to see her for what she truly is to me.

My sister.

No sooner does the newest edition to Heaven's celestial army touchdown then she immediately makes her way over to me, her eyes saying much more than any words she might have wanted to utter. Father had told her about Ryan's current state and in true form she is here now to be with him again.

"Michael, you need to tell me—is he gone?"

There were a million different words I expected to come, but in every scenario I imagined before she had shown up, those words had not been a part of them. I am not sure if it has something to do with her concern for him blinding her to what she should already know or if she's asking because she is in some way testing me, but whatever the reason, this is one question I do not even want to think about, much less answer.

"No he is not gone, but there was a moment or two during the entire process that I was concerned that it would be his fate. I have never seen anything like it and I was of the understanding that I had seen all there was to see."

"You said that he reacted to what happened, but how exactly?"

"Every person that has ever touched your heart, in any capacity, whether by bond or otherwise, he has envisioned it and worse, experienced it firsthand."

The Serenity of old would have broken in that moment and there is a small part of me that still even now awaits it, but when it doesn't come I realize that she has indeed changed. What would have broken her apart before seems to only strengthen her now. The unsure girl of old is gone and in her place is the tough as nails warrior before me.

"Take me to him, Michael. I think we've been apart long enough."

I want nothing more than to bring her to him, but first she needs to be made aware of everything that we have been through in the time they have spent apart. If she is indeed what will bring him back to us then she has to go in knowing everything. It will only secure what Raphael and I have done in her absence.

"You need to experience what he did during our time in Hell before I can take you to him, Serenity. We believe you to be the only thing that can bring him back to us now and that means going in knowing everything."

"Then hit me with your best shot, Michael."

I have always been able to connect to her easily, but now, with all the changes as I take her hands in mine, our minds connect immediately. I can only liken it to the way Gabriel was able to reach her in the intensity of it, but without the bond they share. Where it had actually taken much focus in times past to reach into the recesses of her mind that no one else was privy to, we were easily together as one now.

I brought all of the images of what Ryan experienced and pushed them into her mind and within seconds I hear the sharp intake of breath as the gravity of the situation we faced came at her. Every single incident that he witnessed between both of my brothers and the soul mate all flooding into her subconscious one after the other until even she could take no more and turns her head away from me.

"He saw it all?"

"Yes and in some instances it appears as though he actually experienced it from both your perspective and that of your various suitors. Add that to the jealousy he already felt over the bond you share with Graham and what happened with Lucifer and it is no surprise that it turned him inside out. He somehow

246

connected to the darkest parts of Lucifer and it awakened the darkness in him."

"Were you able to take it away?"

"Only time will tell, which is why Father felt it necessary to bring you here now. There is no one that can reach Ryan in the way that we need, but you."

"I saw his chest before we left you alone with him; he did something to himself didn't he?"

"Yes, Serenity. He tried to rip the heart from his chest in an effort to make it stop."

For all of the changes I have seen in her, it's obvious that the human parts of her still remain as she drops her head to the floor. I can only imagine the upset that she is experiencing, but I could not back down from my position. She had to know everything before going to see him.

"You healed it."

"That did not last as long as I would have liked, I'm afraid. He did far more damage to it again when I brought him here. The darkness in him fighting to get free given where we were, only made him more determined. It stopped being about making it stop and instead about the way the blood falling made him feel."

"He craved his own blood?"

"In a way I have never witnessed before."

"Okay, well I'm here now and I'm not leaving. So if that's all you've got to tell me, I think it's time you take me to him."

"Serenity, you need to prepare yourself, he may not wake up the same Ryan you know and love so deeply, beloved bond or not."

She needs to see what I am trying to tell her. I know that Father already prepared her, but now that she is here and we are about to go to him, she needs to be stronger then she's ever been and prepared for whatever Ryan wakes up when she does what is needed in order to bring him back.

I only hope that everything I did to fix him didn't do more harm than good. I am not sure I want to live in a world where

Serenity loses Ryan, especially after everything she has already done to set everything right and what and who she has lost along the way in her efforts to achieve it.

The world wouldn't be worth living in if these two beings of the light are indeed torn apart by the darkness. It would be like losing Gabriel all over again and that is something I am not willing to face, ever again.

Chapter Twenty-Nine

Ryan

When you're a child, there are things you do that to most adults seem so illogical, yet to you make all the sense in the world. You make your parents invest in nightlights, check your closets for things that go bump in the night, sometimes even taking it so far as to hide under your covers or even spend the night in their room because being in your own is unthinkable. There's a reason for every single one of those actions and it has never been as obvious to me as it is now.

You do all of that because the darkness is terrifying.

Twenty one years, I walked in that darkness. I was the creature that you worried was hiding in your closet, just waiting for the chance to jump out at you. I was the shadow on your wall that the light was supposed to banish. I am the very thing that you hid under the covers to escape and I enjoyed every second of it. In fact, I lived for it.

From being the hunter to becoming the prey has been an extremely hard transition for me to make. The very darkness I embraced so easily, making it my own now scares the living hell out of me. I want nothing more than to run from it, escape its pull before it drags me back down and I become the very thing I've spent the last year and a half breaking away from.

I'm not sure how it's even possible, but sometime between going into Hell and waking up now in Heaven, I have again felt the darkness rise up into my very soul and despite my every attempt at fighting it off, I fall victim to it. I feel every second of the pain I not only inflicted on myself, but on the angels that were only trying to stop me from doing more damage.

Whatever they did to me seems to have made it disappear, but not before leaving scars in its wake and I don't mean the physical kind. It's the ones that are long lasting and that I can't ever be sure will entirely heal. I want to ask what they did just so I know exactly what caused the darkness to rise and even more than that, so I can figure out how it was possible to begin with.

Not only am I an angel, but I am one of the purest in existence. This I know as fact even though I have yet to accept and embrace it. Gabriel had seen to it that in his passing I would be rid of the evil inside of me once and for all, yet that isn't what happened at all. I need to know why.

She's here with me. I can feel her even though just in the air that surrounds me, I can tell she is nowhere close to me. Her scent, the sweet mixture of vanilla and strawberry, wafts its way across the room until it's the only thing I'm able to inhale as I continue to breathe in and out robotically. Her voice as she speaks to someone I can't place is the only sound my ears want to make out. It is like the sweetest music and it's all for me. I want to open my eyes and take her in again as it feels like it's been far too long, but I'm not quite ready yet.

There still seems to be something holding me back, despite the desperate need I have to wake up and go to her, attaching myself to her and never letting go again. Whatever is keeping me from making this a reality really needs to make itself known or screw off once and for all because I'm just not in the mood for it.

I wonder if she had the brand removed, what with me falling victim to the pain and darkness before being able to witness it happen.

Just what had happened to me down there that brings me here now? What had been done to me to bring the darkness back into the light and twist me into pieces from the inside out? Is it still there under the surface just threatening to drag me under or did the angels finally do as they had intended from the moment I arrived here and finally rid the world and me of its power to control?

"It doesn't matter how many times I see you this way, it never changes."

She's close now. So close that I'm almost positive I can reach out and touch her, if only my body would cooperate and give me what I so desperately want.

When she speaks again, she sounds muffled, distant even and I wonder who she's speaking to that causes her to turn away. It's only when the other voice seems to move closer that I realize who it is and the need to wake springs to life uncontrollably inside of me.

"You know what you must do now. Michael has done everything in his power to put Ryan back to normal. I know that it looks bad Serenity, but you must realize that he is at peace now, only sleeping."

"You really expect me to believe that touching him, placing my hand on his and even placing my lips to him, will wake him up?"

"I do not expect you to believe anything. I know how you operate; you are not much different then Gabriel and even Lucifer in that regard. You will always doubt until you see it take form right before your eyes. You know what I have told you, it is now up to you whether or not you do it."

"You make it sound like some sort of fairy-tale. Maybe that's why I have such a hard time believing it. I mean can it really be that poetic?"

"Ryan is your beloved now, just as Gabriel was before him. It is a poetic bond on its own, so why is it so shocking to you that the way in which you wake him up is very much the same? Fairy-tales are fables, of that you are correct, but even the most beautiful fables are based in truth, which is the case here."

"Don't you think it will be too much for him, waking up and finding out everything that's happened?"

I want to answer this question for her because I'm the only one capable of it. They may believe me to be resting, but since

251

I've become more aware, I've learned quite a bit about what's been going on in my absence. I know what happened with Lucifer and the chance that not only Serenity is giving him, but also God as well. I know that what Serenity wanted to tell me in Hell has now taken form and everything has finally reached the most peaceful of endings. I even know that she's been changed by it.

If she would just do as God is telling her, I would get my chance to tell her that no amount of information, especially when it's this kind, can damage me. As the frustration I feel at not being able to communicate with her rises, I feel the press of her lips on mine and almost as if by some kind of magic, I feel the haze begin to lift around me.

What I hadn't been able to do before, I can do now as I slowly open my eyes and take in the sheer brightness of the light that surrounds me. It's almost too much to handle so I begin to shut them, this time awake and aware, but needing the time to become used to it.

"Ry—can you hear me?" she whispers as she moves back from her position over me, her eyes so deeply trained on my body, I don't need to see it to know that she's searching me for some form of awareness.

"No, I think you need to do that one thing again."

"Holy shit!" she shrieks and before I can react, I feel her arms around me and her lips on mine. With just a few short words, the world seems to have spun on its axis and everything I had been experiencing fades away, leaving only the way she makes me feel behind. The emptiness I felt in my chest minutes before is changing and now it feels warm and most of all, full again.

The end result of what I like to call the Serenity Effect.

"Pretty—girl, easy..." I manage to choke out through the tight hold she still has around my neck. "I can't really breathe."

When I said the words, I didn't intend for her to move away, but that's exactly what she did and as I open my eyes again, allowing myself the chance to take every inch of her face in, I see the frightened look in her eye. A look I swore I never wanted to see again.

"Ser, what are you doing?" I ask, hearing the weakness in my voice and wanting to slap myself for it. "You don't need to stop what you were doing."

"But you couldn't breathe…"

"I would rather lose my breath, then lose the way it feels when you're pressed to me that close. Get back over here—now."

It's not lost on me that I sound like a petulant child, but I don't care. All I know is that I need her pressed up against me, connected to me and I need it now.

As I feel her body wrap around mine, I allow my now racing heart to calm. Even though my mind is still flooded with questions, I would not let it affect my time with her. It had done that once before and I'll be damned if I let it ruin the moment again. I can get all the answers I need later; right now all I need is her.

"Ry, I can tell you what you need to know."

"No. Not right now. I don't know how long I've been out, or what the hell actually happened, but whatever it is, it can wait. All I want right now is you, just the way you are."

What sounds like a clearing throat comes through loud and clear, again ruining the moment and I have no doubt just who the offender is. There is only one angel besides Gabriel who had the worse timing in history.

Michael.

"You're kidding me right?"

The vibration of Serenity's laugh against my chest distracts me, but only for a second as the angel chooses the moment I experience it, complete with the wave of heat it slams into my chest, to speak again.

"I know that you do not want to ruin the moment you are in Ryan, but I do believe there are some things that she needs to tell you. Dealing with them now will help speed up the healing process and will also help us determine whether or not what we did to you worked the way we intended."

"Five minutes, Mike. That's all I wanted. Five fucking minutes with the love of my life and as usual, you can't give it to me. If I didn't know any better, I would swear you were my irritating younger brother or something."

The room falls silent with my words and I can't help but smile with the enjoyment I get from it. Seems to me they were expecting a whole different Ryan to be waking up right now. It's nice to shock them for a change instead of the other way around.

"Ryan," Michael speaks again, his tone much more subdued. "I rather enjoy being your younger brother. Annoying you is pleasurable."

"Thanks, asshole." Angels getting the art of the joke, I think I've seen it all now.

"Finally!" Serenity declares and I laugh. Looks like I'm not the only one noticing what just happened with the clueless angel. "It's about damn time."

"I thought you would both enjoy that. I've been holding on to it for awhile now."

"Sure you have, man. Glad you waited until I was awake to do it. I would have hated to miss it."

"Back to the business at hand. As much as I am sure the both of you want to enjoy each other's company, I do feel that you need to be made aware of everything that has happened during your time healing."

"If this is about Lucifer, I already know. I wasn't out for all of it, Mike. I also know that Serenity apparently has a new accessory too, but there is something I don't know and it's really bothering me."

I watch as both of them turn to me, their expressions serious and it takes everything in me not to break.

"What concerns you Ryan? Does it pertain to what happened to you?"

"No, well I mean that is another thing I think I need to find out, but that's not what's bothering me right now."

"Well, we will both tell you anything that you need to know."

"Serenity's new accessory. Is it only visible here or can I play with it when we go home?"

The second the question is out, I break and laugh and not two seconds later, Serenity follows it up with one of her own, again the sound of it making my heart almost flip over inside my chest. That sound will never get old, no matter what we end up going through.

"Don't answer that, Michael. He's being a pervert." Serenity manages to get out in between her fits of laughter. "I'm not the only one with a new accessory though."

I watch as she slides up my sleeve to where the tattoo bearing her name stands out, loud and clear. Something I had done when she was missing and just like every experience with her, one that I would never regret. She would be a part of me, inside and out, forever.

"She's right, don't answer that. I just wanted to keep up the joking you started."

Michael looks between the both of us, as if trying in some small way to figure out the exact moment the both of us lost our minds, which only makes me want to laugh more. He might have been able to joke with us, but he's still very much the stiff angel he's always been. It's actually something I hope he never changes. I don't think I'd know what to do with a more laidback archangel.

"So what happened to me?"

"Ry, when Lucifer stripped me of the brand, it affected you."

"That's where the darkness came from?"

She nods, but her face, that had been lit up and alive seconds before is now serious and sad. Whatever I had been through, it's obvious it hadn't been anything good. Though honestly, when is any interaction with the dark good?

"Is it gone? Or is this going to be something that keeps coming up?"

"We think it is gone. Without that kind of instance happening again it should not make another appearance." Michael answers easily.

Well that's good news. In fact it's the best news. I still might not know everything about what happened, but right now, I don't need to. As long as I know that it won't be coming back anytime soon, I can handle not knowing the rest.

"You need to be made aware that I had to possess you and tap into your emotional attachment to Serenity to do it. It was the only way that I could fix the damage that was done. I know that you didn't exactly give me your permission in the proper way, but I am hoping that you can forgive me for the steps I took."

"If you didn't do it, what would have happened?"

"You would have taken your own life."

"Then you don't need to be saying sorry and asking for forgiveness, Mike. I need to be the one doing something. I need to be thanking you."

"You do not need to do anything of the sort. It is what family does."

The gravity of his statement hit me, but not because it was something I couldn't believe in. It affected me because of the truth in it. It is what family does for each other and for the first time in twenty-three years, it felt pretty damn great to be able to say I had one.

"Is there anything else I need to know?"

Both of them shake their head and I breathe a sigh of relief. I'd been hoping that would be the response. I know that I can handle anything they want to throw at me, but right now I just want a break from the seriousness of it all. I'm here and for the most part I feel okay, which is in no small part thanks to Michael and Raphael, so that's the only thing that matters.

Well that and the fact that I have an extremely sexy angel wrapped up in me, her scent intoxicating as ever and even now, making it extremely hard for me to think straight.

Yes I definitely know what's most important right now and in order to make sure I get what I want, the angel had to take a hike and fast.

"I do believe for the first time, I am in complete agreement with you, brother. We have been through the worst of it and we have come out on top. The light has again triumphed over the darkness and there are no two beings alive that are more deserving of the time alone to enjoy it then the both of you. So with that, I will take my leave."

As Michael vanishes right in front of our eyes, there is only one thought left and it's one that encompasses everything we've been through right from the start.

Finally.

Chapter Thirty

Ryan

If I'm dreaming right now, for the love of all things holy, do not wake me up.

I've been standing here for maybe fifteen minutes and the entire time I haven't been able to control my breathing. There were a few seconds where I thought my heart actually stopped beating, but just as quickly as it came, it passed. At least it did until about thirty seconds ago.

The second Serenity appeared in the entryway, dressed completely in white, wearing a smile as bright as the sun on a summer afternoon, it happened again. It's like my heart dropped straight down into my stomach. I'm pretty sure she's the one lighting the place and I don't mean the lights hanging above us. That's the kind of impact she has just by standing in the entryway.

I've been dreaming of this moment for well over a year and now it's actually happening. She's making her way up the aisle toward me, preparing again to stand here and claim me as hers.

God, she is the most beautiful woman I've ever seen.

She's not alone. When we talked about this day months ago, we assumed that she would be talking this walk alone. She wanted one specific person to walk with her and with what ended up happening, it wasn't possible. Gabriel. He's the reason we're standing here today. He's the reason we're even standing at all. That was her choice and with him gone, there would never be a suitable replacement.

At least until there was.

I've had the last week to come to terms with this, with all the changes that have happened since Gabriel passed and no matter how much I appear to be alright with it, I'm still shocked at just how different it is.

Serenity is not alone walking the aisle because she's got two men with her. One, I know more than I care to admit, the other I'm just beginning to know, but both significant in Serenity's life in ways that are hard to explain.

I've pictured this wedding, this very moment, in my head so many times since standing in Stephenville and asking her to marry me again and never once did I imagine Lucifer being the one to have his arms linked through hers, bringing her to me. Yet this is exactly what's happening and not only that, but Serenity's own father, Gregory, is experiencing it too. It's something I'm sure he never expected either.

The day she brought me to meet him is still etched clearly in my brain. I wasn't sure going in what to expect from the man considering he hadn't been in her life for the majority of it, but I came to learn quickly that he still took his role as father dead seriously.

*****

"So you're the boy my daughter almost died for." He says. He already knows who I am so here's where he tries to make me feel uncomfortable by bringing up history. Too bad he doesn't know me as well as I seem to know him.

"Yeah, I'm also the one that killed her, you forgot that part."

"Oh my god! Ryan stop, you're gonna freak him out!" She cries yet her face betrays her because she's smiling at me.

"He's walking around with the Devil inside him and you think me saying that is gonna freak him out? Come on, pretty girl, even you gotta see that's crazy."

"True! But still, I mean can we not start off with all that stuff, it's not exactly dinner conversation."

"I'm starting to think with the lot our family got in life, this is appropriate dinner conversation." Gregory interjects and I

259

can't help but laugh. I may not know the man, but I can already tell, Lucifer inside of him or not, I like him.

He reminds me of Serenity.

"So Ryan, I have to ask you something and then I believe I need to tell you something."

Despite the abilities I have, I don't want to read him in order to see what's coming for me. It would make things easier because I could anticipate what he wants to hear and give him the right answer, but I've never liked anything that came too easy, this included. So I just nod my head to let him know I'm ready and I wait.

"Despite already being married, which I'm ignoring because of the reason behind it, why do you, at almost twenty-three years old, want to marry her again? Wouldn't you rather wait until after college when things are more secure?"

Great—the speech. I don't have any experience with this, but I do have a lot of people watching to look back on for knowledge in what to say next. Then the TV shows. Thank god for the TV shows.

"I love Serenity. It's that simple."

"Love is never simple, son."

I know it's just a word, but it bothers me. The last person to call me son was Lucifer and somewhere deep inside Gregory, he's there and it makes me wonder if he's guiding the conversation. I definitely need to get used to him being with us when everything in me wants him dead.

"Where your daughter is concerned, it is easy. I mean no disrespect, I know how you feel, but for me, this is something I have to do. More than that, it's something we want to do. When you realize the person you're with is who you want there forever, well ages and times don't mean shit. You just follow your heart."

"And if in the future you do something to screw it up?"

Here's the thing he doesn't get. I will screw this up, it's in my DNA to do it. My mom hated me on sight and saw me as a reminder of what she lost and Dad was Lucifer's most loyal follower for crying out loud; I had screw up written all over me, but I wouldn't let that stop this or end us. I have a wise mans words to guide me through the rough patches after all.

"The fun is in the fixin' sir."

I can tell by the look on his face that he wasn't expecting that answer, but it was just too bad because it's the only one I have and I had his daughter to thank for having it at all.

"Good answer, but here's where we get to the statement part." He says almost as if he's preparing me. "If you ever hurt her in a way that you can't fix, you'll be dealing with me. The damn Devil wants me to add him to this warning, but quite frankly, if you hurt my little girl, I'll make the things he did look adorable in comparison. You hear me boy?"

I have no doubt that he could put Lucifer to shame if something happened to Serenity. They may have been separated for almost her entire life, but love and the urge to protect, it never goes away. I'm living proof of that.

"I hear you loud and clear sir."

*****

Serenity's face during the entire speech her father gave and my responses was cute. She was so afraid things were going to blow up that I swear, she was literally on the edge of her seat the entire time. She might be an angel now, but some things never change and her unease in me meeting her father for the first time was something I never wanted to change because it was a reminder we're still human.

So here he is, twenty years later, walking his daughter down the aisle, giving Lucifer just enough control so he can be here to witness it. Even on the happiest day of my life things are creepy as fuck.

It hasn't been an easy road getting to this point. There were moments where I lost hope that it would ever happen at all. I didn't believe myself worthy of ever possessing someone as pure as Serenity, at least in the way that she does owning

261

me so completely. Even now as I stand here, I find myself questioning just when she's going to wake up and realize that she's gotten in way over her head and take off running.

Judging by the look she's giving as she makes her way closer, that moment won't happen and she's letting me know it without saying a word. The bond we share working as it always has, making the need for actual words non-existent.

As much as I don't want to taint this day with memories, I can't help but notice how different everything is this time. There is no black dress hugging her curves, no shoes that make her look like a streetwalker. The dark makeup is gone right along with the tear stained cheeks. This time there's no threat of death looming over us. It's all just peace and light.

There is only one word that comes to mind as I watch her walking toward me. Angel. She may have started out as Heaven's ball of light, but to me she would always be what she is now. What she has always been to me since the moment I laid eyes on her that first day. My angel. The one being in all of creation that saved me from a life that would have eventually killed me. The angel that brought me into the light where she knows I belong, even when no one else believed in her.

Her dress flows around her, the complete opposite of the black one of our previous ceremony and her hair, complete with the wave I've come to love almost as much as the woman herself, flows wild and loose around her shoulders, completed with a thin veil that rests comfortably on top of her head, shielding me just slightly from capturing the full beauty of her face.

Beautiful isn't even a strong enough word for the way she looks right now. It's made even more powerful with the realization of exactly what her walking toward me this way means.

She is mine—forever.

Nothing is going to keep us apart this time. There is no being, human or otherwise that has it out for us and will tear us apart at the last second. Everything is finally going to turn out the way it's always been meant to. I would capture this angel's heart every single day, just like the first and I would never let her go again.

That hasn't always been the case. Getting to this point last week, had been a dream, but one I almost had to let go of. It hadn't turned out the way it seemed like it would, but it didn't mean letting go hadn't been on the table. Between her fight to do the right thing by the Devil himself, and my short return to the dark side, this moment right here seemed lost forever.

A lot can change in a week though. We survived our trials yet again, coming out of them stronger than ever and now looking ahead, I've got my feet planted firmly on the ground and am looking nowhere but ahead to where everything ends perfectly.

The moment the girl of my dreams becomes Serenity McGregor again.

This time for keeps.

Serenity

He looks so nervous. I want to move faster down the aisle just so he knows for sure that there's no going back this time.

It hasn't exactly been an easy road for us. Even after facing death, Hell, memory loss and a soul mate bond, there's still been more thrown in our path that almost prevented us from reaching this point. It seems that even when you follow through with what you're destined to do, it doesn't solve every problem and over the last couple of weeks I've had that thrown at me more than once.

I love Ryan McGregor more than my soul, heart and mind can even express. There has never been a moment in the last year where that has been in doubt. Even at my darkest point, during my time in hell, it never went away. It was there on the surface always making its presence known and I will forever be thankful for it. I never want to forget the way I feel about him, especially since I clearly remember the point where I actually did forget him, at least as far as my mind went.

My heart will always belong to him and in about ten minutes, he's going to know it even more than he already does. I'm going to live every girl's fantasy and pledge my life to the man standing a few steps in front of me, but more than that, I'm going to pledge my heart and soul to him, the way it's supposed to be. The way it's always been.

The first time we did this, as much as I enjoyed watching him as I made my way in his direction, was also riddled with fear. This time it's completely different. He might be in front of me, in a tuxedo that mirrors the one from a year ago, but that's where the similarities end. His hair is tied back this time instead of falling away from his head and his face is made bright with the light that surrounds him. The smile he wears only adds to it.

He's absolutely breathtaking and even better, he's all mine.

I'm still amazed that I'm not taking the walk down the aisle alone the way I expected to. It's not exactly a secret that before everything happened, I wanted Gabriel to be the one to do this for me. At the time, my father wasn't in my life and I wasn't sure he ever would be and even though I had Michael, who acts like the brother I always wished I could have, it just wasn't the way I wanted it. Gabriel for me was the only person that could do this and even now, there's a void as I'm taking this walk. I still wish he was here.

The pain I feel over losing him is still there, but with everything that's happened since, it seems to have lessened just enough for me to be able to do this without breaking. Where I felt broken beyond repair only a few short weeks ago, I feel differently now. I will always miss Gabriel, but looking around me and seeing the church filled with everything I could ever want, I know in some way he's here.

This was his gift to me and I'm determined to treasure it forever.

The selfishness I displayed a week ago, wanting Lucifer to join with my father, has reached a fever pitch because I'm most definitely getting everything I ever wanted. Not only is my father walking me down the aisle, looking better than ever, but the other person in my life that I need to stay close to is also here.

My relationship with Lucifer will never make sense and that's okay, but right now, as he walks me down this aisle, the same as my father does, I know this is a stepping stone to a new connection between us. He's the only other being alive besides Ryan that understands and accepts me so completely, which makes him the only other person besides Gabriel that can take this step with me now.

There is still so much that needs to happen for him, but I know that as long as we face it together, the way it seems we've been doing from the start, it won't be long before we're enjoying our eternity together bathed completely in the light.

Just the way Gabriel wants us to.

"There's still time to back out of this, my belle. We can run away together where no one will ever be able to find us."

He's joking and I think I love him even more for it. Even though it's coming out in my father's voice, there is no doubt who is actually saying it. Our relationship is different now, but if possible it's more fulfilling than any other one we might have had. He knows how I feel about Ryan and for the first time since all of this began, I believe he supports it completely, without reservation.

He really did mean it when he said he wanted my happiness in the end and if only we could somehow make this walk speed up right now, he might get to see it take shape. There is no other person in the world that can make me happy the way Ryan can and I'm beyond eager to get on with it.

"No matter where we run, he will always find me."

"Then run, Serenity, but run only until you find the place your heart calls home."

His words send shivers through me because in saying them he has proven again that he understands me better than any other. I've known the place my heart calls home for almost two years now and as Lucifer takes his words to heart, moving faster up the aisle, I realize he does too.

It's time now. Everything that we have gone through and faced together has finally brought us to this point. As I position myself across from him much the way I did the first time around, finally lifting the veil and getting to look into his eyes, I am hit with the most powerful of realizations.

Ryan McGregor is the place my heart calls home.

Lucifer

There is one thing I know as I stand here, ready to release Serenity from my arms and into the arms of the man that is prepared to love, cherish and protect her for the rest of her time here and it has nothing at all to do with either of them.

Gabriel is bearing witness to what is taking place and he is smiling. I am not sure how I know this as fact, I just do. Even in our darkest moments, facing each other, he wanted nothing more than a peaceful ending and standing here now, preparing to watch a wedding take place, the sides of good and evil coming together as one, he is achieving that very thing and I can only imagine that his eternal rest will now be that much sweeter.

When she came to me only days before, under the premise of needing to speak to me about something of grave importance, I had been concerned that she was having doubts about what she had agreed to do. Of course, being who she is, I should have known that it was nothing of the sort, but this second chance I am being given is still very new and I struggle with whether I am truly deserving of it.

*****

266

"There's something I need to talk to you about, but—um, also my dad, if that's possible."

"As you are aware, my belle, he is completely aware of everything that we speak about. Nothing remains hidden so anything you say to me now, will also go straight to him and if his response is needed, I can be sure he gets the chance to give it."

"It's about the wedding."

The minute those words fall from her lips, I feel an ultimate level of peace of which I have not experienced since I joined together with this man. My fears regarding just what she needed to speak to us both about had been assuaged.

"What about it? Please tell me that you have not postponed it."

"No, nothing like that. Ryan's doing better now, in fact he's gotten Michael's seal of approval to leave and come back, but I can't go through with it without asking you both something."

"You know how I feel about this Serenity and despite your father's misgivings because of your age; you know he supports you as well. What is it that you need to ask of me?"

"I need someone to walk me down the aisle. I don't really need it, because I was planning on doing it alone, what with Gabriel..."

She cuts herself off and I sympathize with her. Even though we are all coming to terms with Gabriel's loss in our own way, it is still very raw whenever we have to mention him or plans we might have had with him that he is no longer with us to be a part of.

"You want us to walk you down the aisle at your wedding?"

She nods and I smile. The first genuine smile I have been able to display since I experienced the change. I most definitely did not have anything to worry about as far as my position with Gregory went and neither did Serenity. I would do anything she asked of me, even this.

"I cannot speak for your father, but you already know my answer. Wherever you need me, I am there. No questions asked. I want to do this for you."

"Even though I'm marrying Ryan?"

"Because you are marrying Ryan. Serenity, I know everything that has happened between the boy and me, but I think I have always known in the end it would be this way. The way the two of you were pulled toward one another right from the start spoke volumes. I may not understand everything about it, but there is no denying that Ryan McGregor is where your heart calls home."

"You mean that?"

"I have never meant anything more, my belle."

"Well, I guess now I just need to get my dad on board."

"He is already on board Serenity; in fact he is fighting me pretty hard right now in order to tell you that. I will let him do as he wishes."

"Wait!" she calls before I can let Gregory take control. "There's something else I want to say to you before you go."

"Yes?"

"A long time ago, you told me that we were alike and at first I didn't believe you. By the time I did, I was so deep into the way everything was run in Hell that I couldn't be sure it was even me thinking it. I just want you to know, you were right. We are alike."

*****

I am brought back to reality as the minister moves forward, speaking words that require my response. A response that I have been more than a little eager to give, not only for me, but for the man I am sharing this experience with. Gregory and I are both ready to give his daughter and my sister away, to the one being besides the brother not here with us today that would give her the home her heart needed.

"Who gives this woman to this man?"

Releasing the hold I have on Serenity and letting her make her way toward the spot she would take across from Ryan, I give him the answer he is waiting for and in a manner that only I can do.

"We do."

Ryan

Holy shit, I'm going to totally blow this because I don't think I can even open my mouth to speak. I swear the minister is going to turn to me, I'm going to have to say the words I've been going over and over in my head all day and I'm gonna blow it by doing nothing more than some weird squeak or something.

She's making me speechless. She is two, maybe three steps in front of me right now, so close I can reach out and pull her into me, completing me the way she always has and just knowing that is making me lose my shit. It was like this the first time too, but the fear I could sense off her and what I also felt at the time overrode it.

It should be illegal to look this beautiful. So breathtaking that it makes everyone in the room speechless, especially the man that's supposed to be saying the words that will make her his partner in every way possible. Speechless is not a quality that goes over well at weddings, at least I don't think it does, but holy shit, does she ever make it happen.

Please don't screw this up, please don't screw this up, please don't screw this up. I repeat over in my head as the minister opens up the ceremony.

I really want this to be perfect for her, but I swear each second I have to stand here staring at her, the way she looks in her dress and the way the smile on her face just seems to make her even brighter, I'm losing any and all control I might have had to see that through.

269

She's really here and she's really mine.

"We are here today to join Ryan and Serenity in a life of mutual commitment. It is fitting that you, the family and friends, be here to witness and participate in their union. For the ideals, the understanding and the mutual respect which they bring to their life together had their roots in the love, friendship and guidance you have given them. The union of two people makes us aware of the changes wrought by time, but the new relationship will continue to draw much of its beauty and meaning from the intimate associations of their past."

Yeah, it's getting real now and my throat is so dry, I don't even think I'll be able to get the squeak of air out that I'm expecting, let alone the words when it's time for me to say them.

"Ryan and Serenity," he continues which only makes my heart beat that much faster knowing that it's not that long now before I'm actually going to have speak. "Seek from within yourselves, the serenity to accept the things that you cannot change, the courage to change the things that you must, and the wisdom to know the difference. Live each day, one at a time, enjoying your time together, one moment at a time. Seek the wisdom of experience, learning all that you can from each other. Accept hardships as the building blocks of experience, realizing that accepting both the good and the bad are simply a part of being alive. Strive to make as many things right as humanly possible in your life together, that you may be reasonably happy in the life you share together from this day forward."

He finishes and looks between both of us and the smile he wears should put me at ease, but it doesn't. It's only when I feel Serenity's eyes on me that my racing heart starts to calm.

You're extremely sexy when you're scared shitless.

It's those words that make the fear drain away. If Serenity can be calm, firm in the step she's about to take, I can do it too.

I can get through this without screwing it up. I just have to because she deserves nothing but the best.

I have the best, I have you.

"Both Ryan and Serenity have expressed the desire to say their own words to one another before moving on with the exchange of rings, so Ryan, if you would like to begin."

It's do or die time. Here's my chance to stand before, not only our friends and Serenity's parents, but God himself and say everything that I've ever felt as it pertains to this angel in front of me. It's my chance to show the world just how much better this person has made my life just by being in it.

Man, I better not screw this up.

"It seems cheesy to say this considering the first time I ever heard it, it was in a movie and it wasn't even a movie I really liked all that much, but it's the only words I can come up with that really explain the impact that you've made on my life." I say, turning and facing Serenity, taking her hand in mine and making sure our eyes are locked solely on each other. "You complete me, Serenity Richards and no matter what happens from this moment on, know this. You are me and I am you and we are one—forever."

Serenity

How am I supposed to follow that?

If I wasn't about to open my mouth and shout to the world exactly how I felt about this man, I would give some serious thought to kicking him for what he just said. Sure, they're all things he's said to me before, but now, standing here in this church the way we are, all of these people and angels watching us, it has even more of an impact and I'm the one left speechless.

I know the minister is about to turn to me and want me to say my part, but I'm not sure I can. It's only when I hear the voice in my head, the soothing tone that I have come to recognize almost as easily as I do my own, that I know exactly what it is that I want and need to say.

"Speak from the heart Serenity; it will always take you where you need to be."

Gabriel.

I don't know if it's a figment of my imagination or if it's Michael or Lucifer speaking and I'm just wishing so hard for it to be him, but either way, I have never been so thankful to hear that familiar melody, as I am in this moment.

"Before Serenity says what I know she's so eager to say, there's one more thing I need to do."

Holy crap, there's more?

"When you were gone and I didn't know if I'd ever get to see you again, I spent a lot of time writing. I'm not sure if it was supposed to be poetry or lyrics or just ramblings from the mind that wouldn't shut off, but in one of the nights when I couldn't sleep, I wrote this and even though it's probably going to suck, I want you to hear it."

Oh dear god, please tell me he's not going to sing.

My heart calms the minute he speaks again, his voice lower than before, but the familiar rumble still ever present. He's not singing, but there is no doubt with the way he's looking at me as he says them, that he's singing them to me in a way that is distinctly Ryan. Even the simple words I love you sound like music to me when he says them.

**I was broken when you found me,
You lifted me to new heights
Taking the darkness buried so deep inside and bathing it in light**

**As much as I try
I can't seem to fight it.
I'm intoxicated by you**

You're like a hurricane

272

A force of nature that can't be controlled
A path with only one destination
Bringing my heart to life

I can't run, I can't hide
I can't escape it,
I'm intoxicated by you."

Tears are streaming down my face by the time he finishes and again I'm struck with the urge to hit him because this time, he lied. He said that the words would suck and they did anything but. In the simplest of ways, everything he just said explained the impact I've had on his life, which makes them the most beautiful words ever spoken.

Now I really don't know how I'm going to follow that up.

"There have been quite a few times over the years where someone has said something to me that impacts me so much I seem to carry it with me even though I don't have the chance to use it quite the way they did. I can still remember the day, after a pretty big fight between my mom and dad, him coming to my room and telling me that despite all of the bad things I'd heard them say, that the fun was in the fixin'. Flash forward a whole lot of years and I've gotten to say it to the only person that's ever been worthy of hearing it. I said those words to you because they're true of us just as they were true of them so many years before. No matter what we go through from this moment, Ryan McGregor, the fun will always be in the fixin'. Someone that means the world to me, recently told me to speak from the heart, so that's what I'm going to do. You are everything to me, but more than that, you are the one place in all of existence that my heart can call home. You're my beginning and my end and you always will be."

I have no idea where the words came from. When I opened my mouth to speak I had no idea what I'd even been planning to say, but once they were out there, I knew they were the right ones. There could be nothing said now that could explain the way I feel any better than I just did.

Looking at him, really taking in his reaction to everything I've said, I see that I'm not the only one that's been affected to the point of tears. He's also wearing his reaction openly on his face and it takes everything in me not to reach forward now and wipe the tears from his eyes. Ryan has never been more beautiful than he is right now. My broken love put back together again.

The minister steps forward as we pull ourselves together and looking between us one final time he speaks.

"Do you Ryan, take Serenity to be your lawfully wedded wife, promising to love and cherish, through joy and sorrow, sickness and health and whatever challenges you may face, for as long as you both shall live?"

"I do." Ryan answers the words said easily and without any hint of reservation as the minister turns his attention on me.

"Do you Serenity, take Ryan to be your lawfully wedded husband, promising to love and cherish, through joy and sorrow, sickness and health and whatever challenges you may face, as long as you both shall live?"

"I do."

"Ryan, please take Serenity's hand and repeat after me." The minster says, waiting as Ryan fishes the ring out of his pocket, reminiscent of the day he proposed to me outside of this very church, struggling with the ring box and just how perfect I thought it was.

"Serenity," Ryan says, beginning to repeat the words as the man speaks them. "I give you this ring as a symbol of my love and faithfulness. As I place it on your finger, I commit my heart and soul to you. I ask you to wear this ring as a reminder of the vows we have spoken here today, our wedding day."

It takes every single bit of strength I have not to break down in tears again as he slides the ring down over my hand, replacing the one that until earlier this morning had been a symbol of the first time we'd done this very thing. He lingers a few seconds after the ring is placed and I can't help but remember the way he'd done the same thing a year before. Even though this time is so different, I'm glad that there are some things that don't change because that's something I never want to forget.

"Serenity, if you would repeat after me."

Taking the band as Emma reaches forward to give it to me, the ring complete with the dark ring around the outer core, same as his eyes the first time I saw them, I move forward and take his hand in mine, prepared to repeat the very same words that only seconds before he had said to me.

"Ryan, I give you this ring as a symbol of my love and faithfulness. As I place it on your finger, I commit my heart and soul to you. I ask you to wear this ring as a constant reminder of the vows we have spoken here today, our wedding day."

He catches my eye the moment I slide the ring all the way down and I can tell by the way the blue in his eyes glistens that he also sees the significance of the black band that encircles the gold of the ring, a private reminder for the both of us of just who he had been when I fell in love with him.

"And now, by the power vested in me, I now pronounce you husband and wife. Ryan, you may now kiss your bride."

"It's about damn time." Ryan whispers as I smile and before I know it, I'm being swept up into his arms and he's leaning me back, his one hand cradled perfectly on the back of my head. He places his lips to mine and everything around us fades away under the electricity that seems to pass through us both just from the singular motion.

As he breaks away, bringing me back up to my feet and linking his fingers through mine, just as the minister announces us to the room as Mr. and Mrs. McGregor, the brightest light seems to shine in through the stained glassed windows and as we all turn toward it, I'm struck by just what it is that I'm witnessing.

It's Gabriel's approval.

Epilogue

Ryan

It's been three months since the day I married my beloved and in that time I've probably found a million different things out about her that make me love her even more. Every single day with her is a learning experience for me. The Serenity that she is underneath all the glitz and glamour of her Heavenly light, is only a small portion of her and now that we're married, living together in a house just off campus, I'm getting to see everything that I hadn't gotten to before. What really makes Serenity the most beautiful person on the planet.

She sings in the shower and even though she's completely tone deaf, I can't help but adore the way she tries when she doesn't think anyone is around to hear her. She actually snorts when she laughs, which no matter how many times I've caught her doing it still manages to embarrass the hell out of her. The best one though is how even doing the most mundane tasks imaginable, like laundry, dishes and other household cleaning, she still finds a way to make it fun.

I thought I'd seen it all, but I hadn't seen anything, at least until I walked in the door after classes one day and saw her dancing around to the music she had on, singing at the top of her lungs while running the vacuum over the carpet.

Yeah, you have not lived until you see this angel dance around the house happily while she's cleaning.

It's official. I have been so whipped by this woman that no matter what she does, I think I'm going to go on about it like it's as important and life changing as a cure for cancer would be. But that's what love is supposed to be about; at least that's what I believe anyway. That's not to say we haven't had our hard moments already, even this early on in our marriage, but just like she said that day in front of the world, the fun really is in the fixing and we're proving that true every single day.

Gabriel was with us the day we got married, both of us agree on that. We both feel that the light that came shining through the window when the minister announced us married was his way of smiling down on us. Letting us know without question that while he couldn't be there with us, he'd seen and experienced it all just the way we had and he approved. It also didn't go unnoticed that the end of the light landed on Lucifer. I think that's his way of letting Lucifer know he was pleased with the path he had finally taken and I am too.

I may never be able to forget what he put us all through, but I have forgiven him. I think it's made easier because of the fact that he's joined with Gregory. It's a good place for him to be and with the strides he's been making, trying to rectify the things he did while trapped in his true darkness, it will be no time before he gains entrance to Heaven again, something that I'm starting to see now that he wanted all along.

Michael went home after the wedding and though we don't speak as much as we used to, he's never far from my thoughts and most times when I need a break from the classes, the stress of working a full time job and everything that comes with it, I find myself catching up with him in prayer. It's the one thing that during my entire time here so far, has never taken me down the wrong road and with the added bonus of it now being Michael that answers, it's a good way to stay level and connected.

Emma and Graham for all of the pushing I've done trying to get them together, seem to be more distant now than ever before. Graham has his own mixed bag of crap he's dealing with as he struggles to come back from everything that was done to him. Deep down I know that if only he opened himself up again, Emma would be able to help him with that, but just because I got my happy ending doesn't mean that everyone else is meant to so I'm going to bide my time and keep an eye on both of them. When the time is right, they'll get where they need to be and I swear I'll be right there cheering them on.

I still can't believe I'm standing here now. That I'm married to Serenity and we're living such a mundane and normal life together. We cook each other dinner; have date nights, study nights and everything that the both of us wanted for so long when we were alone, but now experiencing together. I was right with what I said to her the day I married her because for the first time, I have everything I've ever wanted and the future never looked brighter.

I'm complete.

Serenity

He's doing it again and he isn't even aware of it.

He's lying on our bed, a textbook in his hand, pretending to read like he always does after everything's been done for the day and we're just enjoying the space together. He's actually lost so deeply in thought that I can see everything in his mind clearly, like my own personal home movie.

It's so freaking adorable.

The first few times it happened, I actually called him on it because of course I found it adorable and wanted to share, even ribbing him a bit with it because it's just another reminder of how alike we are. I finally stopped doing it because I found just sitting and quietly taking in the show is much more fun. It has nothing to do with reading his mind because I don't even need to do that anymore, in fact neither one of us does. It just happens naturally and it's just another way for the both of us to connect.

Ryan has come such a long way since our wedding three months ago. He went right back to school like I did, choosing to skip the honeymoon, since living together here in Stephenville is a dream come true and it costs a whole lot less. He changed his major, choosing instead to take the path where he can help people that suffer the same way he used to. He's working toward becoming an addiction counselor and I couldn't be more proud of him. The things he'd been addicted to might be different then the things that most humans experience every day, but the responses and actions are all the same and no one knows how to help people overcome darkness then someone who has done it himself.

When he's not buried under his course load or with me, he's working his ass off to make sure we never want for anything. I'm not exactly sure what happened, but one day, he went to talk to my dad and after he got home, he started his job search, landing one that he was pretty excited to apply for and has been working his ass off ever since. When I asked him about it, the only thing he'd say was my dad had given him something to think about so he thought about it and did what was right.

I get the feeling that my dad had nothing to do with it, but I don't tell him that. I'll let him continue believing that Lucifer isn't being the sneaky bastard I've come to see that he is.

I've been doing something lately, in an effort to continue with what God says my destiny is. I spend time with Michael, who has taken a vessel for the first time in forever and Lucifer, getting together with the both of them, helping them hash out the problems they have between them. It's actually through helping these two brothers come together again that I realized exactly what it is I want to do with my life. It means a lot of hard work and dedication, but when everything is said and done, I want to be a child psychologist. I want to take everything I've gone through and use it in the right way to help kids who might end up going through a lot of the same things I have.

It's my true gift to the world and with the power of not only Heaven, but the most amazing man in the world behind me, I have no doubt I'll succeed, giving it all I've got.

The only piece that's missing, that would make everything in my life perfect, is Graham. We seem lost to each other again and as much as that pains me because of the very real friendship we've spent years forging, I refuse to give up on him. I will do whatever it takes to get the Graham I know and love back, even if I have to sacrifice myself all over again to do it. No one deserves happiness more than Graham and if the plan I'm putting into motion works, he'll get it. As it turns out, I've still got a lot more gifts I need to give out to the world and the most important one is to Graham himself.

Even God thinks so, which is why he's been helping me.

There's something that happens when you realize your true purpose in life. Everything around you becomes clear. Troubles fade away into the background, true happiness and peace standing in their place. I finally have everything I've ever wanted and while I used to think that I had to be someone completely different in order to achieve it, I'm learning that the opposite is true.

You don't have to be anyone other than you. I'm living proof.

The End

Graham Hudson has been beaten down, broken and doesn't see himself ever being able to recover. Will he ever get over what happened to him during the time he spent as Lucifer's pawn or is he destined to remain in his own personal hell forever?

Coming Spring 2014 – A Light In The Dark
The companion novel to the Love United Series

Acknowledgements

Caleb, Noah, Raine and Isabella, my CNRI. Thank you for being the four most beautiful, amazing and understand children on the planet while I've been locked away in writing mode. You will never know how truly honored I am to be your mother and even at such a young age, have you as my biggest fans. I love you more than words can say.

Joey Reagan what can I say that hasn't already been said? You are truly one of the most important people in my life. Not only do you take these books and go over them until your eyes bleed, offering me advice on what to keep and what to change, but you prop me back up when I feel like pulling my hair out and giving up. I love you just isn't strong enough for what I feel for you. Here's to more pretty girl books in the future!

Ladies of the HMC, who are in no order whatsoever. Jennifer Ankles, Jill Fritz, Faith Walsh, Linda Rabinowitz, Jennifer Hicks, Jenn Lierman, Lisa Morris, Erin Narr, Mariah Newton, Michelle Smith, Portia Lowery and Savanna Decker. Ladies, I'm not sure the pictures of the men are cutting it anymore, not when there's all the amazing photos with you reading books! Soon it's gonna be the MBC with all of the support you've shown me. I love you all dearly, thank you for helping me achieve this dream of mine.

Mallory. Welcome to the Winchester clan. You are official family to me. Never give up on your dreams, I hope one day to see your name in print so I can fan-girl over you the way that you do the world that I've spun here. Thank you for being one of the kindest souls on the planet.

To each and every person that purchases this book or any book that I've written to each person that reviews it and tells their friends about it. Thank you so much from the bottom of my heart for spending not only your hard earned money on this dream of mine but also the hard to come by time. I appreciate it more then you will ever truly know. I love and appreciate you all.

About The Author

Melyssa is a mother of four from Toronto, Ontario, Canada. Previously spending her daylight hours freelance editing for friends and family, she happily traded in her gig for a rewarding career writing young adult supernatural novels. The best part being that in working from home, she gets to spend more time with her own set of real life angels, and maybe a demon or two as well.

She is currently working on Before the Light, a series of novellas that follow the characters from the Love United Series before their lives intersect, as well as Take Me With You, a companion novel to Count On Me.

When she's not writing, you can find her buried under the covers with her portable DVD player, watching marathons of Supernatural and Veronica Mars. When those aren't available, she can be found curled up in a corner with her e-reader and a plethora of books, falling in love with characters written so well she deems them her book boyfriends and girlfriends. If you want to find her, check Facebook or Twitter (@WinchesterBooks) as she may just have an addiction to both. If those don't work you can always keep up with her progress on her personal site where she more than loves blogging about her various endeavors.

See how Serenity and Ryan's story began...

HOLDING ON TO HEAVEN

Love United Series #1

Prologue

Gabriel

Today is a day like no other before it. The preparations are made and the plan now in motion. Heaven is alive with hope at the prospect of what is to come. After careful planning by our Father, change was on the horizon.

"Gabriel, my son, come. Join me and watch as Heaven's greatest gift is unveiled to the world. Today is a day one will not soon forget. You must be a part of it."

I love my father a great deal. More than that, I have the utmost faith in him but there was a small part of me knowing what was to come, that still had my doubts.

"Are you sure she's ready for the magnitude of this endeavor Father? Would she not be better served having more time to prepare?"

"You doubt me Gabriel? Having witnessed what I can do, you fear what we are about to embark on?"

"You know by now that I have the utmost faith in your ability to lead us all sir. I only concern myself with her, as was your intent in giving me my orders was it not? If she is to be the saving grace for the humans and essentially the second coming of Heaven on Earth, should she not be prepared for any and all complications?"

"I would not be secure in sending her if I thought for a second that she wasn't ready. It is her time and she won't be alone. You will be there to guide her down the right path should she falter."

"My greatest achievement has always been the world, as you well know. In recent years, there has been a loss of faith. With her inception we will change that and bring about a better tomorrow for generations to come."

From the moment of my creation, Father told me of the magnificence of Earth and all that inhabited it. In recent years, it seems to be on a rapid decline. Dark forces had begun to descend leaving a great deal of chaos in their wake. After watching and working where we were permitted, it was now time for the bigger picture.

To take the light back from the darkness.

Serenity was such a deserving name for the angelic ball of light that is now set to make her descent upon the Earth. She will restore a sense of peace to a world gone mad and also to a group of Heavenly hosts that were slowly losing their faith.

I have a part to play in this moment as well, more than that of the casual observer. I am to be her guardian. To watch over her as she makes her entrance until the very moment she is called back home. Protecting her and showing her the way. I am tasked just as much as Serenity herself in saving what is left of the world. Not something I took lightly.

It's possible my hesitation was not regarding Serenity and the undertaking at all but centered around my own ability. Could I really follow through and do what Father asked of me? Am I strong enough to hold it all together if for some reason it fell apart?

"My son you must not let the seed of doubt reside within you. Just as I have the utmost faith in Serenity, I also have it in you. Everything you have experienced up until this moment has been to prepare you to take your rightful place by my side. You must not be swayed from that."

It should have come as no shock that he read my mind. All thoughts were visible to the Almighty. There could be no secrets, no thoughts better left hidden. He knew them all. The pride in his voice as he spoke to me from his heart straight to mine was crippling in its intensity.

All any child ever wants is their parent's approval and hearing it from him now, filled with a confidence I had never truly known empowered me. If he believed in me then I could do this. I would do this for him, my brothers and sisters but most of all for the world.

"I will forever cherish your never ending faith in me Father and I will not let you down. I will prove myself worthy."

It is my sacred duty as an agent of Heaven after all.

Chapter One

Serenity

As far back as I can remember I've heard voices. My earliest memory is the day I turned five. My grandma on my mom's side had passed away a week before. It was at her funeral, when my mom made her way to the casket, my little hand clasped tightly in her own that I heard it. Clear as day, the voice of my grandma, telling me things no five year old should have to hear.

"Serenity dear, do not let your mother fall apart. You must not let the demons take control of her."

I was five. What the hell did I know about demons and for that matter, how I was supposed to stop my mother from falling apart was beyond me. I'm still learning how to tie my own shoes for crying out loud. Stopping a grown adult from doing something they would most likely do anyway wasn't even on my radar.

With what I can only explain as childish naivety, I believed she hadn't really passed away. That she'd actually woken up and spoke the words to me aloud. So I answered her back.

"No Nana. You do it."

Well let me tell you, the last thing you want to do at a funeral is talk to the dead, or rather answer them. My mom wasted no time pulling me away from the casket going so far as to pull me completely from the room, all the while checking to make sure no one else heard my outburst.

"Serenity, what do you think you're doing?"

"Talking to Nana." I replied, as if talking to my dead grandmother was something I did naturally every day.

288

Oh come on, I was five, what did my mother expect? It wasn't as if at that point I had a lot of knowledge of death to fall back on.

That was my mother's first glimpse of my 'gift'. I'd like to sit here and tell you that it was her last but then I'd be lying.

From that point on it happened more frequently. It grew from being just family members that I could speak with to the most random people. Hospitals were my worst enemy. Between the sick and the dead, it seemed no one there ever knew when to shut up.

By the time I turned twelve my mom had been through enough with me. The excuses I gave didn't fly anymore and it was then that she brought me to the first doctor. She had to be thinking either I was crazy or that she was losing her mind. Neither option more appealing than the other so finding a cause became her life's mission.

We must have gone through six or seven doctors in the first few months alone, all of whom told her I was a perfectly well adjusted young girl with an over active imagination. My mother just wasn't buying it. I can't say I blame her given that I was the one living with the constant barrage of voices in my head. There was no way I could even dream of making up something that level of crazy.

By the time my thirteenth birthday rolled around, I was officially the patient of a psychiatric treatment center. The mission my mother was on finally paid off in that she found the one doctor in our small town of Summerview that believed something really was wrong with me. Maybe she didn't believe that I was crazy but at the very least, I wasn't adjusting the way I should be. So her method of handling it was advising my mother to have me committed.

Summerview Psychiatric Treatment Center became my home for the next two and a half years. As much as you would assume I hated my mom for putting me in a place like that, I actually found myself thankful she did. It was the one place where the voices couldn't get to me.

In my experience when someone is shown something they don't want to see, or rather what they can't handle seeing, the first inclination is to turn away from it. Well in my case it would seem that the minute I walked through the doors of the center, the voices proceeded to do that very thing with me. It's as if I was too crazy for even them to handle. So they left me alone.

It was the best two and a half years of my life.

While the real reason I was in the center remained under wraps it didn't stop the staff from coming up with an adequate diagnosis for what they believed my problem was. The most popular one being that I was schizophrenic. Apparently being able to hear and converse with the dead fell under the umbrella of that particular ailment. I didn't bother fighting the diagnosis. I figured the sooner they labeled me the sooner they'd leave me alone and find someone else to focus their attention on.

To everybody else I was just the girl who heard voices and it seemed to make my attempts at fitting in go that much smoother. It was in one particular group therapy meeting that I met her, the girl that would become my best friend.

Emma Daniels on the outside seemed like most of the kids I'd gone to school with before I'd been taken away. She seemed happy, well-adjusted and for a while I wondered if she was a figment of my imagination given that I couldn't see just what her problem was. We all had our reasons for being there but with Emma, I really couldn't see it. So of course not knowing ate away at me until I finally gave in and went looking for answers.

I know. I could have easily just asked her but what thirteen year old does that? Asking someone what their level of crazy is, well it just wasn't socially acceptable no matter where you happened to be at the time.

Breaking into the records office I found out she was manic depressive with suicidal tendencies. I have to say, I was shocked by given that she displayed no sign of depression in the times I'd been around her. Not even in group, when you were encouraged to talk about your illness, did she ever make one mention of it. It was then that I decided to get to know her. If I was being labeled incorrectly, I had to assume that she was as well. It just made sense to me that we should stick together. So that was exactly what we did. For the next two and a half years we were stuck together like glue.

It hasn't changed much since either.

The day my mother showed up to get me, about three months after my fifteenth birthday I wasn't ready to go. Having gone the entire time being more than just the girl who heard voices, I wasn't ready to accept the change. The doctors explained my progress to my mom though and after a few meetings with the staff, I'd been deemed healthy enough to leave. Provided of course that I remained on the medication I'd been taking since the day I'd been diagnosed.

I followed the rules when I got home but after a while, I gave up on taking the pills, opting instead for going it alone. If I had been able to go almost three years without hearing a voice, maybe now that I was home I really was cured and I'd be able to live a normal life. Or at least as normal a life as a person like me could actually live.

The normal didn't last long. By the time I turned sixteen the voices were back and it seemed even more powerful than before. I heard them so frequently I had a hard time telling where they began and I ended. We became one.

My mother told me once that there hadn't been a moment where she'd been able to get any peace from me. I'd followed her around everywhere. This is what I likened the voices to. At least with my mother she could shut the bathroom door to get away from me. With the voices there was no door. It was free reign even when I didn't want it to be.

Fast forward five years later and I'm about to start my second year of college. I moved out on my own, got a job and been living apart from my very over protective mother for almost two years. It hasn't been easy but I learned quickly to contain my responses to the voices and have even managed to create a relatively normal life for myself. At least that's how it appeared to someone standing on the outside looking in anyway.

There were only two people that knew the truth and one I didn't speak to anymore. The other is Emma. She remained at the center after I left until her release a year after my own. We managed to stay in touch through letters and phone calls once a week. She was never far from my thoughts. I opened up to her in ways that I hadn't been able to do with anyone else and she did much the same with me. We were closer than friends. We were sisters, bonded by our struggles.

When I went away to college I chose one that was close to her. If I had to go through this life with my so called gift then I was going to do it with the one person that understood it.

Our first week back after summer break I heard it for the first time. A new voice, one that in all of the years I'd been hearing them had never come to me before. This voice seemed different than the others. It's stronger; more distinct. He was able reach me even when I was sleeping which is something the other voices have been unable to do. He seemed to want to help me, listen to my thoughts and make sense of the things that up until that point I'd been unable to understand.

A few weeks after he made contact with me I finally broke my silence and told Emma. As much as I trusted her I always assumed there had to be a limit on her understanding and the last thing I wanted to do was alienate the one person that had been there for me.

Turns out, she must have grown a pretty thick skin when it came to my revelations because in telling her, she gave me an alternate way of looking at things.

"So this guy, he talks to you in your sleep?"

"Yeah he does...well no," I backtracked. "Sometimes he sings to me but most of the time he just talks."

"What does his voice sound like?"

"Ems, what kind of question is that? He sounds like a guy. I don't know how else to describe it."

"You tell me you hear a guy in your head and you don't expect me to ask questions like this?"

She had a point. I suppose to the casual observer this might actually sound pretty cool but for me it's become second nature. I didn't put much thought into the sound of the voice speaking to me, or the fact that I had voices speaking to me at all. It was just something that happened and that I dealt with. Emma wasn't like me though, she found it all fascinating.

"So what does he sound like? Is his voice all high pitched like that one kid on the radio or is it all low, sexy and mysterious?"

I knew she wouldn't stop until I told her. She may have issues but in every other way Emma is exactly like the rest of the teenage population. It all came back to how a person looked, spoke and smelled. It's female hormones at their finest.

"It's not high pitched at all. In fact it sounds pretty low key. It's very melodic, calming even. Whenever he talks to me I feel the most relaxed I've probably ever been. Like nothing can get to me. It almost feels dreamlike.

"Ha! I knew it. You like him."

Huh? How did she come to that conclusion?

"How the hell do you get that from what I just said?" I asked rolling my eyes.

I knew I wouldn't like her reasoning. I never did when she got this way.

"Oh Emma, he sounds so dreamlike. His voice is calming. He keeps me relaxed. It's so completely obvious that whoever this voice is, you like him."

"You're insane."

"No actually I'm depressed. You know this. You aren't denying it though which is interesting. It looks like my best friend finally has her first crush on a guy."

I didn't often admit this but sometimes I wish I could be more like Emma and see the world the way she does. How she could make fun of her own illness and shrug it off as if it wasn't a problem when given our past together we both knew it was. I eventually got to see the issues she faced when we roomed together during our stay in the center. It wasn't pretty.

Her romantic notions aside though she did help me take my mind off just who the voice was and what he really wanted with me, at least for a minute, which is exactly what I had been hoping for.

"I do not have a crush on the voice in my head Ems." I sighed. "Can we drop it now?"

"Sure but I just want to say one more thing first."

Rolling my eyes at her again, I motioned for her to say her piece.

"You said that he comes to you and keeps you calm right? That he has the ability to block out the other voices and that whenever he's around, you feel almost normal right?"

"Yeah I guess. What are you getting at?"

"What if it's not just a random voice? If he has the ability to cut down on the chatter in your head, maybe he's something more specific."

"More specific how Ems? What exactly do you think he is?"

"Maybe he's your guardian angel."